KILL OR BE KILLED

Damn pig farmers! They dropped out of first grade—when they were thirty! Neither Dropiv nor Agayn had a chance to recover. Dropiv couldn't and Agayn was still trying to push Dropiv from him. The Death Merchant finished off Dropiv with a downward *Kekomi* kick, the heel of his left boot crashing into the fifth and the sixth thoracic vertebrae, squarely in the center of the back, about the level of the lower ends of the shoulder blades. Dropiv's spine cracked. The cord broke. The Russian died, his dead weight pushing against a frantic Guerguen Agayn. Agayn didn't remain frenzied with fear for very long. Camellion scrambled his brains with a 9mm GB slug, popping the Ruskie low in the forehead, just below the rim of his combat helmet.

Spinning around, Camellion holstered the two Steyr auto-pistols and started to pull the Oda-Mar knife. His fingers were going around the handle when he spotted three more Russians headed his way. Two were armed with AKM bayonets. The third, an officer, had a Vitmorkin machine pistol in his right hand—and he was raising the weapon straight at the Death Merchant.

THE DEATH MERCHANT SERIES:

56 in the incredible
adventures of the

DEATH
MERCHANT
AFGHANISTAN CRASHOUT

by Joseph Rosenberger

PINNACLE BOOKS   ◎   **NEW YORK**

DEATH MERCHANT #56: AFGHANISTAN CRASHOUT

Copyright © 1983 Joseph Rosenberger

An original Pinnacle Books edition, published for the first time anywhere.

First printing, August 1983

ISBN: 0-523-42000-5

Cover illustration by Dean Cate

Printed in the United States of America

PINNACLE BOOKS, INC.
1430 Broadway
New York, New York 10018

I tell you this, American: the Russians are lower than animals. An animal will kill to protect its young, to eat, to live. The Russians kill because they enjoy it. They are using chemical warfare against us. The skin blackens and falls off the bones. They are very vicious against our children, thinking that we, as a nation, will surrender to save our little ones. They have dropped toys from the air that are booby-trapped with explosives. Hundreds of our children have been blinded by these devices, or have been killed, or have lost their hands and arms.

We will never surrender our freedom to monsters of evil.

Warn your people, American. The blood flowing in our nation will someday flow in yours—unless you are very very careful. . . .

Khair Bahauddin Ghazi, in a conversation with Richard J. Camellion.

CHAPTER ONE

By the big black beard of Boob McNutt, this just isn't my day!

It hadn't been Richard Camellion's "day" for the past six weeks, ever since he had landed in Delhi, India, and, by a complicated route, had finally arrived at the mountain base of Khair Bahauddin Ghazi, the Afghan partisan leader with the largest following.

Like all Afghans, Ghazi, his son, Ismail, and the rest of the freedom fighters were brave, proud, cruel, hospitable, backward by Western standards—and stubborn. It was that adamantine firmness of will that piqued the Death Merchant, that irritated him worse than a tack in the toe. Their stubbornness, plus their bravery! Yet there was a difference between courage and recklessness.

"We must be daring," Khair Bahauddin Ghazi had said to Camellion and the other Westerners. "We must make up in bravery what we lack in arms and other equipment. We will never submit to the Russian animals from the north."

At the time, the Death Merchant had replied only in thought—*The great virtue of the stupid is that they don't live long!*

Very true. Very logical. The area around Kabul did have to be reconnoitered, if Camellion were to rescue Werholtz and Hemschire from Kabul Central Prison. The Death Merchant and the three other men had started out from Ghazi's base high in the Hindu Kush Mountains.[1] For seventeen days they had struggled across the rocks, moving through deep

---

[1] Means "Killer of Hindus." The Kush is an extension of the Himalayas, although some say it's an independent system.

1

valleys and around dangerous gorges, all the while hiding from Soviet air patrols. Whenever possible they traveled at night, for there was always the possibility of meeting a Soviet ground patrol.

Now, at two o'clock in the morning, they had! The glow in the distance, beyond the low hills, wasn't coming from the lanterns of a troop of Boy Scouts.

It would not have been difficult to bypass the Soviet patrol, a tactic the Death Merchant had suggested to Ismail Mohammed Ghazi. Rodney Hooppole had reinforced Camellion's proposal.

"There's only four of us," Hooppole said, "and we don't know how many Russians. We are not supermen, *kuvii*[2] Ghazi."

"The more Russians we kill, the greater will be our revenge in the eyes of Allah," Ghazi had said firmly. "We will ambush them. We would go to our graves with dishonor were we to ignore such an inviting target. Allah wills that we destroy them."

That was still another irritation to the Death Merchant: the fact that the Afghan warriors were Shi'a Muslim, the same kind of religious fanatics who were subjecting Iran to a daily bath of blood. Like the moronic fundamentalists in the United States who saw the hand of God in everything, the Shi'a Muslim fundamentalists saw their Allah lurking in every tree and bush. Unfortunately for them, Allah had not prevented the Soviet Union from invading Afghanistan. To the Death Merchant there was little difference between the Russians and the Afghans. Both could rationalize murder: the Soviets in the name of Communism, the Afghans in the name of Allah. The planet would have been better off without both. Then again, the planet would be better off if the whole human race vanished!

Even worse—in Camellion's opinion—the Afghans loved dog fights and delighted in watching two poor animals fight to the death. To Camellion, who thought more of animals than he did people, this was the unpardonable sin and marked the Afghans as brutes without hope of redemption.

Finding it difficult to control his temper and not chop Ghazi, "Jr." in the throat, Camellion glanced up at the starlit

[2]"Friend."

2

sky with a thin slice of moon. He then turned to Ismail Ghazi, a handsome dark-haired man in his middle twenties.

"Our job is to evaluate Soviet strength around the east side of Kabul," Camellion said, speaking calmly. "We shouldn't do anything to endanger that mission. We're only eight kilometers from the city. We have forged papers. We are only a few kilometers from the old caravan road. The plan is to wait close to the road then join a passing caravan. We should go around the Soviet patrol and stick to the plan."

Mului Jalai Imu, the other Afghan, jabbered in Pushto[3] to Ghazi. Ghazi something back to Imu who didn't speak a word of English, and turned his eyes to the Death Merchant.

"We will go forward and see how many Russians are there," Ghazi said stoically. "If they greatly outnumber us, we will go around them. We must see for ourselves. It is most unusual for the Russians to have a patrol this far from the city at night. Come, Allah is with us."

Turning, he started on his way. Without a second glance at Camellion and Hooppole, Imu followed—*A puppy following his master!*

A professional mercenary who was built like a brick shipyard, Rod Hooppole shook his head dispiritedly, a look of pained disgust and apprehension on his narrow face that sported a long handlebar mustache.

"That bloodthirsty bloke is going to get us killed," he said in a low voice to Camellion who had unshouldered a silenced Ingram MAC-10 submachine gun, fitted with a metal-frame stock, and was also carrying a Soviet AKM assault rifle.

"The bugger does have a point though," Camellion said. "What are the pig farmers doing here at this time of the morning. It does make you rather curious, doesn't it. . . ."

"Not me it doesn't," the practical Hooppole said. "I don't give a fiddler's fig what the ivans are doing here. Let them be I say. We could have gone around them."

"I agree, but we can't unring a bell. Ghazi 'Junior' insists on having a looksee, and there isn't any way we can talk him out of it."

The four carefully made their way up the rocky slope, the incline thick with chunks of granite, scattered spearmint bushes

[3]The leading language spoken in Afghanistan.

and mountain scrub trees. All the while the glow beyond the hills grew brighter.

The summits of the hills were uneven, as barren as the dark side of the moon and strewn with rocky rubble. Tall, slab-like rocks leaned every which way at odd angles and here and there were weathered pinnacle rocks. In some places there was gritty soil, in other places naked granite.

In a strange sort of way, Camellion admired Ismail Mohammed Ghazi. For a young squirt who had never been out of Afghanistan, the hillbilly haven of Asia, Ismail had a lot of savvy; and while he was as daring as a drunken tightrope walker, he was by no means foolhardy. He was not a raging bull crashing about in a china shop, as evidenced by the way he had gotten down on his belly and was wriggling forward between two large rocks. Camellion and the two other men were soon down beside him, staring at the flat plain at the bottom of the slopes. What they saw did not fill their hearts with joy. There were three Soviet Army vehicles, parked in such a way that they formed a triangle. The point of the triangle, facing the north, was a BTR-40 armored car, its turret pointed south, as was the 7.62mm SGMB machine gun in the turret. Two soldiers were leaning against the vehicle, both smoking cigarettes. The southeast point of the triangle was an eight-wheeled BTR-6 armored personnel carrier. It too had a SGMB-MG protruding from the roof forward. The small glacis plate in front of the driver's compartment had been removed and four Russians appeared to be working on one of the GAZ-48B gasoline engines. The southwest point of the triangle was an armored BD-4 command car; its bump of a turret was open and a soldier was standing in the opening and slowly observing the surrounding area through a NSPT infrared night vision device. Within the triangle three soldiers were behind automatic grenade launchers. The bright light came from seven battery powered floodlights placed on top of the three vehicles.

Hooppole broke the silence as he adjusted his Nikon IF hard-rubber armored binoculars. "They're a night patrol," he whispered. "It's almost two-forty-five. They couldn't have been working on that engine since yesterday afternoon."

"Keep down," warned Camellion, "Or we'll be spotted by the goon with the NS device. We're well within range of those grenade launchers."

4

"Those launchers are the kind I was telling you about," Hooppole said. "It's a 30mm weapon, with a circular drum magazine that holds forty rounds of frag stuff. Soviet infantrymen call it the *Plamya*. It's very effective. It can fire either a shaped-charge antitank round or a cluster of beehive type missiles."

Ismail Mohammed Ghazi dropped the verbal bombshell, saying mechanically, "We will send those Russian savages to the devil they worship. I have worked out a plan."

The Death Merchant pulled back from between the two rocks; so did Ghazi, a grim but determined expression on his face.

"*Kuvii* Ghazi, we can't attack," Camellion said patiently, recalling that Courtland Grojean had told him the Afghans would be "difficult to the extreme." "It's five hundred feet down the slope. We'd be spotted by the man with the night sight scope before we were a fifth of the way down."

"There are plenty of cover rocks to the east and the west," Ghazi pointed out morosely, sitting up and putting his AKM across his lap. "There's also ample cover rocks to the north. We can approach from those three directions. Movement will be very slow and it will take us several hours to get into position, but I know we can do it."

"Four AKMs and one MAC-10 against two SGMBs and a pack of Russians with three armored vehicles!" Hooppole's voice was as angry as his face. "I didn't come to these mountains to commit suicide." Having backed away from the two rocks, he rolled over on his left side and sat up.

Ghazi went on forcefully, "Each of us has three fragmentation grenades and three thermate grenades. We have the element of surprise and automatic weapons. We can kill them all in less than two minutes."

The Death Merchant tried his best to sound casual, even friendly. "I'm not saying it's impossible. I am saying that attacking them is not necessary. I'll give you one good reason: once the Soviet high command in Kabul discovers a wiped-out patrol, it will send out any number of ground and sky patrols to comb these mountains. That will turn us into spiders trying to crawl without legs, my friend."

"Damn it! Even if we did snuff all those Russians, we'd have to turn around and head back to the base," Hooppole said urgently. "We wouldn't have a chance to wait and link up with any caravan, much less get into Kabul. Furthermore, where are the rest of the Russians? I counted only ten. But an armored carrier alone holds sixteen plus two crew members!"

Ghazi smiled tolerantly at Camellion. "I was raised in this section of the Kush. I know these mountains the way you are intimately familiar with the area of your childhood. I assure you, the Hind gunships will not find us."

"You heard what Hooppole said." The Death Merchant glared pitchforks at the Afghan. "Once we terminate the Russians—assuming we can and do—the mission would be finished. He has a point, too, about the number of Russians. Ten Russians and three vehicles don't add up. They wouldn't send out a patrol with only ten men."

"It is night," said Ghazi. "The others are probably asleep in the vehicles. It's only good security that not all of them would expose themselves to a possible ambush. You, *kuvii* Camellion, cannot deny that."

The Death Merchant couldn't. "But I can't go along with you. What you propose is far too dangerous."

Mului Jalai Imu, who had also wriggled back from the rocks, spoke rapidly in Pushto and gave a low, snickering laugh, his manner, tone, and chuckle telegraphing an insult directed at Camellion and Hooppole.

In turn, Ghazi rattled off a stream of Pushto at Imu, after which he looked at the tense, angry faces of Camellion and Hooppole and said slyly, "Mului said that in his opinion all infidels from the West are cowards. Could he be right? Is it possible that the two of you are too terrified to attack the animals below us?"

Detecting that Hooppole was about to explode from rage, Camellion reached out and placed a firm hand on the British merc's arm. Camellion knew that he had been very neatly trapped. Either he helped Ghazi or, after they returned to the F.F.A. base, the word would quickly spread that—*Hooppole and I are cowards. The Afghans are nuttier over 'macho' than the refried bean boys south of the border. My effectiveness would be ended. I'd never get to Werholtz and Hemschire. I don't think I ever will anyhow. But that's not the point, not now. . . .*

"Attacking the Russians below is not nearly so dangerous as your proposal to go into Kabul and free those two men from the Central Prison," interjected Ghazi before Camellion could speak. "Therefore, you must be afraid of the patrol. . . ."

Camellion did the unexpected: he smiled without humor.

"And what did you reply to friend Imu?"

"I told him that you and Mr. Hooppole would prove you were not cowards by helping us kill the Russian pigs."

Hooppole's eyes flashed in bitter anger. "You can tell Imu I'll prove my bravery by snapping both his arms at the elbow!"

"Relax, Rod," Camellion said sharply. "As the prophet said, 'When the dogs are sated they make presents to each other of what remains.' " In a softer tone to Ghazi—"We'll help you attack those pig farmers, but we'll do it my way, or we won't do it at all. That's final. . . ."

Ismail Ghazi smiled.

Hooppole didn't argue. He only stared at Camellion, Ghazi and Imu. He had been outvoted and realized it would take four men to do the job. Only three men—should he refuse to go? If the two Afghans and Camellion tried and failed, how would he get back to the base alone? He wouldn't. He couldn't.

"Very well, here is how we'll do it," Camellion began.

The eastern sky was scratched faintly with streaks of dawn by the time the Death Merchant and the three other men were in position and ready to massacre the Russians who were *Raydoviki*—tough, well-trained veterans.

Camellion had worked straight west through the rocks. He had turned and gone northwest, then in a straight line to the southeast, sometimes moving standing up, but mostly he crawled, careful not to let his AKM or MAC-10 clank against any rock. Now he lay only thirty feet north of the BTR-40 armored car, in a position that enabled him to see the front and both sides of the vehicle. He could also see the ends and the north side of the BD-4 command car and the front end and north side of the personnel carrier.

Ismail Ghazi and Mului Imu were in the rocks to the southeast, Rod Hooppole to the southwest, all three hidden in the rocks, only a short distance from the *Raydoviki* who were not exactly in the same positions they had been a few hours ago. Two pig farmers had come out of the rear of the armored carrier and had joined the four who had been working on the engine. All six were drinking coffee from thermos bottles and eating sandwiches.

There was still a man behind each automatic grenade launcher, but the ivan who had been monitoring the NSPT infrared scope had dropped down inside the command car.

Three men were now by the east side of the BTR-40 armored car. The third man had crawled out of the vehicle from the hatch over the driver's compartment and had brought with him a large thermos jug and an ammunition bin of an SGMB machine gun. The bin had been filled with mugs and whatever the four were eating for breakfast.

For a time, extreme apprehension had weighed heavily on the Death Merchant. Always he studied a situation from all sides, weighing the advantages against the disadvantages. This time it was different. Because of Ismail Mohammed Ghazi he had been forced to make an instant evaluation. There was the possibility that the Russians had set up a seismic intruder alarm system and had sensors scattered in the rocks surrounding the plain. Probably not, since a man had been at an infrared scope. If there had been a SIA system Camellion and the other three would have been helpless against it. There hadn't been—*Or we wouldn't have gotten this far*.

Both his AKM and MAC-10 ready—all he had to do was switch off the safety levers—Camellion waited, thinking of the Afghans and their code of *tureh*—bravery—which dominated every waking moment of their lives. Just the same, it was that fanatical *tureh* that had given the Soviet Union its own "Vietnam" in Afghanistan. The Kremlin had thrown in two hundred thousand crack troops and still hadn't conquered the half desert, half mountainous nation that covered a high, landlocked patch of central Asia and was almost the size of Texas. Scattered along fertile valleys between the sands and the snows, most of the fifteen million Afghans farmed and grazed livestock, seared by one hundred twenty degree heat in summer and twenty below zero in winter.

The Soviets controlled the important cities, such as Kabul, the capital, Kandahar, Baghlan, Charikar, and lesser cities. The Russians were firmly entrenched in the major towns and larger villages, but in many of them they found themselves in a situation analogous to the U.S. Cavalry in the Old West, one hundred ten years ago. They held the "fort," but the "indians" had them surrounded. And in hundreds of small villages, especially those in the mountains, there was not a single pig farmer.

The plan of attack was not complicated. It would take the Death Merchant the longest to get into position. Once he was ready, he would signal the other three on his German-made Voglax Y-4 walkie-talkie. The other three would have the volume of their receivers turned very low so that the beep-beep wouldn't carry to the Russians. It was that simple. And at the same time that dangerous.

I get involved with the weirdest of people! He pulled the Voglax from underneath his black cotton robe, wished he had a thick steak—well done, switched on the W-T, and twice pressed the call button. He thought of the armored car only a short distance away. A BTR-40 normally carried a crew of four. Three of the crew were sitting on the ground, leaning against the vehicle and feeding their faces. Did the car have only three crewmen on this particular patrol? If not, where was the fourth Slavic son? Inside the vehicle?

Just as Camellion was pushing off the safety of the MAC-10, the southeast quadrant exploded with gunfire, with the ugly roaring of AKM assault rifles.

The show was on the road! The curtain had just gone up. *But it beats being an oboe player!*

The deadly MAC-10[4] in his hands, Camellion jumped up from the rocks and, with an expert eye and smooth reflexes, swung the muzzle of the Ingram's noise suppressor on the three Russians by the side of the armored car. In that shave of a second, hearing the two AKMs shatter the early morning stillness, the three were in a frozen limbo of surprise, an astonishment from which they would never recover.

The silencer on the Ingram whispered *PHYYYYTTTTTTTTT* and a swarm of 9mm FMJ slugs buzzed into the Russians, killing them so quickly they were stone dead before even God received the news!

No sooner had the third freak fallen on his face than Camellion—the AKM strapped securely to his back—was sprinting toward the armored car, his eyes watching not only the side areas, especially the one to his right, but also the

---

[4]The MAC-10 fires either a 9mm or a .45 round. The MAC-11 uses a .380 cartridge.

turret. He had to make sure of the fourth hog in the barnyard. If there was a fourth crew member.

There was—inside the armored car. Igor Bucheksky, the commander, had been napping. Hearing the gunfire to the southeast and thinking that the patrol was under attack by Afghan partisans, he had only one thought: to get the other three men inside the vehicle and get it moving. What Bucheksky didn't know was that the rest of the crew was dead. He had not heard the silenced MAC-10 to the north and the three crewmen had died so quickly they hadn't uttered a sound.

Accordingly, Bucheksky stepped up on the commander's platform and thrust his head and shoulders through the open hatch of the turret. He spotted Camellion at the same time the Death Merchant saw him, brought up the Ingram and got off a short burst, all of it happening so quickly that Camellion could not even be sure that he had hit Bucheksky. He had. Two projectiles had ripped the Russian in the head as he was dropping down and he was one hundred percent dead by the time his body crashed onto the commander's platform.

Not knowing whether the target was dead or wounded and waiting, the Death Merchant raced to the west side of the vehicle and pulled a V40 fragmentation grenade[5] from a leather pouch beneath his robe. He was too experienced in the ways of staying alive to leap onto the rear of the armored car in order to decrease the range. Not about to expose himself unnecessarily to enemy fire, he put down the MAC-10, pulled the pin, and gently flipped the grenade up and into the open hatch of the turret; he then dropped and wrapped his arms around his turbaned head.

Deep within the car the grenade exploded with a hollow barrel-sounding *berroommmmmm*. Picking up the Ingram, Camellion crawled to the front of the vehicle—which was actually its rear—and looked around the huge wheel, a strange uncomfortable feeling on the back of his neck.

Playing it professional, Rod Hooppole had not fired a single shot. He had had good reason not to. He was lying

---

[5]The smallest grenade of current known manufacture, yet very lethal at close proximity. It produces 400 to 500 fragments with a lethal radius of five meters and a max. effective zone of twenty-five meters.

only twenty-five feet from the BD-4 command vehicle and knew that sooner or later the man—or men?—inside would get the machine into action. The nice part about the setup was that the vehicle had to be pointed east in order for the SGMB machine gun to fire east. That meant that the driver would have to turn the vehicle around since it was pointed west. To do so, he would either have to swing to the north or the south, then turn around and head east. "Which way?" is what worried Hooppole. Should the command car swing north before it turned, it would be out of range of Hooppole, yet still not close enough to Camellion to enable him to fry it with thermate. If the vehicle turned south—fine. The end of the swing would place it only fifteen feet from Hooppole who reasoned that whoever was inside the vehicle must have heard the V40 explode. It followed that the driver wouldn't want to drive close to whomever had thrown the grenade.

Ismail Mohammed Ghazi and Mului Jalai Imu went into action the instant Ghazi heard Camellion's beep-beep on the Voglax walkie-talkie. So excited over the prospect of killing Russians that they were almost shaking with anticipation, both men jumped up from the rocks and started to run forward, Imu reaching for a P-18TH3 thermate canister, Ghazi raking the six Raydoviki in front of the BTR-6 armored personnel carrier with a stream of AKM fire. While they ran, both men screamed curses at the Russians, calling them every obscene name in the Pushto language.

The six pig farmers who had been eating breakfast didn't hear them. The hail of 7.62mm AKM slugs butchered them faster than their minds could register either pain or shouted words. Only one man uttered a short cry as the steel-cored slugs slammed him back to the grass, wet with cool dew.

The six kills were only the beginning for Ghazi and Imu, both of whom ran straight toward the armored troop carrier in which there were two more Russians. Josef Lyalin had been calling Kabul on the radio and Boris Zhegolov had been catnapping on one of the side benches. The roaring of the AKM had alerted Lyalin and awakened Zhegolov, both of whom realized immediately that their six comrades outside were dead and that they soon would be, unless they were very lucky.

Lyalin quickly closed the hatch over the driver's compart-

11

ment, yelling at Zhegolov, "Secure the rear door. We'll use the side ports to fire through. We'll have to do the best we can until help arrives."

"Best" was not good enough for the two Russians. The next thing they knew there was a loud *whooshing* sound and a tiny bit of hell was splashing over Zhegolov and Lyalin. Imu had thrown the first TH3 grenade and it had exploded over the south side of the troop carrier, some of the molten iron jumping through the gun ports and grabbing the two Russians.

Thermate becomes a miniature foundry when ignited, the thermate turning to molten iron which will burn through the toughest armor plate and eat flesh as fast as fire consumes tissue paper.

Only a few drops splashed on Lyalin and Zhegolov. Eating into the flesh of the two Russians, those few drops were enough to turn them into pathetic creatures who could only shriek in agony, flop about like fish out of water, and finally fall to the floor.

Whooshhhhhhhhhh. Mului Imu's second thermate canister exploded on top of the carrier, the dazzling blue-white fire glowing eerily. Within minutes the molten hell would be dripping into the interior of the vehicle.

Ghazi and Imu had not lost track of the three Ruskies behind the automatic grenade launchers. Neither had the Death Merchant or Rod Hooppole. As for the three Russians, they had dropped to the ground in confusion, debating what course of action to take. The owl-faced Bogdan Cherpensky, the man behind the launcher that was closest to the now burning BTR-6 armored personnel carrier, hesitated on firing in the direction of the vehicle. He could not be sure that all the men inside were dead. Worse, he didn't know how many of them had gone with the mine-laying force. Mikhail Uttkin, the G-launcher operator to the northeast, was in the same limbo of indecision. He didn't dare fire and he had more sense than to move.

Aleksandrovich Amosinov was the man at the launcher that was closest to the Death Merchant. He had also heard the hollow explosion from the bowels of the BTR-40 armored car. But what could he do? He knew the crew was dead and he had caught a brief glimpse of a figure darting to the west side of the wrecked vehicle. Was the man still there, waiting, or had he moved west, keeping the car between himself and the open space? To fire off a barrage of grenades this close to the armored car—the vehicle was only fifteen meters away—was entirely too dangerous. A 30mm fragmentation grenade was lethal within a radius of eleven meters, its maximum effective zone eighteen meters.

The engine of the BD-4 armored command vehicle roared into life. Concurrently, the Death Merchant cut loose with the MAC-10 and Mikhail Uttkin, deciding that all the comrades in and around the personnel carrier were dead, began throwing grenades at the burning vehicle and at the rocks beyond.

BERRAAAM! BERRAAAM! BERRAAAM! In rapid succession, ten 30mm grenades exploded with roars that might have cracked the sky.

Ismail Ghazi and Mului Imu, knowing that they had done their job, had turned and darted back to the rocks southeast of the area. However, they were not safe from the *Plamya* launcher which had a range of ninety-two meters.

The first two grenades detonated by the south side of the demolished personnel carrier in which machine gun cartridges were now popping off like a string of large firecrackers. The second, third, and fourth grenades exploded on the north side of the carrier, the concussions making the wreck quiver. The last six grenades exploded in the rocks—two to the south of Ghazi and Imu, four in a line even with the two Afghans, both of whom had pasted themselves to the ground like postage stamps and were praying loudly to Allah to save them.

Allah was either half awake or lazy because he heard only the frantic, silly supplications of Ismail Ghazi who didn't even get scratched. In contrast, Mului Imu was killed outright by the eighth grenade, the hundreds of pieces of shrapnel turning him into bloody Afghanburger, the tremendous concussion tossing him seven feet into the air.

PYYYYTTT-PYYYYTTTTT-PYYYYTTTTTT! The Death Merchant's first stream of 9mm rounds blew up Aleksandrovich Amosinov. Six more slugs terminated Mikhail Uttkin and saved the life of Ismail Ghazi, for if Uttkin had lived, he would have continued to fire his *Plamya* and one of the grenades would surely have found Ghazi.

Bogdan Cherpensky was not a coward; he wasn't a fool either. The Russian who runs away today lives to kill tomorrow—only Cherpensky did not flee fast enough. *PYYYYTTTTTTT!* Two 9mm projectiles popped him in the left buttock, five more in the small of the back, all seven kicking him forward so fast that he tripped over his own feet and fell flat on his face. He didn't get up; he didn't move.

Wondering how many laughing angels could dance on the head of a thermonuclear bomb, the Death Merchant shoved a fresh forty round magazine into the Ingram MAC-10 and looked toward the south. He didn't like what he saw. . . .

The three ivans inside the BD-4 armored command car were enraged over the Death Merchant's having snuffed their three comrades at the *Plamya* grenade launchers and intended to make short work of the lone individual who had created so much destruction. Unaware of Rod Hooppole, Igor Septinn, the driver, turned the command vehicle to the north while Vyatcheskov Katrimorkin opened the hatch in the forward "bump"—just behind the driver—and reached for the SGMB machine gun[6] mounted on the roof. The third ivan, Stefen Bolingu, opened the single gunport in the rear of the vehicle, just on the chance that there might be another terrorist behind the vehicle. It was the biggest mistake of Bolingu's life and his last.

A terrorist was running behind the command vehicle—Rod Hooppole, who was cursing "this goddamn nightgown of a robe" almost entangling his long legs. Only moments earlier, as soon as he saw that the car was going to turn north, he had decided he had to take the chance, chase after the vehicle and whack it out with a thermate grenade before the machine gunner killed Camellion. The canvas sling strap of his AKM assault rifle over his left shoulder, a .45 MatchMaster auto-pistol in his right hand and a P-18TH3 canister in his left hand, Hooppole began closing in on the command car. He was only twenty-three feet behind the vehicle as Stefen Bolingu opened the armor plate across the rear 13" X 7" port and started to look out. By this time it was full dawn and, due to the light from the east shining fully on the opening, Hooppole saw clearly Bolingu's Oriental-like face. In that split second Hooppole knew that if he failed to kill the ivan the man would no doubt chop him to bits with either an AKM or a

[6]*Sydmaki-Gork Mochem Brojovka*—refers to the state factories of the USSR.

machine pistol. Hooppole pulled up short, raised the Match-
Master, snap-aimed and began pulling the trigger. Six times
he fired. Two of the big flat-nosed round .45 slugs missed
the opening, hit the metal and ricocheted. A third round sped
half an inch to the right of Bolingu's head, narrowly missed
Katrimorkin standing on the gunner's platform and hit the
armor plate to the right of Septinn. The fourth and fifth slugs
caught Bolingu in the face, one in the upper lip, the other
below the left eye. The sixth slug missed because the dying
Bolingu was falling back to the floor. Again there was a loud
ricochet from the projectile's striking armor plate.

Having stopped to fire the MatchMaster, Hooppole found
that the armored command vehicle was now almost out of
range. Nonetheless, he threw the thermate canister, hoping
desperately it would explode on top of the vehicle. It didn't.
It missed the rear part of the four-wheeled fortress by less
than 0.9 meters (3 feet), struck the ground and went off two
seconds later, with the result that only a part of the rear of the
car was washed with burning thermate.

Hooppole, feeling miserable over his failure, turned and
started running toward the largest rocks to the southeast. Six
seconds and twenty-nine feet later, he heard the familiar
snarling of AKMs far to the north—at least four or five of the
bloody damned weapons! A bullet cut through the right side of
his flapping robe, narrowly missing his hip. Several more
projectiles zipped through the lower part of the robe on the
left side. Two more cut through the folds of his turban,
jerking it to the right front of his head. His lungs begging for
air, Hooppole reached the rocks, raced around a car-sized
boulder and flopped down, inhaling and exhaling as rapidly
as a bellows.

The Death Merchant didn't have time to wonder what
Hooppole was doing and why he hadn't burned the BD-4
command car when he had had the chance, before it had
begun moving. The instant the vehicle got under way,
Camellion suspected he was in for trouble and that he'd end
up a cold cut if the machine gunner ever got him in his sights.
Camellion dropped, crawled under the wrecked armored car
and scooted back several feet from the front end. Projectiles
from the SGMB on the command car could not reach him.

But suppose one or two of the ivans get out of the car? Mercy mercy, Mother Percy! I'll be up the stinky creek!

Pulling the first TH3 canister from the leather pouch, he saw the telltale blue-white flash behind the car that had turned and realized that Rod had tossed a thermate grenade—and missed. There was only a twenty-inch clearance between the ground and the bottom of the armored car—*Not much room in which to get the canister started, but enough*. The BD-4 was coming straight on and Camellion began considering its speed—*About twenty-five miles per, I'd say*. Another danger was that if he didn't roll the canisters far enough, some of the hot mix would splash back on him. He pulled the second and the third canisters from the pouch, then picked up the first canister and pulled the pin, keeping his right hand down firmly on the curved metal handle.

NOW! With a flipping motion, he half-rolled half-threw the first thermate canister when he estimated the command car was seventy feet away. As fast as he could he pulled the pin from the second TH3 canister and rolled it from underneath the armored car. The third thermate grenade was next— Camellion rolling it like the second one, to his left. At the same time he heard AKMs firing to the north, the sound carrying with preternatural clarity in the mountain air. *Damn that nutty Ismail Ghazi!* Hooppole had been right. There were more pig farmers. But what had they been doing all this time. There were only more rocks, a narrow road, and the ruins of an old fortified *qala*[7] to the north. No time to worry about that now. He looked at the approaching command vehicle.

Igor Septinn saw the first TH3 canister and turned the vehicle sharply to his right in an effort to escape the deadly cylinder. He did—almost. The thermate ignited into a hideously beautiful ball of burning iron that, for only a fraction of a moment, spread with amazing rapidity, some of it splashing on top and against the right side of the vehicle.

Septinn did his desperate best to escape the second canister that had rolled to the right of the BD-4's original course, which had been to the north. Septinn couldn't escape. He was moving too fast. The thermate ignited only eight feet from the front of the vehicle, a lot of the molten iron sloshing on top and against the front of the command car, some going

[7]Castle.

16

through the driver's slot and hitting both Septinn and Katrimorkin whose head and shoulders were protruding through the forward opening in the roof.

Instant excruciating agony, the thermate eating first into the flesh of the two Russians, then right into their facial bones. Screaming, clawing at his face, Igor Septinn fell sideways from the bucket seat in the driver's well while Vyatcheskov Katrimorkin dropped from the gunner's platform onto the metal floor.

The command car, moving east, continued through the burning thermate of the second and the third canisters, its speed decreasing, since Septinn's foot was no longer on the gas pedal.

Camellion crawled hastily from underneath the armored car, leaving from the front of the vehicle so that it would be between him and the ivans approaching from the north. He didn't take the time to look around either side of the car to see how far away the enemy might be. From the sound of the firing, the Ruskies couldn't be more than several hundred feet to the north—and that had been more than a minute ago. Straight as an arrow he ran south, hearing the firing of two AKMs to his right, ahead, to the southeast. The sounds of the shots were very close together, indicating that two men were almost side by side. But only two. Either Hooppole, Imu, or Ghazi had Gone West.

Eventually, close to the jumbled mass of rocks, Camellion felt slugs tearing through his robe and redoubled his effort. Much to his relief he was soon behind the boulders and moving east toward Hooppole and Ghazi.

He found them firing short bursts at the rest of the Russians who were now well within the north section of the area. Three had succeeded in reaching the armored car and were tossing projectiles from its west side. The group from the north-central section was trying to keep the command car that had stopped between them and the rocks to the south. Seven more pig farmers were trying to use the same tactic with the BTR-6 armored personnel carrier.

Ismail Mohammed Ghazi shoved another magazine into his AKM and glanced at the Death Merchant. "Imu is dead," he said offhandedly. "A grenade got him."

"I didn't think he was out for a coffee break," replied Camellion, his voice cold. He had taken the AKM from his shoulder and was switching off the safety. "We have ourselves to worry about." He paused as Hooppole got off a short burst, the slugs killing one Russian and making the other three fall flat. "If the pig farmers ever get to those *Plamyas* we'll have had it in spades," Camellion continued. "Concentrate your fire on those three launchers. Aim for the magazines. Eventually one of our slugs will explode a grenade."

"It had better be soon, mate," Hooppole said tensely. "I've only two magazines left and we might need ammo on the way back to the base."

Camellion didn't reply; it wasn't exactly a morning for talking. He picked his way through the rocks, going west for thirty-five feet, and snuggled down by the side of a rounded boulder. He was in time to see five Ruskies belly-crawling toward the automatic launcher that was east of the BTR-40 armored car. Farther to the east he saw seven Russians—crouched so low they appeared double-humpbacked—running toward the *Plamya* that was farthest to the east, several of the enemy loaded down with enormous bags that bumped against their hips—filled with what?

Camellion aimed with all the precision of a newly married virgin bride reading a marriage manual, lining up the tube sight with the center of the *Plamya* magazine. *It should be a snap. The launcher can't be more than fifteen to sixteen meters east of the armored car. Just a wee bit closer, you sons of Mother Russia . . . another few feet.*

The seconds clicked off. The Death Merchant's finger gently squeezed the trigger, the AKM assault rifle spitting out a dozen 7.62 X 39mm projectiles that cut into the magazine of the automatic launcher and exploded four 30mm Vezkop grenades. The big blast was beautiful, an explosion that tore apart the launcher on its tripod and scattered its parts for hundreds of feet, some of the smoking bits and pieces falling even in the rocks protecting Camellion and the two other men. The sheer concussion killed three of the Russians and knocked the others into unconsciousness.

The Death Merchant didn't have time to congratulate himself—not that he wanted to. He had never wanted to be there in the first place. Ten seconds after he fired, Ismail Ghazi and Rod Hooppole fired, the former at one of the Russians who had a large bag on his hip, the latter at the launcher that was in the northeast sector of the area.

BERRRROOOOUUUUMMMMMMMMM! The blast sounded like a five-hundred pound high explosive bomb going off, the flash of a ball of fire almost thirty feet in diameter, the concussion so violent that it rocked the personnel carrier to the south. Even Camellion and the two others felt the wave of concussion pushing against their faces.

Immediately following the explosion all sorts of wreckage began raining from the sky, bits and pieces of junk. Of the Russians there was not a trace.

Pon my soul! That had to be more than grenades going off!

Other than the blowing of the *siah bad*—the "black wind" still cool in the early morning—there was the thick burning smell of cordite, of burnt TNT, and that particularly sweet, sick odor that is always present when men are torn apart by explosives or mangled to pieces in other ways.

The Death Merchant started to move east through the rocks. Ghazi and Hooppole began moving west. They were all halfmoon smiles when Camellion met them, especially Hooppole, who was carrying in his left hand a small green object which he thrust out toward Camellion.

"This is the reason for the last big bang," Hooppole explained happily. "The explosion blew this all the way over to us. It's a Soviet anti-personnel mine.[8] As you can see, it's only about five inches by maybe three-and-a-half or four. It's made of plastic and non-detectable. Here, see for yourself. Don't worry; there's no fuse in it."

Ismail Ghazi said proudly to Camellion who had accepted the mine and was examining it, "I suspected that it was small mines that the pigs were carrying in those large bags. For that reason, I fired into one of the bags." He added, his voice now bitter, "The logic of the Russians is as flawless as it is deadly. They know that blowing off someone's foot is better than killing them. They know we have few medicines and almost no men of medicine. It requires two to three people to carry a casualty and, within a week, the wounded will probably die from gangrene."

"Pretty deadly," Camellion said and handed the small mine back to Hooppole.

---

[8]Nicknamed "Squashy," this is the Soviet "Dremba" APNDPM mine. Made in green and white for purposes of camouflage, the mine measures 4½" X 2½" and is made of plastic.

"The animals from the north were planting these small mines in and around the ruins of the old *qala*," Ghazi explained. "They are using them all over my nation. The Russians know that we Afghans often hide in *qalas*." A terrible look of hatred dropped over his dark face. "That is one ruin we will avoid when we attack Kabul."

Attack Kabul! The Death Merchant didn't try to conceal his surprise. He knew that the Afghans were daring to the point of recklessness, but he had never believed they were suicidal. Even Hooppole was astonished.

"How can your father's group attack Kabul?" Camellion inquired steadily. "It numbers less than three thousand fighters, and they're scattered all over the Kush. There's only a hundred fifty men at the main base."

"Why Kabul?" asked Hooppole. "The Soviet's puppet government is in Herat."

"We'll have more than five thousand men once Abdullah Saljoonque and Mohammad Malikyar unite their groups with ours," said Ghazi whose full name was Ismail Mohammed zai Ghazi.[9] "We will attack Kabul because the Soviet high command is in Kabul. Herat is the capital in name only. It means nothing. Once Kabul falls the people in Herat will rise and slaughter the Afghan traitors who are licking the Russian boots and sinning against Allah."

Hooppole glanced at the Death Merchant, both thinking the same thing: that to attack Kabul was total insanity. Not only did the Soviets have light and heavy armor in and around Kabul, they had scores of HIND-B and HIND-C helicopter gunships and perhaps twelve thousand troops. The Death Merchant and Hooppole knew two other facts of life: the idea to attack Kabul had not been born in the gray matter of Ismail Ghazi. He was not that large of a thinker. The second fact was that it would be totally useless to try to talk sense to any of the Afghan leaders. all of whom were convinced that Allah would eventually lead them to total victory over the Soviets. Never mind that the only weapons the Afghans had were those they managed to steal from the Russians or the ones the CIA managed to get to them— which, due to certain complexities, was not often.

[9]The Pakhtun are named after an ancestor from their father's line of descent. Their names bear either *khel*, meaning "group," or zai, meaning "son of."

"Hear that sound?" Hooppole cocked his head and was on instant alert.

Camellion and Ghazi both heard the faint *flub-flub-flub-flub*.

"Choppers," said Hooppole. "Coming from Kabul. One of the ivans must have gotten off an SOS. Let's get the hell out of here—fast."

With a final look at the bright morning sky, they started south toward the bigger rocks. Only five minutes away there were small ravines and a mish-mash of caves, ledges, and jumbled pinnacle rocks that would protect them from gunship fired air-to-ground missiles.

Cow patties! Why am I surprised? What can you expect from a people who think the reason for a half moon is that Allah sliced it in half to please the Prophet?[10]

As disgusted as a crackpot gun control advocate at a pro-firearms convention, the Death Merchant had the feeling that Fritz Werholtz and Stewart Hemschire might as well be on another planet. At the present time, the Central Prison in Kabul was—seemingly—that far away—and in another galaxy. . . .

CHAPTER TWO

10.00 hours of the same morning that the Soviet armored patrol was destroyed. The five story office building of the Afghan Textile Company which the Soviet High Command has commandeered for its own use.

Major Andrew Pytyr Sogolov of the KGB and Colonel Gregor Voukelitch of the GRU, the only two men at the large conference table in the third floor meeting room, waited impatiently

---

[10]For the same reason, a crescent appears on Islamic flags.

for Major General Pavel Vasily Mozzhechkov and his staff officers to appear for the usual morning briefing.

Sogolov and Voukelitch had exchanged only the briefest of amenities and then had sat down at the table, each man, because of a mutual dislike, careful to avoid the eyes of the other.

Their enmity was more than professional, because each belonged to a different intelligence service.[1] They despised each other on a personal basis, as different individually as day is from night.

Sixty-two years old, Colonel Voukelitch was of the old school, a rigid, pure military man who firmly believed in morality and in the decent treatment of an enemy. Privately, within his own mind, he considered the Chairman and the members of the Central Committee nothing more than gangsters. His duty lay not toward such *nachal stvo*;[2] he fought only for Mother Russia, for the idea, for the land.

Major Sogolov was cut from a different bolt of cloth. Only thirty-six years of age, he was a ruthless opportunist whose sole ambition was to rise in the KGB, the kind of man who would send his own mother to prison.

A tall, blue-eyed man with a square jaw, Sogolov would like to have caught Voulkelitch doing something adverse to Marxist theory, then report him. He couldn't. *Chort vozmi!*[3] The *sookynsyn*[4] was always correct and proper, never saying or doing anything that could evenly faintly be misconstrued as being anti-Party.

Sogolov suddenly felt uncomfortable, a wee voice telling him that he had better worry about himself, that his own position within the KGB was none too secure. Nor had it been since the attempt on the life of Pope John Paul II had failed. Sogolov, remembering how he had been in Sofia, Bulgaria at the time, recalled with a feeling of extreme discomfort how Moscow Center had ordered him back home, the order coming in not more than ten minutes after the

---

[1]It's the KGB that controls Soviet life. Without the KGB there wouldn't be a Soviet Union. The GRU is strictly Soviet military intelligence; it does operate world-wide.
[2]"The Bosses."
[3]Literally "devil take it." The Russian equivalent of "Damn."
[4]"Son of a bitch."

Vatican had announced to the world that John Paul II would live.

No less than Andropov[5] himself had blamed him for the failure to terminate the Pope.

"Comrade Sogolov, it was your assignment," Andropov had raged. "It was your responsibility. It was you who planned the elimination of that damned religious troublemaker. The failure lies on your head."

"Sir, it was Agca's fault,"[6] Sogolov had protested weakly. "I was told he was a crack shot. He wasn't. And the two men who were supposed to create a diversion, so that Agca could escape, lost their nerve and ran off."

Andropov was not a man to accept excuses. Colonel Sogolov became Major Sogolov and was posted to Khabarovsk, an industrial city close to the northeastern border of China. There he had remained until six months ago.

He didn't consider Kabul a step up the ladder. Over 1,524 meters above sea level, Kabul was made beautiful by the contrast of its rich gardens and fertile fields with the barrenness surrounding it and the backcloth of high mountains on the skyline. Once it had been a walled city close to the Kabul river and protected by mountains, swamps and its magnificient citadel, the Bala Hissar. But that had been a long long time ago.

Now Kabul was essentially a cosmopolitan city and had been thriving and expanding until the arrival of the Soviet Red Army. With its houses and industrial areas stretching into surrounding farmlands and grazing areas, Kabul and countryside had been merging, but no more. No longer did people come to Kabul, the population steady at 800,000.

In many respects, the city was very modern. Since the end of the 1940's the traditional town center had been replaced by new roads, squares, parks, government buildings, hotels and shopping centers, cutting through the remnants of the old town.

[5]Yuri V. Andropov, the former Chairman of the KGB. The KGB made plans to kill the Pope because he had sent a letter to the Central Committee, stating that if the Soviets moved into Poland, he would come to Poland and stand with his people.
[6]Medhet Ali Agca, the Turkish terrorist who tried to kill the Pope.

One could still wander through Kabul and find small shops where tea was available, bakeries where flat wheat loaves were made and sold, butchers, fruit and vegtable sellers, milk and cheese shops, and street hawkers. The traditional bazaars were open streets lined by single-room shops, with *serais* or courtyards behind. At one time there were covered streets, but no longer. The older shops were usually just a single square room open to the street by day and shuttered at night. Yet Kabul had kept its own characteristics from earlier times and earlier purposes. There were still specific living quarters for the different people living in Kabul. The Qizil Bash and the Hazara, both of whom are Shi'a Muslim, live in one area while the Chandawul, the Hindus and the Sikhs live in another; both these areas are on the edge of the city where most activities are dominated by the Tajik, who are Sunni Muslim of the Hanafi sect, the state religion. There were different quarters too for silversmiths, coppersmiths, shoemakers, salt and sugar dealers, and other trades.

Sogolov's face became hard when he thought of the Pakhtun, the most numerous people of all in this dreary country. *Da!* All of them were a *ne kul'turno*[7] people, but the Pakhtun were the worst of all. *Da—printsipial'ny narod!*[8] Ironically, they were not even city dwellers. In Kabul their jobs were connected with their old caravan and transport occupations, so that they dominated lorry transport and mechanical workshops. And they were fierce fighters.

At times a solitary man, Sogolov would have liked to explore the old streets and shops of the city. He didn't dare. Even members of the Soviet forces who ventured out in twos and threes often disappeared. My God! Being stationed in Kabul was like living in a prison. His bitter thoughts were interrupted by the opening of the double doors at the far end of the room. An instant later, General Pavel Vasily Mozzhechkov waddled into the room, accompanied by his six staff officers. Without even saying "Good Morning" to the two intelligence experts, the seven Red Army men pulled out high-backed chairs and sat down at the table, several of the staff officers opening briefcases.

A double-jowled man with a red face, a small mouth with

[7]Uncivilized.
[8]A people with little principle.

thick lips, and brown hair turning gray, General Mozzhechkov was supreme commander of the 6th Shock Army in Afghanistan and was a recognized expert on antipartisan warfare. As usual, he was not bubbling over with good cheer and friendliness. He had good reason to be morose—the old men in the Kremlin were not happy. The entire Soviet force in Afghanistan was bogged down. Stalemate. No end in sight. The rebels continued to resist and more than hold their own. Oh sure, there were the successes. Soviet troops, supported by armor and aircraft, would often secure a village. But for how long could they hold it? A week, two weeks, a month later, the rebels would attack—always with speed and surprise—and retake the village or villages. There was constant sabotage. Trucks blew up. Even tanks and aircraft. Trains were derailed. There were the constant desertions from the regular Afghan army. Now this new mess, the attack on the mine-laying patrol.

"Gentlemen"—General Mozzhechov's little gray eyes swept down the length of the table to Major Sogolov and Colonel Voukelitch—"both of you are aware of how an armed patrol of the 116th Division was ambushed early this morning—and practically on the outskirts of the city!"

"Yes, Comrade General," Voukelitch said in a serious tone. "My office received the news while the attack was still going on. The main radio center contacted my office as soon as it received the call for assistance. Only three men escaped."

"Damn it! I'm not interested in how many men survived!" Mozzhechkov said angrily in a loud, deep voice. "I want to know why that patrol was ambushed."

He turned his shaggy head to Captain Gorkin Lyushbik who, anticipating the question, was taking a sheet of paper from his briefcase.

"Captain, were we not assured by the GRU that they hadn't spotted any rebels in that sector for weeks?" demanded Mozzhechkov.

"That is correct, Comrade General Mozzhechkov," responded Lyushbik, looking at the paper in his hands. "It was Sector 14-L-5D. Headquarters was assured by the GRU that the sector was safe for general operations."

Folding his arms, Mozzhechkov looked steadily at Colonel Gregor Voukelitch. "Well, Comrade, you are the head of the

GRU in Kabul, are you not? Perhaps you can explain why cleared areas are suddenly full of murderous Afghans!"

"Comrade General. My office did give clearance to that sector. But I should like to point out that the clearance was only partial, based on the possibility that the rebels could filter back any time. Apparently that is what happened." Voukelitch, who wasn't impressed with rank, looked right back at General Mozzhechkov. He could tell that Mozzhechkov was not satisfied, yet under the circumstances could not complain. The GRU had done its job.

Major Fedorovich Grohenen cleared his throat for attention and said in a polite voice, "Comrade General, five men from the ranks were murdered last night before 24.00 hours. Three in the Hazara section of the city, one in the Chandawul, and one in the Hindu section. This is the first time one of our people has ever been killed in the Hindu section."

"Surely those men weren't alone?" Mozzhechkov said crossly.

"All five were with groups, sir. Three were shot from a distance. Two were stabbed. No one has been apprehended. I have taken the liberty, sir, of having a hundred Afghans arrested. They will be executed as soon as you sign the order."

Captain Lyushbik said mechanically, "Two of our people were also stabbed last night near the Pul-i-Hesti mosque. The last report I had was that the two men would live. The hooligans who attacked them escaped. Other acts of terrorism against us include"—he looked at the sheet of paper in front of him on the table—"iron filings in the gas tanks of six trucks, the derailment of the supply train from Baghlan, and twenty-six RPG-7 anti-tank rocket launchers and ten cases of 85-millimeter projectiles stolen from the supply depot toward the center of the city."

He changed sheets and looked at the figures on the second piece of paper. "Statistically, Comrade General, acts of terrorism against our liberation forces have risen 9.2 percent in the last four months of the same period last year."

"The Central Committee and the General Staff will love that," declared General Mozzhechkov. "All we've been reporting for months is one disaster after another. He focused his attention on Major Andrew Sogolov. "Well Major, what do you have to say about this mess, or have you forgotten that you and your KGB 'experts' are responsible for security in the city." His voice was one big sneer. "Don't tell me you don't have enough men. You have almost three hundred agents and more than three thousand men of the *Kah Gay Beh's*[9] Armed Forces Directorate,[10] and that's not counting your counterintelligence people. Yet the damned Afghans seem to come and go at will. The next thing you know they'll be 'stealing' one of us!"

Sogolov's face underwent a series of contortions. "I should like to know how the filings were found inside the tanks of the vehicles," he said drily, all the while looking at General Mozzhechkov. "I should also like to know where the sentries were, and what they were doing when the rocket launchers and the cases of missiles were stolen. They were army sentries, Comrade General—your own people, not mine."

A realist, Sogolov didn't entertain any false ideas about General Mozzhechkov or any of his officers. They all hated him. Sogolov couldn't blame them. No one likes to be spied on constantly, and the entire Soviet armed forces was honeycombed with KGB agents whose sole duty was to supply the Party with an ideological appraisal of individual officers as well as a political evaluation of individual units. The slightest hint of ideological deviation in any man, no matter his rank, was enough to bring swift KGB retribution.

For a short moment General Mozzhechkov stared at Sogolov; then he turned his head to Captain Lyushbik. "Comrade, I'm sure you have the answers in your report."

Lyushbik consulted the report on the table. At length he looked at Sogolov. "The filings were discovered when the trucks were checked this morning at 06.00. The army Investigative Committee conducted an inquiry into the sabotage of the vehicles and the theft of the rocket launchers and their projectiles. The sentries never left their posts; they performed their duty. The results of the investigation are inconclusive. There is simply not an explanation how the rebels managed to

[9]KGB: pronounced *Kah Gay Beh* in Russia, where it is known by its initials to Soviet citizens. However, most Russians have never heard of the GRU—*Geh Eh Ru*. The Soviet government denies its existence.

[10]The Armed Forces Directorate oversees the Ministry of Defense, the General Staff, the GRU and the conventional air, naval and ground forces.

gain access to either the trucks or the ordnance. The I.C. people did decide that the sentries were not at fault."

"Does that satisfy you, Sogolov?" taunted General Mozzhechkov, sugar-sweet politeness dripping from each word. "Or would you prefer to question the sentries yourself?"

"*Nyet*, that won't be necessary, Comrade General," replied Sogolov pleasantly, acting as if he hadn't noticed Mozzhechkov's verbal superciliousness. "There is only one way we're ever going to control these sadistic savages, and that's with brute force, by using stern methods."

Lieutenant General Yevgenni Barancheyev, sitting to the left of Mozzhechkov, uttered a laugh. "It seems to me we have been using stern methods. We've executed thousands of them. We're using chemical warfare. You have eighteen hundred men and women in the Central Prison, Comrade Sogolov, and have learned nothing from them. All we know is that Khair Bahauddin Ghazi is the leading rebel leader. So suppose you tell us what you mean by 'stern' measures."

"We destroy their self-confidence, their belief in themselves," Sogolov said fiercely. "The first thing we'll do is hit at their faith in their damned Allah. We'll begin by blowing up their precious Pul-i-Hesti mosque, right here in Kabul. We'll show them once and for all how powerful their 'god' is."

"I doubt if it works," sighed General Mozzhechkov. "The Afghans are religious fanatics of the worst kind. If anything, destroying the Pul-i-Hesti mosque will only intensify their resistance."

"And I'll get some answers from the trash in the Central Prison," snapped Sogolov—"starting today. . . . ."

CHAPTER THREE

Kabul Central Prison. 14.00 hours. Three days after the Soviet armored patrol was ambushed in the foothills of the Hindu Kush.

Three tremendous squares, two of the smaller squares within the largest square—this was Kabul Central Prison. The smaller square, in the center of the complex, contained the administration building, offices, and main control center. The middle square, four stories tall, was the prison; the outer square was the twenty-one foot high stone wall. There was a guard tower at each corner of the outer square and another tower in the center of each wall. Lights in the hundreds of cells burned day and night. Food was little more than slop.

The lights never burned in the torture cells of Unit-K which was in the east wing of the prison. The basement of Unit-K also contained the Special Interrogation Rooms, or torture chambers, and the Behavior Conditioning Cells—cells so tiny that the victims could neither sit, stand, or lie down comfortably. The KGB guards and their turncoat Afghan helpers laughingly called these cells "the dog houses."

Hadji Wakul and Sinah Mugamkurl sat against a wall in a cell that contained twenty-eight prisoners. During the fourteen weeks that the two men had been incarcerated, no one—neither the other prisoners nor the KGB—suspected that Wakul and Mugamkurl were anything but two ignorant and very unlucky Pakhtuns who had been in the same bazaar when a Soviet officer was shot. The two assassins had been found and executed on the spot an hour later, but not before 184 bystanders had been rounded up by the KGB and carted off to Kabul Central Prison. Wakul and Mugamkurl had been among the 184, of whom seventy-two had been released. The other 112 continued to rot in filthy cells. Eventually the KGB would either release them, shoot them, or keep them as slaves for construction work.

To add to the tension and the severe psychological torture of uncertainty, Wakul and Mugamkurl could not even talk to each other, much less to other prisoners. High sensitivity microphones, concealed in the walls and ceiling of each cell, carried the slightest whisper to the Central Control Center and brought instant punishment from the brutal guards—savage beatings and even worse misery. Prisoners' arms would be handcuffed behind their backs; a rope would be tied around the links of the cuffs, and the victims hoisted off the floor by means of ropes suspended from eye-hooks in the ceiling. There they would dangle, often for days, crying piteously for water or for release in death. Burning with cigarettes and kicks in the genitals were common. One sadistic Afghan guard, nicknamed "Mr. Lard-Butt," specialized in pouring battery acid into the ears and noses of his victims. There was no segregation of the sexes, men and women tossed in cells together, there to perform their necessary bodily functions in front of each other. A hundred billion lice fed off the prisoners, and in the "dog cells" prisoners were often attacked by rats the size of cats.

The irony was that the KGB had two of the biggest prizes in all Afghanistan and didn't know it!

In reality, Hadji Wakul was Fritz Rupert Werholtz, a thirty-seven-year-old West German mercenary. Stewart Hemschire, or "Sinah Mugamkurl," was a British merc. Both men were a godsend to the CIA because they spoke perfect Pushto and had had experience in covert operations. Werholtz had been an agent in the West German *Bundesamt für Verfassungsschutz.*[1] Hemschire, a "private contractor," had worked on and off for the CIA.

Both men had been sent into Kabul to obtain vital intelligence estimates. Using special dye supplied by the Company, they had dyed their hair and beards black and had darkened every square inch of their skins. Company men had told them the truth: capture would mean torture and certain death.

[1]Means Federal Office for the Protection of the Constitution— West German counterintelligence.

Accordingly, each man had been fitted with a hollow molar in which was an L-pill. One bite and unconsciousness would be instant; death would be complete in seventy-two seconds.

Werholtz and Hemschire couldn't talk to each other, nor to the other prisoners, at any time. Prisoners were never taken from cells, except for questioning. There were no exercise periods, no showers, no washing of any kind. Meals were served in the cells. Elimination of body wastes were performed in the cells, in buckets that often overflowed, the stench overpowering.

But Werholtz and Hemschire could communicate—by code, by resting their hands on each other's legs and "pressing" out code with a forefinger—as they were doing now. . . .

Something is going on, Werholtz "said." *For the last three days the KGB has been dragging people out of here left and right. I've seen twenty men and six women taken past our cell this afternoon.*

I know, replied Hemschire. *Sooner or later they'll get around to us. You know what that means. And if they discover we're not Afghans . . . I hate to knock myself off with a damned pill. I'd rather go out fighting.*

All we can do is wait, said Werholtz. *We can't depend on the Company to rescue us. They can't even get a man to us, or he would have silenced us forever by now.*

You're right. We wait. We can always kill ourselves as a last resort.

Both men broke off communication in Morse when they saw two guards dragging a naked victim past their cell. The man was unconscious, his body black and blue.

Hell must be like this, thought Werholtz. Constant . . . never ending.

CHAPTER FOUR

Happiness is more often remembered than experienced. At the moment, eating *korma*[1] and *sawad*,[2] all that Richard Camellion felt like remembering were the past twenty-two days that he and Hooppole and Ismail Ghazi had struggled over rugged mountainous terrain. Their destination had been the mountain stronghold of Khair Bahauddin Ghazi and his band of *mujahideen*.[3]

They had arrived, only to find that the mountain base no longer existed. They had found only seven mujahideen waiting for them, with the explanation that *Malik*[4] Khair Bahauddin Ghazi and his force had moved to Bashawal, a town to the south, close to the Pakistan border. The men had been left behind to act as guards and to escort the Death Merchant and the two other men to Bashawal.

It had become apparent at once to Camellion and Hooppole that Ismail Ghazi was not surprised to learn that his father had moved.

"You knew all the time, didn't you?" Hooppole accused the Afghan. "You knew even before we left here weeks ago. Why didn't you tell us?"

"Suppose one of you had been captured by the Russians?" Ghazi said reasonably. "You could not have told them what you didn't know."

Camellion and Hooppole had not been able to argue with such logic.

Seven days after meeting the seven men, the Death Merchant and the others arrived in Bashawal—twenty-four hun-

---

[1] A stew with vegetables.
[2] Bread soaked in chicken broth.
[3] A fierce freedom fighter.
[4] A title that means an Honored Man.

dred souls clustered in wooden and stone buildings on such a jumble of narrow, twisting streets that all of it looked as if it had fallen from the sky. It was 21.00 hundred hours, and the streets were deserted, the night as dark as Satan's heart; yet intuitively the Death Merchant felt hostile eyes appraising him and Hooppole.

The seven *mujahideen*, led by a huge bearded man named Fazal Bhutto, went on their way, disappearing into the deep shadows and leaving only Ismail Mohammed Ghazi with Camellion and Hooppole.

"Follow me, *kuviis*. I will take you to Mr. Kinsey," Ghazi said. "He is in a small dwelling at the north end of the town."

"Damn you, Ismail," laughed Hooppole. "You even knew weeks ago that El would be here. I suppose you guessed he wouldn't return to Peshawar."

"No, I knew nothing about his plans to return to Pakistan," Ismail replied seriously. "Fazal Bhutto told me that Mr. Kinsey was here in Bashawal."

"When will we be able to confer with your father?" asked the Death Merchant, following Ghazi who had turned and was walking rapidly along the cobblestones of the street.

"Where are he and his men?" said Hooppole.

"Tomorrow morning I will take the two of you to his new headquarters," Ghazi said just above a whisper. He didn't say where his father was at the moment and Camellion and Hooppole, suspecting he didn't want to tell them, did not press the issue.

As they hurried along the narrow, dark street, Ismail Ghazi did explain that his father moved to a new location every few months, or even every few weeks, depending on information ". . . supplied by our intelligence network." He said that there was little danger that Bashawal—". . . this out of the way town"—would be attacked by either Soviet copter gunships or paratroopers. The nearest Soviet force was ninety-six klicks to the northwest—"And there isn't much danger those Russian sons of old sows will even venture out of their stronghold, much less come this far."

That same night, as the Death Merchant and Rod Hooppole sat eating *sawad* and *korma* (and drinking some of Kinsey's precious coffee), Elrod Kinsey, the CIA observer and "dirty tricks" expert, confirmed Ismail Mohammed Ghazi's words.

"We are fairly secure in Bashawal," he said. "Soviet forces have failed to suppress the anticommunist revolt and are very much in a defensive position. They seldom venture out of their bases, and when they do, it's always a necessity, such as their attack last month on the Panjsher Valley *mujahideen* who threatened the road back to the Soviet Union."

"Then there is always the danger of an attack, even here," Camellion said, sipping his coffee. "The Afghans must have some sort of warning system—haven't they?"

"They sure have and you'll shudder when I tell you what it is."

Kinsey explained that the "warning system" consisted of strings of one-man observation posts on prominent features and ridgelines, lines as far as five klicks from the town. When helicopters or armored vehicles were sighted, Yusef would yell to Abdul, "Helicopters are coming!" Abdul would holler to Mohammed, Mohammed to Rashid, Rashid to Hassan, etc., etc., etc.

"That makes me feel just great!" said Hooppole with outraged dignity. "Here we sit like three turkeys depending on a bunch of Allah-lovers yelling at each other. Man! That's what I call 'security.' I know: it's the best they can do. The world has to give them a lot of credit. They've brought the forces of one of the world's superpowers to a complete halt."

"The warning system works too," Kinsey said. "Well, it does halfway." Thoughtfully then, after he lit a cigarette, he said that the CIA estimated there were at least seven thousand partisans operating in Afghanistan, but that there were only three main organizations of which Khair Bahauddin Ghazi and his men were the largest and the best organized.

"All three groups operate pretty much the same way," Kinsey said.

First there were urban operations, carried out by three to six members . . . the cutting of phone lines, the placing of explosives, etc. Around the major cities—Kabul, Herat, Kandahar, Baghlan, et al—*mujahideen* from the suburbs would attack the rear of Soviet columns leaving the cities, usually acting on information supplied by informants within the Soviet-controlled Afghan army.

"The Soviets don't trust the Afghan army anymore than they trust the freedom fighters," Kinsey said with satisfaction. He chuckled. "You know what used to happen when the partisans surrounded a Soviet outpost? Afghan puppet troops would wait until the food and ammo ran low, then they'd slit the throats of the Russian advisors and surrender."

A third method used by the guerrillas was to attack modern government apartments specially built for the Soviet invaders, and bridges, power stations and military posts around the cities.

"It seems to me that they Soviets aren't making good use of their helicopters," offered Hooppole. "Their Mil-24s[5] are among the best choppers in the world."

"The HINDS carry a lot of firepower," Camellion said. "I've seen them in action. Another thing is the psychology of the Russian mentality. The Russian will fight like a maniac when his own land is invaded, but he's not worth a tinker's damn outside his own border. Russian patriotism stops at the border. I'm talking about the average pig farmer on the street who has basically a peasant outlook on life. He's too stupid to want anyone else's land."

"The Russian passion for secrecy is another minus for them," Kinsey said. "They're paranoid about any foreign power learning about their equipment. It's that intense secrecy that makes them hesitate about committing choppers in numbers, unless they feel it's to their advantage."

"There have been cases—so I've heard—of the Russians destroying damaged Mil-24s with the crews trapped inside," Camellion said. "The Russians did it to preclude military secrets from behing compromised."

"It's true," confirmed Kinsey. "I don't have to tell you what that does to Soviet morale. According to reports we've been getting, morale among Soviet troops is almost zero." He stared at the flames in the firepit dug in the hard ground that was the floor of the stone hut. "We can be sure that the big shots in Moscow are frantic," he said in amusement. "They know the world is watching and that the West is laughing at how they're bogged down. God, how I love it! The biggest land army in the world and it can't conquer partisans armed with a hodgepodge of weapons, old weapons, such as Lee Enfields. Most of the *mujahideen* equipment is captured Soviet Simonev rifles, AKMs, and what have you, although the Red Chinese are supplying them with Type-56

[5]NATO names: "HIND-A" to "HIND-F."

AK-47s[6] and Egypt is sending small amounts of Egyptian-made copies of the Carl Gustaf SMG."[7]

"I understand that the Chinese would send a hundred times more equipment if the Pakistanis would let them," Camellion offered, watching Kinsey shift the wad of cutplug in his mouth, then spit a stream into a coffee can.

Short, bald, and with a very smooth face, Kinsey looked more like a birdwatcher than a professional career employee of the CIA. When he wasn't smoking, he was chewing tobacco and could spit juice like a grasshopper, with an accuracy that was uncanny. Well educated, an authority on Eastern philosophy, he and the Death Merchant had had some interesting discussions on Hinduism, Zen, Buddhism and the basic differences between the philosophies of Lao Tzu and Kung Fu Tzu.[8] Kinsey had been pleasantly surprised to find that Camellion was very familiar with the *Rig Veda* and the *Bhagavad Gita*,[9] and had admitted that he ". . . never thought that mercenaries were interested in such profound subjects."

"That's another paradox," explained Kinsey. "The Red Chinese want to get back at the Soviets by helping the Afghans. The crack in the glass is that the Pakistanis are afraid of both the Soviets and the Chinese. The Paks don't want to stop all Chinese supplies from coming through their country, but they're not going to let the Chinese have a totally free hand either. They don't dare, or the Soviets could invade Pakistan to stop the shipments."

"No way." Rod Hooppole flipped his cigarette into the firepit. "The way the Soviets are messed up in Afghanistan has taught them a lesson, the same way we learned in Vietnam. They're not about to invade Pakistan. If you think the Af-

[6]A copy of the soviet AK-47.
[7]The Swedish 9mm Model 45.
[8]Known in the West as Confucius.
[9]There are four *Vedas*, the oldest being the *Rig Veda;* they are the highest religious authority for most sections of Hinduism. Part of the *Vedas* are the *Upanishads* that contain the very essence of Hinduism's spiritual message; however, the great masses of people receive the teachings of Hinduism through hundreds of popular tales and myths collected in huge epics. One of these epics is the *Mahabharata*, in which is contained the beautiful poem of the *Bhagavad Gita*.

ghans are hell on wheels, you should see the Paks in action, especially the Pathans!"[10]

Kinsey nodded slowly. "Ah, yes . . . it isn't likely that the Soviets would want to make fools of themselves twice. But who knows? Anyhow, the possibility does exist."

"I can tell you one possibility that is almost nil," the Death Merchant said flatly, "and that's the possibility of our rescuing Fritz Werholtz and Stewart Hemschire. They could be dead by now. Even if they're alive, Kabul Central Prison is enormous. How could we find them?"

"Assuming we could even get to the prison," interjected Hooppole sadly. "Not to mention getting them out, and then leaving the city."

"Gentlemen, I suppose now is as good a time as any to tell you the news." Elrod Kinsey sat up straight and shifted the wad of tobacco to the right side of his mouth. "Khair Ghazi intends to attack Kabul! How does that grab you?"

"We know. Ismail told us," Camellion said, his tone glacial. "We're not going to count on a wild scheme like that to help us get to Werholtz and Hemschire. Let's assume for the moment that Ghazi is serious. It would take four or five months for all the Afghan fighters to organize and get to an assembly point. By then, Hemschire and Werholtz would be dead or have been tortured into telling all they know."

"Wrong, Camellion," Kinsey said quietly. "I don't know it until a week ago; that's when Khair Ghazi told me that the various *mujahideen* have been on the move for the past five months. The attack against Kabul is scheduled to take place in roughly three weeks."

Camellion felt as if he had just sniffed ammonia. He and Hooppole stared at Kinsey, Hooppole's eyes widening with amazement.

Kinsey went on with "Khair Ghazi will tell us about the plan tomorrow. And that reminds me: a few days ago I talked with *Redwing* in New Delhi. As soon as we have the details of Ghazi's plan, we'll contact *Redwing* and the Company will decide where to make the airdrop. *Redwing* said they're going to drop a couple of thousand assault rifles, grenades and a lot of other stuff to Ghazi."

---

[10]The warrior tribe that lives near the Khyber Pass, some in Pakistan, some in Afghanistan.

The Death Merchant slowly shook his head—*This is getting more ridiculous by the minute!*

Hooppole was frankly disbelieving. "You're saying that the Company is going along with Ghazi's nutty plan! I can't feature Grojean and the rest of the 'brains' going along with such a crazy scheme."

Kinsey got up, went over to the coffee can and spit out the tobacco. After wiping his mouth with a handkerchief, he laughed slightly and said, "It's the practical method of joining them if you can't talk them out of it. God Himself couldn't dissuade these Afghans from changing their minds about anything. Look at it this way: if the attack is a success, a lot will be gained and the Russians will have egg on their faces. We might even get to rescue Werholtz and Hemschire. If the attack fails—it probably will—the Russians will still have been dealt a severe blow. Either way, the CIA can't lose!"

"We can!" Hooppole said contemptuously. "We might end up dead in Kabul." He made an angry face. "Of course, the Company couldn't care less. We're expendable. At least Camellion and I are. You're a 'Career' spook. You can stay back here where it's safe."

"Nobody twisted your arm to take this assignment," Kinsey murmured. "You can always pack your bags, back out, and go home."

"Bullshit!" sighed Hooppole.

Camellion scratched the left side of his face. "Personally, I'm a bit curious as to how Khair Ghazi thinks he can attack Kabul and win. These Afghans are headstrong, but they're not stupid. They never throw away men recklessly."

"We'll find out tomorrow morning," Kinsey said. Standing up, he was suddenly all smiles. "By the way, how would you two like to have a nice, hot bath?"

Khair *khel* Bahauddin Ghazi and one hundred and ninety-two of his men had taken up residence in a series of natural caves in the lower hills of the Karakorum range, the underground base four klicks north of Bashawal, close to the *ziarat*—or tomb—of Hadji Mukib Naqaswar, a local saint.

Ismail and two other freedom fighters came right after dawn to the small house where Kinsey was staying. On the way Ismail explained that while the caves had only one

38

entrance on the lower ground, there were numerous openings on top of the hills, these serving as chimneys and, if need be, escape hatches. Ismail said too that there was the ruins of a fortified *qala* on one of the hills.

Drawing close to the area, Camellion could see that the *qala* consisted of a tall stone tower surrounded by a round stone wall, the immense size of the ancient fortification indicated by the wall that was several feet taller than some of the ten-foot pine trees nearby. Resembling a Scottish broch,[11] the *qala* had not been used for ninety years.

Within several hours after leaving the house where Kinsey had been staying, they were in the largest cavern that was lighted by sheep's-fat lamps and facing Khair Bahauddin Ghazi who was sitting on a thick carpet. On either side of him were Sebghauullah Mahlik and Torak Adjar, his two lieutenants. All three stood, Khair Ghazi putting out his right hand and smiling.

"*Kuvii* Camellion. *Lesta sha* ("How are you?")?" the Afghan chief said.

Shaking hands with Khair Ghazi, the Death Merchant returned the greeting, adding, "*Kor yenji, Kaa unji,*" which meant "Where are you going? What are you doing?" Camellion was not prying; these inquiries were part of the normal greeting ceremony.

Adjar and Mahlik used the very formal "*Staray ma-shi*" ("May you be not tired") greeting, Mahlik also saying that they were just in time for *iftar*—literally "breakfast."

Men and women were not idle in the underground stronghold. Shy women in black dresses—some with eyes outlined in red mascara—hurried by, lugging baskets of firewood. Camellion was surprised by the light complexions of many of the men and women, some of whom even had blond hair and blue eyes. He noticed too that none of the women were wearing the *chaudry*, or outdoor veil, so common in Muslim countries.

As the lights from the flames of the sheep's-fat lamps cast shadows over the rock walls and ceiling, the Death Merchant felt that he was on a time trip—any period during the past 2,500 years. The shadowed gaunt faces of the turbaned Afghans, many of whom had the lower part of their faces

[11] A dry-stone construction, without any kind of mortar in the joints. Used about 500 BC.

covered with a dark scarf, could have been part of the Afghan forces that had resisted Alexander the Great's invading army in 327 B.C., or the conquering Mongol hordes of Genghis Khan in the twelfth century, or the armies of Timerlane in the fourteenth century, or the British in the nineteenth century. Only the modern weapons, including several captured Soviet 12.7 M-38/46 DShK Degtyarev HMGS, indicated this was the Thermonuclear Century of Mass Destruction.

During the breakfast of *qaymaq* and *kabili*—clotted cream over mutton heaped with rice, carrots and raisins—Khair Ghazi congratulated Camellion and Hooppole on helping his son Ismail destroy the Soviet mine-laying patrol.

"Allah was kind in sending the two of you to us," Khair Ghazi said. "Ismail told us how both of you fought bravely against the Russian tyrants. This is good."

"Oh, *kuvii* Hooppole and I are just a collection of mirrors reflecting what everyone expects of us," Camellion said diplomatically. He reasoned that Ismail had told his father the entire story, including how Camellion and Hooppole had wanted to ignore the Soviet patrol in preference for the recon of Kabul. Accordingly, Camellion added, "We had wanted to complete the mission and go to Kabul. However, Ismail insisted that we attack the Soviets. He and Mului Jalai Imu would have attacked the patrol by themselves if we had not helped them."

"Our honor as men demanded that we help Ismail and Mului," Rod Hooppole said solemnly. "We know you are very proud of your son."

Busy stuffing rice and mutton into his mouth, Khair Ghazi nodded vigorously, the Death Merchant detecting that the Afghan chief was very pleased, not only with Ismail—*But with me and Rod. We've proved ourselves. The Afghans now know we're not cowards.*

Secure in the knowledge that he now had more leverage with Khair Ghazi, the Death Merchant thought of *pakhto,* the strict code of honor that controlled the lives of the Afghans. Bravery in battle was only a part of *pakhto* that all were expected to maintain. Those who did not were ostracized and, in extreme cases, killed.

Pakhto demanded that one retaliate against offense or injustice regardless of cost or consequence. It was *pakhto* that demanded that an Afghan offer "guest friendship," this meaning he must receive, feed and protect by every available means anyone who might come to his house, even an enemy. The guest is temporarily accepting his host's authority and superiority—*just as we are accepting Khair Ghazi's authority and superiority while in his camp.*

While he ate, Camellion studied Khair Bahauddin Ghazi and the rest of the Afghans. In spite of their customs and beliefs that would have been alien and frightening to the average American, in reality there was little difference between any of the national groups and/or "races"—including the ordinary Russian. All that any of them really wanted were the basics: security for the family, a better way of life, peace of mind. It was the various customs of Humanity that created all the gulfs and the barriers, customs from tradition and various beliefs; and the worst offender of all was the difference in religious beliefs. *Try to tell Khair Ghazi that the demands of his precious Allah are unrealistic, against all human nature and murderous—and he'll try to kill you! The Jews will bow only to God, and sincerely and honestly believe they are "His Chosen!" And an American Fundamentalist will insist that the world was "created in six days." A difficult job, too. God had to "rest" on the seventh day! Ah, but when the Pope speaks, he speaks for God! The Hindus worry about moksha, or liberation, from "karma."[12] And the Buddhists believe that "trishna"[13] is the cause of all human misery. A man could think about it and start talking to himself and walking into walls for the rest of his life! All these religions have never learned that the "secret of life" is life itself. The "secret" of death? There isn't any. It is only a change of consciousness . . . a slip-over from the "here" to the "there."*

The Death Merchant waited until breakfast was over and everyone on the rug was sipping coffee, sweetened with peppermint, before bringing up the subject of Khair Ghazi's full-scale offensive against the Soviet forces in Kabul.

The Death Merchant used Khair Ghazi's full name and title in beginning the probe. "*Malik* Khair *khel* Bahauddin Ghazi, *kuvii* Kinsey has told me of your intention to organize the

---

[12]This is the very essence of Hinduism.
[13]The clinging or grasping of life based on a wrong point of view which is called *avidya*, or ignorance.

three largest groups of *mujahideen* and attack the enemy in Kabul,'' Camellion said in any easy manner.

Khair Ghazi put his tin cup down on the rug and looked at Camellion.

"That is true. We would have informed you and Mr. Hooppole sooner if you had not undertaken to go to Kabul. To have possessed that information would have been too dangerous for you. Every man has his pain level and should the Russians have captured you and Mr. Hooppole, both of you would have been made to confess. I am sure you understand, and you also, *kuvii* Hooppole.''

Hooppole readily agreed, nodding slowly.

"It will be a shock and a deadly new surprise to the Soviets when you attack Kabul,'' Camellion said enthusiastically. ''I doubt if the Soviet high command has ever anticipated such an eventuality.''

"There is nothing that is new except what has been forgotten,'' Khair Ghazi said slowly, as if turning many things over in his mind.

"I told him the plan was suicide,'' a man said, speaking to the Death Merchant. ''We don't have the firepower!''

The man who had spoken was not an Afghan. Tall, muscular, with a short beard and hair so long it was tired in back in a pony tail, the man, in his middle thirties, wore Chino military pants. West German *Fallschirmspringerstiefel* paratrooper boots, and a black turtleneck sweater on which was printed in white letters and in English: *KILL FOR PEACE. WAR FOREVER.* Between the *KILL FOR PEACE* and the *WAR FOREVER* was a grinning white skull. On each side of the skull was a thunderbolt, the ends pointed inward toward the lower jaw of the skull. Above the skull was what appeared to be an inverted ''U,'' a small curl on both ends—the Greek letter, Omega.

Jugen Werner Wesslin was a member of Colonel ''Mad Mike'' Quinlan's *Thunderbolt Unit Omega* army, the deadliest bunch of merc killers in the world, a member in the sense that he would respond to a call anytime Mad Mike needed him.

A West German, Wesslin was a good friend of Fritz Werholtz and, at present, was in Afghanistan as a military adviser to Khair Ghazi, his four thousand dollar a month fee paid by the CIA.

42

A pair of Smith & Wesson .41 mag M-57 revolvers were buckled around his waist. A Walther P-38 autopistol was in a left shoulder holster.

Short on protocol but long on resoluteness, Wesslin was determined to make his point. "We can't fight Soviet armor with only automatic rifles, grenade launchers and shoulder-fired missiles," he insisted, speaking with a faint accent. "I tell you, Khair Ghazi, the plan will fail. Half your force will be slaughtered."

Ismail Mohammed Ghazi, sitting next to Torak Adjar, who in turn was next to Camellion, leaned forward, looked past the Death Merchant and glared at Wesslin. "One can never succeed at the smallest of tasks if he thinks only of failure," he said sternly. "My father has planned the offensively most carefully. You have admitted that portions of the plan are good. Yet you would have us continue to run from the Russian wolves like frightened puppies."

"I'm trying to keep all of you from being slaughtered!" Wesslin's voice was brusque. "I keep telling you that the Soviets are already well entrenched in Kabul. They have the advantage. By holding key positions, they can force us into killing zones. Once that would happen—*kaput!* It would all be over for us. Not only do we do *not* have weapons for such a massive assault, if the Russians managed to outflank us and come at us from the rear, they'd butcher us. *Ja*—it would be a 'Stalingrad' in this part of the world."

Camellion put down his cup and turned to Wesslin. "I'd appreciate knowing what part of the plan you consider tactically worthy of consideration."

Wesslin shook his head in disgust. "If you think we can construct some kind of logical plan from the good features, forget it. The bad far outweighs the good."

"I'd still like to know!" demanded Camellion, showing his annoyance.

"*Gott!* Another optimist!" snapped Wesslin, scowling at the Death Merchant. "If you were out driving your car and had a flat, you'd probably get out and congratulate yourself because the other three tires were still up! That kind of rose-colored Pollyannaism does not win battles. The only thing in favor of the Afghans is that they have an intimate knowledge of the terrain in and around Kabul, plus assistance from the people in Kabul, and morale. But have you seen morale stop a round from a Soviet 122mm D-30 artillery piece?''

Seeing that Ismail Ghazi was about to lose his temper, his father silenced him with his eyes, then said pleasantly enough to Camellion, ''*Mujahideen* hold all of the Kabul valley and its suburbs between three o'clock in the afternoon and the end of curfew at seven o'clock in the morning. The exception is the center of the city. In Chewakee alone, seven hundred fighters are already in position and waiting. Chewakee is a suburb of Kabul; it is less than five kilometers from the center of Kabul. Another thing in our favor is—''

Listening to Khair Bahauddin Ghazi, the Death Merchant again thought of why Fritz Werholtz and Stewart Hemschire were so important to the CIA and why the Company wanted the West German and the British mercs either rescued or silenced forever. Posing as photographers, the two ''private contractors'' were working in Afghanistan for the Company and had extensive knowledge of CIA operations in the country. Worst, they both knew the name of a highly-placed Soviet officer in the Afghan occupation force who was selling information to the CIA, in the hopes that eventually he could defect and be taken to the United States. The only thing that Werholtz and Hemschire didn't know was the chain of contact by means of which the Soviet officer was sending the information to Company agents in Pakistan.

Should the Russians ever learn of the two prizes they had and forced Werholtz and Hemschire to talk, the entire CIA network in Afghanistan would collapse.

''—that Soviet helicopters never fly at night. When they do, the area is always brightly lighted by flares.'' Khair Ghazi smiled, showing very white and even teeth for a man approaching sixty-seven summers. ''They are afraid of their own DShK heavy machine guns we have captured and are using against them.''

Maintaining an agreeable expression, the Death Merchant surveyed Khair Ghazi, a lot of speculation running around in his mind. The Afghan leader's face was a network of wrinkles above a hawklike nose and a short black beard. Dressed in an old brown suit, a faded white shirt and Soviet officer's boots, he was bareheaded and using one half of his broken spectacles as a monocle. Around his waist was strapped a webbed Soviet cartridge belt and a holster filled with a Colt

.45 auto-pistol. Stuck in his waistband was an AKM bayonet, the red handle and the red scabbard standing out starkly against the white shirt. Before the invasion, he had been a camel breeder.

"*Kuvii* Kinsey no doubt has told you that the *mujahideen* have been moving into positions for the past five months," Khair Ghazi said heartily to the Death Merchant. "You are wondering how it was made possible—is that not so?"

"Not really." Camellion noticed slight surprise in Ghazi's eyes. "It's well known that the Soviets control only the major cities and don't even venture out of them at night except when they feel it is safe, which is seldom. I should think that by moving at night and remaining in hiding during the day, thousands of men, in four or five months, could move to positions close to Kabul."

Elrod Kinsey said, "I suppose that during the day they hid in villages and small towns along the routes?"

"No, never in villages," replied Khair Ghazi. "Should the Soviets surround a village and start a house to house search, there would be no escape. Only the hills and mountains were used in the slow migration."

"Our religion would not permit the freedom fighters to hide in villages and towns," intoned Sebghatullah Mahlik rather sullenly. A heavily-bearded man with a long face, he was suspicious of all Westerners. Before the invasion, he had owned and operated a small clothing store in Barak, a suburb of Herat. "Allah would not smile on us if we endangered innocent people in the villages . . . women and children, the sick and the handicapped."

The Death Merchant interrupted, saying with a weary patience, "I am curious about how all the groups maintain communication, *Malik* Khair Ghazi. Radios are in very short supply and the last three hundred walkie-talkies and spare batteries that were air-dropped couldn't do the job."

Khair Ghazi, his son Ismail, and Mahlik and Adjar smiled cagily, making Camellion and the other three Westerners feel uncomfortable, as through the Afghans considered them fools.

"*Kuvii* Camellion," said Torak Adjar, "you are suffering from the disease that affects a lot of people from the West, the disease of luxury and convenience. To communicate over long distances you are used to short wave radios and other modern conveniences. We would use them too if we had

45

them. As it is, we use runners and carrier pigeons. Granted, such methods are slow, yet equally as effective as the best transceivers."

Human runners and carrier pigeons! To coordinate an attack against Russian armor in Kabul! So incredibly fantastic it might even work. But . . . there isn't any way they can win.

Camellion didn't put his thoughts into words. He was getting ready ro ask Elrod Kinsey about the forthcoming air drop when Khair Ghazi said, "Speaking of walkie-talkies. We have put twenty of them into special use. We are using them in our warning system. As you know, each device has a range of eight kilometers or five of your American miles. We have five men stationed on high ground in a line that extends from here, northwest, for thirty-four kilometers. Another five sky and ground watchers are in a line stretching to the southwest. Should the Soviets come from either direction the men would use their walkie-talkies to relay a warning to us.

The Death Merchant glanced at Elrod Kinsey, a slight smile on his lips—*No more of Ahmed yelling to Hasmid and Hasmid to Yousef and Yousef to Mohammed and Mohammed to. . . .*

Rod Hooppole said in a serious tone, "Khair Ghazi, you have said that the *mujahideen* are in position around Kabul. Surely those thousands of men could not have surrounded the city without the Russians suspecting what is going on, even if the fighters are in the mountains!"

"My words exactly!" Jugen Wesslin said bleakly, his voice icy. "Already the Soviets have had to decide that an attack is imminent. Soviet choppers don't fly at night, but their recon planes do, at heights of fifteen thousand feet, where they're safe. Their high resolution cameras, using infrared film, can always get a full story of ground activity. They have had to have spotted many of the *mujahideen* on the move at night. I tell you, Khair Ghazi, they will be expecting us and waiting with any number of traps."

"That's logical," Elrod Kinsey said slowly, rubbing his left cheek with his right hand. "The latest intelligence reports indicate a slowing of ground traffic both in and out of Kabul; however, air traffic has increased. AN-22's have been flying in all sorts of material."

Wesslin stared hard at Khair Ghazi who didn't seem at all

concerned by the West German's dire warning of disaster. "And don't even think of attacking the Soviet airbase. It's surrounded by light and heavy Russian armor, including T-64 tanks and M-1973 153mm self-propelled guns!"

"There is a time for everything; there is even a time for the times to come together." Khair Ghazi sounded annoyed and impatient. "The Soviet airbase will be attacked by three thousand men. The other four thousand will attack from the south, the north, and the west."

The Death Merchant and the other men from the West were stunned—*Seven thousand men! Pon my soul! Henry Ford was right!*

Torak Adjar continued with an explanation of objectives. "The columns from the south and the north will head for the Soviet headquarters complex near Fazwah Square. The goal of the column from the west will be the Central Prison." He smiled first at Camellion, then at Rod Hooppole. "With the help of Allah you will be able to rescue your two good *kuviis.*"

"If they're still alive," Camellion said drily.

"I will be in charge of the column from the west," Ismail Ghazi said proudly, a grandiose ring to his voice. "We will rescue your German and your English friend. I give you my word."

"The two men are still alive—as of five days ago," Khair Bahauddin Ghazi said positively. "They were questioned briefly by the KGB who believed their story that they were merely innocent bystanders to the shooting of Captain Vadim Norsenkin. The Soviets have put them to work with other prisoners, building fortifications around the city. Every night they are returned to the Central Prison."

"It's madness!" Jugen Wesslin said hoarsely, his eyes boring into Khair Ghazi. "Half those men will be slaughtered and you know it."

Even the Death Merchant was surprised by Khair Ghazi's reply:

"More likely than not," he promptly admitted. "We estimate that eighty percent of the force will be killed in the assault; and every single man knows that there is small likelihood of his surviving the attack."

Calmly he surveyed the shocked faces of the Westerners. "Yes, I know. You are thinking that we Afghans are barbarians, that we do not love life, that we are willing to make cannon fodder of our young men.''

No one answered, except the Death Merchant. ''Speaking for myself, *Malik* Khair Ghazi, I think that while your moral efforts are honest and worthy in the eyes of Allah, none of you have sufficient training in military matters to make a realistic judgment and evaluation of the situation. I believe you will come very close to conquering Kabul. But I think that in the end you will lose, that you'll be beaten back. In my opinion, those men will have died in vain.''

''No, *kuvii* Camellion! There will be victory in their deaths!'' Torak Adjar said vehemently, his little black eyes flashing at the Death Merchant. A heavyset man in his middle forties, he was dressed in baggy Afghan pants, baggy Afghan shirt and wearing a blue turban. Before the time of the troubles, he had been a *powindah*—a sheep herder—and a member of the *Jirga* in his village—village council. ''We discussed the situation with Zia Khan Nusisnary, of the Afghanistan Islamic Nationalist Revolutionary Council. He agreed with us and with *Malik* Abdullah Saljoonque and *Malik* Mohammad Malikyar; they agreed that five or six thousand dead is a small price to pay if those deaths succeed in getting us the attention of the world and making known to humanity what the Soviet Union has done and is doing to this nation!''

Thinking that deliberately sending five thousand men to their deaths was a peculiar and brutal way to get publicity, Camellion said candidly, ''I should think the world press would be interested in Soviet sadism in this part of the world. However, I must confess I haven't seen much in American newspapers and magazines.''

''The American media has given us little space,'' replied Khair Ghazi. ''*The New York Times* has only scratched the surface; this is true also of *The Christian Science Monitor, The Washington Post* and *The Los Angeles Times*. None of their reporters have been to the front.''

''Have you presented your plea to the United Nations?'' said Rod Hooppole.

''The U.N. did not even have the courtesy to respond!'' Sebghatullah Mahlik snorted angrily. ''The United Nations is the Mecca of hypocrisy. And the same can be said for the American State Department.''

Elrod Kinsey, shifting uncomfortably on the rug, spoke for

the benefit of Camellion and Hooppole as much as he was speaking to the Afghans: "I've explained that it's the policy of the United States not to become involved. The United States can't risk World War III. It's the same with Pakistan. That nation had cordial relations with the Soviet Union and doesn't want to risk war, and the Paks are Muslims, the same as you. You yourself, *Malik* Khair Ghazi, have said that you would not want to embarrass the Paks because there are four hundred thousand Afghans in Pakistan. I should also like to point out—"

"A wise man does not depend on the United States for anything!" interrupted Torak Adjar. "It is that way with all infidels!"

"That's not true, *kuvii* Adjar!" snapped Kinsey, showing a resistance, a backbone of iron, the Death Merchant didn't think he had. "All the revolutionary groups have been supplied by my government. Think of all the air drops the CIA has made." His voice rose in anger. "Who in hell do you think is going to drop two thousand assault rifles and grenades and anti-tank missiles? The CIA that's who!"

"*Kuvii* Kinsey," began Khair Ghazi apologetically.

"I'm not finished! Since you have criticized the United States, *kuvii* Adjar, suppose you explain why your own Muslim brothers have not helped you, with the exception of the Egyptians and, to a certain extent, the Pakistanis. Where are the Saudis and the United Arab Emirates with all their billions from oil? Not one weapon have they sent. Not a single damned bullet! Not one grenade!"

"We did seek help from the U.A.E., in March of 1982," Adjar said heavily. "They promised to help. They did not. We later found out that they didn't because the Saudis wouldn't move. The Saudis refused because they didn't have any assurance from the United States. We were told that the decision not to help came from the White House."

"That is true, *kuvii* Kinsey," Sebghatullah Mahlike said gruffly. "Your President doesn't realize that the Soviet Union's invasion of our country is a major international disaster which in the long run will adversely affect the United States. The U.S. is failing to keep the Russians from the Persian Gulf, the Indian Ocean, the oil of the Middle East and the population of India."

"Well now, it certainly wasn't the U.S. President that

49

prevented Iran and Jordan from helping you! They haven't sent any aid," remarked Kinsey, biting off each word. "I happen to know that the Iranians wouldn't even discuss the matter. All you got from the Jordanians was the run around."

"*Malik* Khair Ghazi," Camellion said loudly, "you mentioned that Hemschire and Werholtz are still alive. The only way you could have that information is by having an informer who is highly placed in the Soviet camp. Is that not so?"

"The name of the agent must remain a secret," Ghazi said softly, a look of respect and admiration in his eyes. A clever man, he sensed that Camellion had deliberately changed the subject to avoid a violent argument between Kinsey, Mahlik and Adjar. He was grateful. If the men had been in his own house, he could have demanded that Mahlik and Adjar apologize to Kinsey. But the camp was shared by all. Adjar and Mahlik had equal status in regard to "guest friendship."

Khair Ghazi was more than aggravated when Jugen Werner Wesslin jumped verbally all over the Death Merchant, saying sharply:

"Camellion, what did you mean when you said the attack would succeed but that it would fail in the end. I demand an explanation."

You demand! Watch it, kraut!

"Those who demand are not apt to get what they want," Camellion said politely. "In your case I'll make an exception to save time. I must also correct your contradiction in terms. If the attack succeeded that would be it; it couldn't fail. What I said was that the *mujahideen* would almost win; then they would be beaten back. I also said that thousands of men—in my opinion—would die in vain."

"*Damen! Mein Gott! Damen!* I was told you were an expert in strategy. How can you make such absurd statements?"

"Let me tell you about a man named Henry Ford. He had—"

"Who is this Henry Ford?" asked Khair Ghazi.

"Henry Ford was the American who first mass-produced the automobile," explained the Death Merchant. "In mass-producing the Ford car, it was necessary to have window glass cut rapidly, the way you make cookies with a cutter. Ford went to the glass cutters. 'It can't be done,' these experts told Ford. 'Impossible. Forget it.' Henry decided to go to people who didn't know anything about the cutting of

50

glass, people who weren't aware of all the technical impossibilities and, therefore, wouldn't let them get in the way of solving the problem. Well, these amateurs finally figured out a way to mass-cut glass.''

Hooppole, perplexed, scratched the side of his head behind his left ear. ''I say, what does that little success story have to do with the attack on Kabul?''

''*Ja,* what does that have to do with it?'' repeated Wesslin.

''The Afghans don't have all the technical rules of military warfare telling them it can't be done. They're willing to sacrifice thousands of men to gain their objective. On that basis, they'll probably come close to gaining that objective. But like I said''—he looked straight at Khair Ghazi—''the attack will fail. They will not conquer the Russians in Kabul.''

''I won't be there to find out!'' sneered Wesslin. ''I'm not about to commit sucide. I'm also reporting to Redwing what I consider to be stupid action on your part.''

''Gee golly gosh!'' Camellion gave a snickering little laugh. ''Be my guest. Report any damn thing you want. While you're at it, you can also report your main talent: that you think you know it all but keep proving that you don't.''

His rage making him momentarily speechless, Wesslin stared at the Death Merchant, a knot of frustration forming in his stomach. Before the West German could reply, an Afghan came out of the shadows, hurried over to Khair Ghazi and said something in their native tongue. At once, Ghazi, his son, and the other Afghans were on their feet, concern on their faces.

The Death Merchant and the other men got to their feet. They knew that something was seriously wrong.

''Our lookouts have sighted a Soviet armored column thirty-two kilometers to the northwest,'' Khair Ghazi said ominously. ''The warning just came in over the walkie-talkies.''

''I trust you have a defense plan?'' sighed Camellion.

''We have. And then some.''

CHAPTER FIVE

Success is, an amazing amount of the time, a positive manipulation of failure. In the case of the Afghans, success involved lessons well-learned from past failures.

For one thing, they had learned that the Russians were not only extremely vicious—the Soviets had slaughtered two hundred fifty thousand Afghans—but also extremely tricky. The freedom fighters had also learned that the Soviets could and would attack anywhere in Afghanistan if the Russians felt the assault was to their advantage. And because the Afghans had learned their lessons well, Khair Bahauddin Ghazi and his men were prepared for the Soviet armor that had been sighted thirty-two klicks to the northwest.

Over a large well drawn map, scaled 1:40,000, Torak Adjar and Ismail Ghazi, the "official" strategists, explained the defense measures to Camellion, Hooppole, and Kinsey. Jugen Wesslin watched, after explaining that it was he who had planned much of the strategy.

"The gunships will come first," Ismail Ghazi said. "They will arrive shortly before the Soviet tanks and the other armor are within range of this sector of the mountains. The helicopters will firebomb the town and use missiles against the larger buildings. They will then use missiles against the top of these hills and drop their fire bombs."

"Can you be positive that the Russians know we're holed up up here?" asked Hooppole, studying the large map and wondering what the scattered red "X's" meant.

"Don't be naive, *Amerikaner!*" admonished Wesslin. "The Soviets have carefully reconnoitered this area from the air. They have seen some of the *mujahideen* in these hills. Believe me, the Soviets know we are here."

"He is right, *kuvii* Hooppole," said Torak Adjar. "If the

Soviets were not positive of our presence, they would not be attacking."

"Well, if they're attacking this far from Kabul, I shudder to think what they are doing to the fighters gathered around Kabul," said Kinsey in a low, sad voice.

"Our problem now is here," Ismail Ghazi said, placing his finger on a section of the map. "In this position we have four Grails.[1] However, we have only five missiles for the weapons."

Although the words on the map were in Pushto, Camellion and the others could see that the hill Ghazi was indicating was only a short distance from the town.

Hooppole swept his left hand over the map. "These red X's. They are northwest of the hills and scattered over a wide area."

"Our main defense against the tanks and other vehicles." Ismail smiled. "Each X indicates a concealed dugout. They are placed in such a manner that the Soviet armor will have to come straight at them; it is the only way the tanks can approach the northwest side of the hills and get within range."

Added Jugen Wesslin: "There's a similar set-up southwest of the town." His voice had lost much of its bitterness. "You see, the Russians know we have some of their weapons. It would be like them to mount a two-pronged attack and have a column from the southwest come in five or six hours from now."

"There are two men in each dugout," Ismail pointed out. "They have anti-tank weapons, one missile for each launcher. They will concentrate on the tanks."

"Would I be wrong in saying that those men constitute a suicide squad?" offered the Death Merchant, admiring the sheer boldness of the Afghans. "They can hardly retreat after they fire their RPGs."

"You would be and are wrong." Ismail gave Camellion a hard look. "We never order a man to deliberately die. There is a tunnel that extends down from each dugout for two meters. Since each dugout is one meter deep, this means that the tunnel is three meters underground, or ten of your feet

[1]The SA-7. A shoulder-fired surface-to-air missile. The range is 11,500 feet. Of Soviet manufacture, "Grail" is similar to the U.S. REDEYE and is a tail pursuit weapon, deadly against low-flying helicopters and subsonic fixed-wing aircraft.

underground. Another tunnel extends for thirty meters from the short tunnel that angles down. The men will be safe in these tunnels. This is a trick we learned from reading about the Vietnam War.''

''Yeah, the gooks were damned good at building tunnels,'' said Hooppole. ''How safe your men will be is another question. Of course, in this hard ground, it isn't likely that the tanks will cave in the tunnels.''

''The Soviets will drop grenades into the dugouts,'' Ismail said, ''but they're not going to bother with tracing tunnels they don't even know exist. They won't have the time; they'll be under fire.''

Torak Adjar grinned at Camellion, Kinsey, and Hooppole.

''These blue circles.'' His finger moved along the crinkled map. ''They are Soviet anti-tank guns concealed in dugouts in the side of a hill. They are thirty meters apart. Blessed be Allah! There are only six shells between the guns. . . . Allah will have to be merciful to us.''

A tall, bearded man, his chest crisscrossed with cartridge belts, walked up and speaking Pushto, said to Ismail, ''The helicopters have been sighted. Word just came in. They are less than ten minutes away.''

The man moved off and Ismail explained what the man had said, adding, ''We'll go to one of the lookout points above. We can always duck back down through an opening before the choppers can fire on us.''

Ismail in the lead, the small group raced several hundred feet to another portion of the huge cavern, rushing past *mujahideen* checking assault rifles and other equipment. Going through an opening so low that one had to stoop over, Ismail led them through another cave, this one much smaller—another hundred feet to a ladder constructed of small logs (six-inch thick oak)—lashed securely together with rawhide ropes, the rungs—each end of each rung in a cutout portion of the ''runners''—much smaller, only three inches in diameter. The forty foot ladder was held in place by ropes extending from both sides and wrapped around various rock projections in the cave.

''Do not worry; it is safe,'' Torak Adjar said and started up the ladder to the opening in the rocky ceiling.

The ladder didn't lead to the top of the small mountain. Beyond the opening was another cave and another ladder. At the top of this sixty-foot ladder was the outside which the men soon reached, the opening surrounded by boulders, some ten feet high, the large rocks covered with long poles over which were tree limbs and other brush.

The roaring of helicopters was very loud.

Once the group was on the mountain top, Ismail Ghazi motioned to another group of rocks a short distance away, to the southeast. "Over there," he said. "From there we can see Bashawal. The swine Russians are about to attack the town."

The Cosmic Lord of Death descended on Bashawal. Eleven MiL-24 (HIND-C type) Soviet helicopters roared in from the southeast at only seven hundred feet, their five-bladed rotors making a thunderous noise that seemed to shake the very mountains. One after another the HIND-Cs fired off their "Spiral" missiles, as well as 57mm rockets, from the pylons on the stubby wings. *Whooosshhhhhhhhh!* Hell exploded in the town, entire sections of Bashawal seeming to explode and turn into masses of flame and smoke. And when the fire and smoke was blown away by the stiff wind there was only rubble, shattered stone and parts of walls standing. The Afghans that had been in the town had not been harmed. They had been warned and had fled to the hills to the south.

Seeing the mass devastation, the men with the Death Merchant felt cold hatred for the Russians. Camellion did not. He was too much of a realist to let emotion interfere with the facts of life. Besides, one never hates a low form of life. To the Death Merchant a Russian was about equal with a *spirochete*, the microorganisms that cause syphilis. A doctor doesn't "hate" *spirochaeta;* he merely kills them because they are a danger to man.

"When will the men with the Grails fire?" whispered Kinsey in a small voice. "I know that the copters are too far away at present."

Ismail Mohammed Ghazi's voice was as cold as ice. "When those Russian killers are finished destroying the town, they'll swing this way. When they pass over our people, at least five of the gunships will be destroyed."

"That is another reason why the Soviets do not like to employ helicopters against us," explained Torak Adjar. "They know they always lose some of their craft."

"We will not see the Grails destroy the HINDs," Ismail Ghazi said offhandedly. "As soon as the Russians start fire-bombing what's left of the town, we'll go below. It will take only minutes for the choppers to swing this way."

By now, three fourths of the town was gone and there were only mounds of stones, fires, and a lot of drifting smoke. Nonetheless, one of the HINDs veered off, swung in low, and again, at only two hundred feet, started a run over the western section of the town. A dark object fell from the underside of the gunship; ten seconds later and another object fell. *Voska* fire-drums, or what the Afghans called "Dragon Fire." Slightly large than a fifty-five gallon oil drum, each *Voska* contained several hundred thermite sticks, each about eight inches long and half an inch in diameter. The detonator, shaped charge, and igniter for the thermite were in the rounded nose of the "Dragon Fire."

The first *Voska* exploded and sent two-hundred-fifty firesticks soaring outward, and since the drum was a hundred feet above the ground when it burst, the sticks were carried almost five hundred feet before they began falling to earth. It was truly a shower of burning death, each glowing stick of thermite burning at almost three thousand degrees.

Altogether the first HIND dropped four *Voskas*. It then roared off, banked, and started toward the northwest hills while the second gunship made its run on the town.

The Death Merchant and the other men did not see the deadly copters. No sooner had the first *Voska* left the HIND than Ismail Ghazi said, "Time to return to the caves." By the time the Russian gunner on the first gunship was sighting in on the summit of the first hill, Ghazi, Camellion, and the other men had scrambled down the first ladder and were below ground, running toward the second opening that led to the second level.

Whhhooooosssshhhhhh! A series of explosions in a four hundred-foot long line, the "Spirals" and the 57mm rockets going off so simultaneously as to be almost indistinguishable in time. Another *whhhooossshhhhhh!* and another line of violent explosions that blew up trees and demolished rocks and boulders, including the covering over the rocks surrounding the opening. Three of the enormous boulders were turned into rocks the size of washtubs, almost half a ton of the blasted debris falling through the opening and breaking a dozen of the wooden rungs of the ladder. However, the Death Merchant and his group were safe. Already they were starting down the second ladder at the end of the cave.

The four *mujahideen* with the shoulder-fired Grails were on the side of the first hill facing the blasted town, in a cleverly concealed dugout only fifty feet from the top of the mountain; and they were worried. Always the Soviets attacked with masses of choppers, usually five or six, two at a minimum. But now, only one had flown over. Only one! *Ya Allah!*[2] Could it be that the Soviets had finally wised up and were adopting a new tactic? Were the HINDs no longer going to attack together, but come over one by one? If the latter, then the task of the four men would be impossible. They would only be able to bring down one chopper before the other gunships located them with sensors and began throwing missiles and rockets at them.

"What do we do?" asked Muammer Geris, looking at Melih Yegen, the leader of the tiny group. "The second helicopter is approaching."

Yegen thought for a moment. "It could be a test. The Russians might be waiting to see if anyone fires at them. We'll let the first five pass over, then see what happens."

"What will we do if they come over one by one?" asked a worried Cihat Esenbel.

"In that case we'll start shooting down the last five, beginning with the first of the five to fly over us," replied Yegen. "We'll get one, maybe two, before the animals from the north kill us."

"May Allah help us," murmured Huseyin Akinci.

The third HIND made its run over the string of mountain-tops which by now looked like a World War I battlefield. Trees were burning; boulders had been turned to rubble; and there were numerous craters. The blue-gray smoke was so thick it looked solid!

There was no fourth gunship! Apparently Melih Yegen had been right: the Soviets had been making a test, for now, while the third gunship that had flown over flew to the northeast to join the first two, the remaining eight HINDs roared toward the hills, all eight strung out in a line, preparing for saturation

[2]"My God!"

fire. The eight Soviet gunships were only three hundred feet above the ground.

The four *mujahideen* in the dugout threw off the covering of branches and fired their Grail missiles when the eight helicopters were directly overhead. The four missiles shot upward, looped, turned, and streaked straight toward the nearest four gunships. At once Cihat Esenbel loaded the last missile into a Grail and Muammer Geris raised the launcher, aimed, and pulled the trigger.

The first four missiles exploded almost concurrently, the tremendous blasts making even the bushes on the ground bow earthward. It was a beautiful sight to the people of Bashawal watching from the safety of the hills to the south. For only a second there were four bright balls of smoke and red/orange fire after which parts and pieces of HIND-Cs rained from the sky, along with parts and pieces of sixteen Soviet corpses, the crews of the four destroyed helicopters.

A fifth HIND became a casualty, due to some of the wreckage from another gunship smashing into its main rotor and the tail rotor. There was a grinding sound as the main rotor went out of sync and began to wobble, all the while spinning slower and slower. The tail rotor had stopped completely. Out of control, with its pilot in a panic, fighting the controls, the gunship dropped like a cannonball, struck the rocks and exploded, the big bang ten times louder than a thunderclap, the wave of concussion moving boulders that weighed a ton. Not only had the fuel of the gunship exploded, but with it its missiles and rockets; and when the smoke was gone there wasn't a trace of the chopper. There was only a ten foot deep, forty foot wide crater—and several tons of rock that had fallen from the ceiling to the floor of the cave below the entrance on the mountaintop.

BBBERRRRUUUUUMMMMMMM! Half a minute after the first four Grail missiles exploded, the fifth missile struck another HIND-C and turned the gunship into many thousands of smoking pieces of debris. The four man crew was ripped apart, parts of their bodies interwoven with twisted metal that fell to the rocks.

The five HINDs that were left didn't bother to finish fire-blasting the remainder of the mountaintops, nor to swing back and attempt to missile-kill the Afghans who had, in only a few minutes, destroyed six of the helicopters. The Russian pilots had flown into a trap and they knew it. How many more traps did the sneaky Afghans have? The Russian pilots didn't want to find out. They roared straight up, banked steeply to the east and soon were gone.

Unable to believe their good luck, Melih Yegen and the three other Afghans hurriedly crawled into a tunnel at the back of the dugout, a tunnel that slanted downward to a tiny cave that connected to another cavern that, in turn, opened to one of the larger spaces on the first level below the surface of the mountain.

Although missiles had come close, they had not destroyed the main surface entrance to the complex of caverns. With caution, the Death Merchant, Khair Bahauddin Ghazi, Ismail Ghazi and six other men went through the opening and looked around, the strong odors of burnt thermite, hot rocks, burnt wood and leaves assailing their nostrils. Many of the pine and chinar trees had been turned into blackened, smoking stumps, and in numerous places the thermite sticks were just burning out.

Khair Ghazi extended the antenna of a Voglax walkie-talkie, to contact observers in the south hills.

"The bastards sure did a good job of 'clearing' this mountaintop," said Elrod Kinsey in a voice that vibrated with resignation.

"You should see what those 'Dragon Fires' do to a village!" Torak Adjar said savagely. "Those Russians are devils; they destroy everything."

Kinsey and the rest of them soon found out what "Dragon Fire" and missiles could do to a town. The observers from the south mountains reported to Khair Ghazi that Bashawal had been destroyed, that not a single building was standing, and that much of the rubble was in flames.

"Let's return to the caves," Khair Ghazi said sadly, putting the walkie-talkie into his coat pocket. "There isn't anything we can do out here." He turned to one of the *mujahideen*. "Ahmed, you have a walkie-talkie. Stay out here and pick up the reports from Kamal and Abdullah."

Sometime earlier, Jugen Werner Wesslin had explained to Camellion, Kinsey and Hooppole the tactics that the Afghans would use against the Russians advancing from the northwest. As the Afghans viewed the situation, the Soviet tanks were not the principal weapon in the Russian arsenal: the *Raydoviki* troops in the armored carrier were. The tanks would use their big bore guns to lob shell after shell on the side and the top of the area. However, they wouldn't be able to shell the mountains once the Soviet troops had advanced and were on the mountains, attacking. The Afghans would remain in the caves and wait. When the Soviet troops were almost to the summits of the mountains, the *mujahideen* would come out of the mountaintop openings and fire on the Russians.

Two observers to the east, at the base of one mountain, would relay by walkie-talkie the positions of the enemy. Ahmed Gubarsi would pick up the messages from Kamal din Buhzid and Abdullah Gomunlq, the two observers, and would relay them to the "front" by means of thirteen men, calling out to each other—another Rashid would call out to Miam, Miam to Fazal, Fazal to Yasir . . . and on down the line. . . .

"We'll have to hurry," Torak Adjar said as the group entered the cavern. "Rocks tumbling through the openings must have damaged many of the ladders. The ladders will have to be repaired."

"There is time," Ismail Ghazi said. "It will be another hour before the Soviets are within range. They never like to fire from a distance. By the time they fire we'll be ready. There are spare rungs for the ladders and ropes in the caves."

The Soviet column moved steadily forward—nine rows of armored steel death. In the first row were four T-64 MBTs,[3] their 125mm smoothbore main guns level with the turrets. Three BRDM-1 armored cars were in the second row. The next six rows were composed of BTR-70 armored personnel carriers, five carriers to a row, fifteen troops to a carrier, although four carriers carried only spare ammo and supplies. In the ninth row were two ACRV-2 command and recon vehicles and two more armored cars.

The Death Merchant, Rod Hooppole and Ismail Ghazi had climbed a ladder, moved through one of the natural openings on the mountaintop and were in a group of rocks where they could watch the advancing Soviet force, the deep blue-gray vehicles appearing apocalyptic in the bright sunshine.

[3]Main Battle Tanks.

The four men were not in any great danger, not at the moment. The chance that the first rounds from the T-64s' guns would fall on them, or even come close, was one in a thousand. Once the tanks lobbed the first few shells at the mountains, the four men would go back down the opening to the second level of the cavern complex. To remain on the first level would be too dangerous; an explosive shell in the right place, especially if it fell into a topside depression, could bring down tons of rock from the ceiling.

"That's a lot of death out there," Kinsey said tightly through clenched teeth. "Those T-64s are good. Did you know a T-64 has an automatic loader for its big gun? That automatic loader lets the Soviets reduce the crew of each T-64 to three. That's rather interesting in an army that's not short of manpower. But it's practical. The reduction of the crew by twenty-five percent saves ninety-five men in every tank regiment."

The Death Merchant was not in any mood to discuss the merits of Soviet tanks. He lowered his binoculars and gave Kinsey a quick glance. "You're sure the short-wave is in a safe place?"

"Of course!" Kinsey sounded insulted. He transferred his gaze to Camellion. "Listen! I do my job and I do it damned well—and if the Ruskies get through it won't make any difference about the radio. We won't need it. . . ."

Major Vsevolod Anatoly Filatorsky, the commander of the column which was part of the 10th Armored Regiment, didn't like riding in an ACRV-2 command car. The low silhouetted vehicle was too cramped, too hot, and the armor too thin. Major Filatorsky enjoyed being stationed in Afghanistan even less. But he couldn't do anything about that either.

This present operation against the Afghan *chernozhopny*[4] irked him even more. In his opinion it was a mistake, a serious miscalculation on the part of General Mozzhechkov and his staff. The operation was against all logical tactics, in the main violating the master principle of *Ne Po Shablonu*.[5]

[4]A vulgarism—in the plural—used by the Russians to insult any person(s) with dark skin. Literally it means "black asses."
[5]A phrase that appears often in Soviet military writing. In English it means not by pattern or not by stereotype.

The force was advancing by pattern. *Da*, the entire battle plan could have been conceived by idiots! The Force-in-Force ratio was nil. In any engagement the *total force* had to include all maneuver units and ground and air support elements that the commander could bring to bear on an enemy, this force relative to the *total force* that an enemy could bring to bear to oppose him. But there wasn't a shred of intelligence regarding the Afghan force waiting in the mountains. The enemy might number two hundred or two thousand! As for weapons, already six good gunships had been destroyed.

Soviet military theoreticians always emphasized a need for the rejection of a breakthrough achieved by massed troops, as well as attacking on multiple axis and carrying the battle deeply into the enemy's rear. More important was the need for rapid concentration and dispersal of combat power on a rapidly changing battlefield.

Every single one of these principles was being violated! Major Filatorsky told himself. The troops were massed in the carriers and would remain bunched up. Massed, they would have to storm up the side of the mountains. Multiple axis? Carry the battle to the rear of these cursed savages? Impossible. Dispersal of combat power? From the carriers to the mountains would be the only dispersal possible.

These terrible flaws had been discussed in depth with General Mozzhechkov who explained in his usual bellicose manner that the fighting in Afghanistan presented a "unique situation" and "demands that we throw away the books on tactics."

The bottom line was basically simple: the only way to smash the rebel trash was to race straight in, open fire with the heavy stuff, then send in the troops.

Lieutenant Sergei Edemvo turned from the radio. "Sir, it's Captain Pobenco. He reports that we're only three kilometers from the lower regions of the mountains. He requests information on when to open fire."

"Tell him I'll call him back as soon as I look over the terrain," said Filatorsky who was pushing himself from the commander's chair. He stepped up onto the platform and started a complete circle scan with the turret periscope. All he saw was desolation piled on desolation . . . the rocky plain, then the mountains to the southeast. A hot blue sky overhead.

Not a single sign of the Afghans! Damn them! Those *chernozhopny* were waiting.

Filatorsky moved back to his chair and motioned to Lieutenant Edemvo. "Give me the phone."

"Comrade Filatorsky, we can achieve accurate fire at even three thousand meters," Captain Krylov offered nervously. "There's no reason why we should get close to those mountains."

"He's right, sir," said Captain Birnovovitch all too quickly. "The closer we get to those mountains, the more danger we risk."

Accepting the telephone of the field radio from Lieutenant Edemvo, Major Filatorsky didn't reply. He didn't blame Captain Krylov and Captain Birnovovitch for being edgy. The Afghans were human devils and, like flying snakes and Jesus Christ lizards[6], could do remarkably well with remarkably little.

Filatorsky spoke into the phone. "Comrade Captain Pobenco, this is Major Filatorsky. Stop your vehicles when you're fifteen hundred meters from the mountains and open fire. A full spread. First the sides of the hills, then the top. The armored cars will accompany the carriers and set up a cover fire while the troops get out and while they charge the lower rocks. Confirm."

"Confirmed, sir. Fifteen hundred meters," replied Captain Pobenco.

Captain Krylov and Captain Birnovovitch exchanged worried glances but wisely held their silence.

"How far away do you think they are at present?" asked Hooppole, staring through his binoculars at the advancing Soviet column.

"I'd say about a mile and a half," murmured the Death Merchant. "Give or take a few inches maybe."

"A mile and a half." Kinsey thought for a moment. "Roughly that's two thousand four hundred and some meters. That's getting close." He pushed back his reversible tweed hat and looked up at the sky. Once you could see past the

---

[6]No disrespect meant here. This is the actual name of a lizard in Central America. It's called the Jesus Christ lizard because it can walk on water—very rapidly for about ten to fifteen feet.

drifting smoke the sky was all azure. There wasn't a single cloud.

What sounded like a half-snarl, half-chuckle came from Ismail Ghazi. "A few hundred meters more and those tanks will get their big surprise for the day. May their crews rot in hell!"

They continued to watch the armor move toward the line of mountains, even the Death Merchant, waiting for the ten Afghans in the five camouflaged positions to fire, feeling the tension. Carefully, methodically, he scanned the entire area through mini Zeiss 8 X 20mm binoculars. All he could see were billions of pebbles and larger rocks—*A seabed maybe, a couple of hundred million years ago, or it could have been created during the last glacial period.*

Search as he might, however, he could not detect anything that even faintly resembled the covering of a dugout.

He and the others didn't have long to wait. Although they expected it, it was still that kind of jumpy surprise when they saw what looked like a small trap door flung open and back, not more than three hundred feet, or 91.44 meters, in front of the two middle tanks. Suddenly another cover—several hundred feet to the left of the first one that had opened—was tossed back. Just as rapidly the four men in the last two dugouts pushed back the frameworks of poles, covered with thick canvas and pebbles, and quickly went about aiming their Soviet-made RPG-7V anti-tank rocket launchers.

A mistake! Camellion could see that the dugouts, spread out in a four hundred foot long line, had been poorly positioned. They should have been on the sides, on each flank. If the dugouts had been placed on the flanks, the Afghans would have been able to shoot off their projectiles without being spotted—*The way they are now, in front of the tanks, is suicide. The pig farmers won't be napping.*

The Soviet observers in the T-64s weren't!

The *mujahideens* had to stand up to aim the RPGs, and it was during those ten seconds that the observers in the commanders' cupolas of the turrets saw the Afghans and opened fire with ShKAS light machine guns.

Two of the Afghans, directly in front of the tanks, were chopped apart with 7.62mm slugs before one man could even aim the launcher.

The Afghan in the first dugout to the right of the one in

which the two men had been killed was very fast. He pulled the trigger of his rocket launcher at the same instant the observer in a T-64 opened fire, a score of 7.62 projectiles blowing him apart a micro-moment after the 85mm projectile shot from the tube. The muzzle velocity of the projectile was 300 m/sec, with the effective range being three hundred meters. In several seconds the projectile found a target and exploded. But not against one of the Soviet tanks. The projectile had missed one of the tanks and, instead, had hit one of the five BRDM-1 armored cars. A big *BANG,* a flash of fire and smoke, and the vehicle was wrecked, its insides blown out. Two of the crew were dead. The last two were dying.

The *mujahideen* in the next dugout to the right didn't consciously fire his launcher. ShKAS steel stopped him, twenty-one hydraulically swaged slugs blowing off his head and chopping open his chest, the TNT shock forcing his finger to jerk against the trigger of the RPG. *Whooosshhh!* The rocket was on its way. *BLAMMMMMMMM!* The rocket exploded against the mantlet[7] of the turret of one of the middle of the line tanks, the crashing sound like a giant clap of thunder. The observer was pulverized, the ShKAS light machine gun torn from its mount and thrown twenty feet into the air. The mechanism of the 125mm cannon was wrecked, including the hydraulic lug-lifts. With a loud, ringing clang, the long barrel of the gun dropped to the top hull of the tank. The T-64 came to a halt, its blasted turret and armor plates, twisted inward like ripped scabs from a gaping sore, smoking.

Another Afghan fired his launcher—he was in one of the dugouts to the left—but it was by reflex, a micron of a moment after machine gun slugs dissolved the upper half of his body, the sudden shock of contact of slugs with flesh forcing his finger against the trigger as the corpse fell backward, the launcher tilted upward. The rocket shot out, upward toward the sky, and was soon out of sight.

Another freedom fighter—in the last square hole in the ground to the left—aimed at an angle at the last tank in line, fired and missed. The rocket streaked right by the big kill-machine, shot between two armored cars, struck the side of a BTR-70 armored personnel carrier and exploded, the blast

[7]In the front of the turret. That part of the turret that moves up and down with the gun.

sending pieces of armor plate and bodies of troops soaring upward.

Only seconds after the Afghan fired, 7.62mm slugs from one of the turret-mounted ShKAS machine guns splattered the Afghan and his partner all over the dugout.

In his command a car a pessimistic Major Vsevolod Filatorsky ordered the column to increase speed and Captain Pobenco to begin firing at once as the tanks moved toward the fifteen hundred meters position. Vaguely, Filatorsky wondered what that son of a bitch Sogolov and *Glav*PUR[8] would try to make of the lost of the tank and the armored car. The KGB was filled with nothing but bastards. All their mothers had four paws and barked.

Far more disappointed than Major Filatorsky, Ismail Mohammed Ghazi cursed, took the binoculars from his eyes and reflexively hunched down when the 125mm gun of a T-64 roared. The shell, streaking through the air, made a noise similar to ashes being shaken in a metal container. Moments later the shell exploded eight hundred feet below and two hundred feet to the left of where the group was standing, the violence of the giant blast making the earth tremble.

"It figures," Rod Hooppole said. "They're using HE stuff."[9]

"They'd hardly use any other kind for this kind of job," the Death Merchant said. "They want to cover a wide area."

"At least this beats being with the 'home division' back in the States," commented Elrod Kinsey. "But come to think of it, we are involved with the local police, aren't we?"

BLAMMMMMMMMMMMM! There was another crashing explosion on the lower ramparts, this blast much closer to the group.

Hooppole and Kinsey shifted nervously, giving Ismail Ghazi darting little glances. Ismail, closing his binocular case, didn't seem to notice the two men, neither of whom wanted to be the first to suggest the group get the hell off the mountain.

---

[8] *Glav*PUR: the Military Political Corps of the Soviet Union. The organization used by the KGB to exercise the Party's direct control of the armed forces.

[9] HE: high explosive. The T-64 also fires armor-piercing, fin stabilized, discarding sabot (APFSDS) and high-explosive antitank (HEAT) rounds.

An amused Richard Camellion said in a matter of fact voice, "Friend Ismail, I suggest we do a vanishing act before a shell does the job for us."

"We go now," Ismail said harshly. "It is now up to the gunners below to destroy those tanks. With the help of Allah they will. . . ."

He turned and hurried toward the rocks concealing the opening to the ladder. Kinsey, Hooppole, and Camellion followed, all three thinking the same thing: the *mujahideen* at the two guns below would be extremely lucky if they weren't blown into nothingness after they fired the first two rounds.

With the help of Allah! Camellion wondered how Ismail would react if—*I told him that many "great" religious holidays were founded on superstition, on astrological time. The Christians call the winter solstice Christmas and the spring equinox Easter. The Jewish religion depends on the spring equinox for Passover and the autumn equinox for New Year holy days. Good ole boy Ismail wouldn't believe any of it any more than he would believe that the exception is Ramadan, the ninth month of the Muslim year. Ramadan is founded on the moon cycle and wanders all around the solar year. . . .*

The two guns concealed in dugouts were Soviet 122mm anti-tank D-30s. The breech of a D-30 was of the vertical, sliding wedge type and was semiautomatic in operation. The D-30 A-T was a fine weapon in other ways, the neat and practical mounting enabling a crew to change targets quickly and accurately, that is, trained crews.

The two dugouts, a hundred feet apart, were in the hillside at almost ground level, dug so deeply that only a foot of the barrels protruded from the tree-covered hillside.

By means of a series of ropes, fastened to a framework of branches, the crews of the D-30s pulled the coverings from the front of the barrels and went to work. They rammed shells into the breeches, aimed and fired. The 122mm shell from the gun farthest to the east fell short. It landed twenty yards in front of the T-64s, exploded, and dug a useless crater in the hard ground. The shell from the second anti-tank gun also missed the tanks—in the opposite direction. It fell among the personnel carriers, the concussion violently rocking four of the vehicles.

The response of the Soviets was predictable. Captain Josef

Pobenco barked orders into the field radio. The gunners responded by redirecting the computers, and the guns of the tanks were brought to bear on the two anti-tank weapons in the hillside dugouts.

The Russian gunners were well-trained. The first 125mm shell exploded only 9.1 meters (30 feet) from the D-30 to the east. Tons of rock and soil were thrown into the air and concussion rocked the anti-tank gun slightly; otherwise it was not harmed. Neither were the four Afghans who were the crew. The explosion in such close proximity had deafened them. Now they couldn't have heard a brass band in a clothes closet.

The second and the third 125mm shells landed even closer to the other anti-tank gun which got off another 122mm round a few moments after the east D-30 fired its shell. Once more the shell from the east D-30 fell short by thirty meters, or one hundred feet, in front of the tanks which had stopped and were facing the mountains. The round from the gun to the south fell much closer to the tanks, but still missed by twenty-one meters.

The Soviet gunners now zeroed in with a vengeance.

BLAMMMMMM! BLAMMMMMM! BLAMMMMMM!

One 125mm shell exploded only seven meters above the dugout of the east tank gun. The explosion sent tons of slate and boulders crashing down on the gun emplacement, the landslide burying almost all of the crew and almost all of the D-30 anti-tank gun. Only one man of the crew was alive and he was dying. His lower body was covered with rocks, his stomach, intestines and legs pulverized. As for the gun, only half of its barrel remained uncovered. But not for long. . . .

WOOOOOOOOO . . . Another 125mm shell screamed through the air.

BLAMMMMMM! The shell burst less than two meters below the gun, the gigantic blast digging out tons of earth and rocks beneath the emplacement. The weapon and its crew of corpses crashed downward and were quickly buried in a man-made grave that would not be opened for centuries: in another time, another civilization. . . .

BLAMMMMMM! BLAMMMMMM! Two 125mm HE shells slammed dead center into the position of the south side anti-tank gun, the double explosions of such raw power that the nine-ton gun was lifted up and tossed ten feet into the air, the long barrel torn loose from the mountings, one horizontal brace leg ripped off. Blobs of flesh and gore and blood, splattered all over the rocks, the only evidence that human beings had once been in the vicinity.

Now that the Soviet force had silenced the pesty *chernozhopny*, the three T-64s concentrated on the mountainsides. The metal monsters carried forty rounds each for the 125mm cannons, the usual mix being 12 APFSFS, 6 HEAT and 22 HE. Not on this trip. Each tank carried 5 APFSFS and 35 HE, the latter of which they now used to bombard the hillside for a length of two hundred meters, one 125mm HE shell after another, the guns firing methodically, each monstrous crash shaking the small mountains—it was only 1,180 feet from the rocky plain to the mountaintop—and often making dust and small rocks fall in the cavern complex.

The Afghan force waited impatiently in the caves on the second level, each man ready, including the Death Merchant, Hooppole and Kinsey. Other than two 9mm 19-shot Steyr GB auto-pistols in leather holsters secured to a canvas individual equipment belt (part of the A.L.I.C.E. system), Camellion carried a Oda-Mar knife[10] and a 9mm Carl Gustav Model-45 SMG. Six spare magazines for the SMG were in a canvas pouch strapped to the belt behind the left side holster. He had three other weapons: two 7.65mm Walther *Polizei Pistole* (PPK),[11] one in each pants pocket, and "Baby," the ice pick with a lead handle. "Baby" rested in a special holster strapped to a harness between his shoulder blades.

Hooppole was armed with two .45 MatchMaster pistols in hip holsters, an M1 carbine bayonet and scabbard, a Soviet AKM assault rifle and spare magazines.

Elrod Kinsey was all prepared to go out on the mountaintop and die with two 9mm Hi-Power Brownings and a 9mm Port Said SMG that was identical to the SMG the Death Merchant carried—identical because the Port Said was the official name of the SMG copied after the Carl Gustav submachine gun.

Camellion looked toward Khair Ghazi who, with his son and Torak Adjar, was talking frantically to a runner who had

---

[10]Made by master knifemakers, Oda Kuzan and Al Mar. The name of the company is *Al Mar Knives*.

[11]The "K" in the Walther PPK stands for *Kriminal*—German, of course.

brought another relay message from Kamal din Buhzid and Abdullah Gomunlq, the two observers at the base of the mountains, far to the east, out of harm's way.

Rod Hooppole dropped his cigarette butt and ground it out with a heel of his leather boot. "It shouldn't be long now," he muttered. He cocked his head to the left when three more 125mm shells exploded topside, the explosions deep, sounding as if they were coming from the bottom of a deep, deep barrel. The rock walls vibrated ever so slightly, and fine dust fell from the ceiling. "Yeah, anytime now. The ivans have been throwing HE stuff at us for fifteen minutes." He peered questioningly at Elrod Kinsey. "El, you ever been in a fire fight before, maybe in 'Nam?"

Kinsey shook his head nervously. "No. I was never in service." He tried to sound casual, but his voice betrayed his deep anxiety.

Jugen Wesslin, his hands resting on the butts of his twin S & W .41 Model 57 mag revolvers, gave Kinsey a sympathetic look.

"You're a fool then if you go out there," he said, a note of finality in his voice.

Surprised by Wesslin's bluntness, Kinsey blinked at the man and waited for the West German merc to amplify his statement.

"You're an adviser," Wesslin said in an unconcerned manner. "Advisers aren't required to fight. Why risk your life if you don't have to? Camellion and Hooppole will tell you the same thing."

"There's no profit in dying," Hooppole said.

"A fire fight is as impersonal as nature," the Death Merchant said. "There aren't any villains in a fire fight, only survivors. You have to be more than an expert at killing. You have to be lucky."

Kinsey reddened. "We're short of men as it is—and no man fights my battles for me."

"It could be your one and only battle, your last battle," Hooppole said tonelessly.

"I'm going," Kinsey said stiffly. "That's all there is to it."

The Death Merchant glanced across the area. "Here comes the 'Lone Ranger' of the *mujahideen*."

"And 'Blackbeard,' " mused Hooppole. "I'd hate to meet that bearded joker in a dark canyon. . . ."

It occurred to Camellion that Ismail Ghazi was built similarly to Hooppole. Both were of medium height and well-muscled without a gram of fat. There the resemblance ended. Thirty-six years old, Hooppole was Ismail's senior by ten years. Hooppole was also a careful thinker and far too experienced to let emotion interfere with logic.

An AKM in his right hand, Ismail, Fazal Bhutto trailing behind him, walked over to the Death Merchant and his group, Ismail's thick mustache dotted with sweat. The Afghan went straight to Wesslin.

"*Kuvii* Wesslin, my father wishes to know why none of the shells have been falling on top of these hills. What are the Russians up to?"

"They aren't up to anything," Wesslin explained without rancor. "They won't start throwing shells at the top until the troops start up the hillsides. The guns will stop firing when the troops are halfway up."

"We won't have much time to get out there after the shelling stops," the Death Merchant said, "and we can assume that half of the entrances will be destroyed. Either we get out there in time or the *Raydoviki* will bottle us up down here."

Ismail stared hard at Wesslin. "You are positive of your words?"

"I'm sure that's what the Russians will do if they have any sense, and they'll spread the shells in a wide pattern," Wesslin said.

"Oh, they pig farmers have plenty of sense in some things," Camellion drawled. "Fact is, they have more common sense in some things than we Americans."

A curious look fell over Kinsey and Hooppole's face.

"You mean the arms race?" offered Kinsey.

"Yes, and in other matters. The Soviets send their people with crazy political ideas to Siberia. We send ours to Washington."

A robed Afghan ran over from Khair Ghazi to the group and spoke rapidly in Pushto to Ismail. The man then moved off and Ismail said, "The observers have reported that the Soviet troops have begun the advance up the hill. I suppose shells will begin falling at any moment?"

71

BLAMMMMMMM! The first 125mm shell exploded. From the sound, Camellion estimated it had fallen a quarter of a mile south of their present underground position. The next explosion was closer.

For thirteen minutes the shelling continued, gigantic blasts and bursts that shook numerous rocks from the ceiling, some the size of basketballs. When the barrage ceased, there was a deathly, eerie silence, the kind of stillness, frozen in time, that comes before a tornado or an earthquake.

Hooppole sighed. "I suppose it's time to go out and shake hands with ivan. . . . ."

CHAPTER SIX

Well-ordered and well-trained, the Soviet troops started up the sides of the large hills that ran together, the 375 men and officers confident that they would reach the summit without too much difficulty. Not even the Afghans, for all their daring and bravery, could withstand a bombardment from 125mm guns. If the swine had not had the good sense to retreat, they were surely dead. What few remained alive would be too *bov'ochnoye*[1] to offer any resistance. Even so, the *Raydoviki* proceeded cautiously, each man scanning the tops and sides of the larger rocks untouched by the HE shells whose power was unbelievable—except to military men. Hundreds of pine and chinar trees were only blackened stumps. Hundreds more had vanished completely. Blown into pieces that were next to nothingness, they had been replaced by craters, immense shell holes still smoldering. Surprisingly there was little smoke. The wind was too brisk.

Major Vladislav Gregorevitch, the officer in charge of the infantry troops, had urged his men to move with all possible

---

[1]Literally translation is "shell-sound." The closest word in the Russian language to describe shell-shock.

speed. Since he and the other officers didn't know about the openings on the top of the hills, he had reassured the troops that the Afghans would be bloody corpses. Even so, Gregorevitch was feeling the tension. Like all Russians in Afghanistan who were there to "pacify anti-communist elements," Gregorevitch harbored a healthy fear of the Afghans. How could one fight a people who didn't have the sense to know when they were beaten, fanatics who weren't afraid to die. They were ten times worse than those damned Poles!

During these times, just before a battle, it was life rather than death that tended to fade with each step. Like the other men Vladislav Gregorevitch automatically settled into a state of non-feeling, of non-thinking of nonessentials, all his concentration focused on the rocks, on the top of the mountains. The men around him were robots as he was a robot.

Vladislav Gregorvitch stared at the top.

Only another thirty meters to go. . . .

Bursting 125mm shells had caved in not only seven of the topside escape openings but had filled with rock four caves below on the first level. In spite of this setback, not unexpected by the *mujahideen*, eighty-five percent of the Afghans crawled through the available outlets and, as quietly as they could, took positions behind rocks. Others crawled into shell holes. The rest of the force continued to climb out of the vents, every man knowing that the element of surprise was on his side.

Torak Adjar was technically in charge of the defenders, although there weren't any orders he could give that he had not already given—stay down, don't make any noise, and fire only after he did. After that it would be every man for himself. May Allah help them all. . . .

Khair Bahauddin Ghazi and Sebghatullah Mahlik remained in the caves on the second level. Not only was Khair Ghazi too important a rebel leader to risk capture, but should the Russians win, he and Adjar would destroy the complex with explosive charges planted within days after the force had moved into the caves.

The Death Merchant lay next to Ismail Ghazi who was on his belly to the left of Torak Adjar. To the right of Adjar were *mujahideen*. To Camellion's left were Hooppole, Kinsey, and Wesslin, as well as the other knots of Afghans, behind jumbled chunks of dark marblelike basalt that were three hundred feet from where the hillside merged with the summit.

Under different circumstance it would have been tactically advantageous if the *mujahideen* had been behind rocks on the rim and could have fired down on the Russians. The guns that had the highest position usually had the advantage. But not in this case. Should the Afghans have fired while the Soviet troops were still advancing on the hillside, the Russian would have pulled back, the incline being too steep for any kind of charge. The 125mm guns of the T-64 tanks would have then resumed their shelling, with such speed that the Afghans wouldn't have been able to reach the caves fast enough.

Under present conditions, if all went as planned, the Russians wouldn't have time to retreat. They would have to fight.

Jugen Wesslin, who had fought Soviet-trained black troops in various parts of Africa, had explained to Khair Ghazi: "That's why the Russians are so nervous in Kabul and in other cities. They're on the defensive, and that's unnatural to them. The Russians have a horror of retreating. Once we open fire, they'll charge. They won't have a choice. They're not going to settle for us pinning them down in the rocks. And once they're among us, the 125s can't fire."

At least it was hoped the T-64 tanks wouldn't fire! The Soviet hand was every bit as brutal as the old peasant gangsters running the store in Moscova. There had been instances when Soviet planes and tanks had fired on Russian soldiers fighting with rebels, killing Soviet troops as well as *mujahideen*, but only after it was a certainty that the Soviet soldiers would lose the fight.

Should the *Raydoviki* go down in defeat on this particular mountaintop would the Soviet commander of the column order the T-64s to open fire again? It was a risk the Afghans had to take.

The area ahead of the guerrillas, from their positions to the uneven, jagged rim, was filled with shell holes, revealing raw rock, boulders of various sizes, geodes formed by aqueous metamorphism, and blackened tree stumps still smoking.

Watching the area, Camellion decided within his own mind that Wesslin was right; previously he had had his doubts. No longer. The Soviet soldiers would have to fight—those who weren't chopped to bits in the first blast of slugs. Otherwise, the entire conflict would develop into a Mexican standoff. Once the Russians got down behind the rocks, they'd have no choice but to remain there, or get their heads blown off—*There aren't enough big rocks between us and the rim for the pig farmers to keep between us and themselves during a retreat. Those mothers will have to charge. I wonder . . .*

Camellion nudged Ismail Ghazi. "Ismail, tell *kuvii* Adjar not to fire until the Russians are within twenty-five feet of us," he whispered. "By then, every piece of Russian trash should be on top. Tell him that the smart thing to do then would be to charge them—hit 'em while they're still disorganized."

Ismail turned and looked wonderingly at Camellion. "Charge them?"

A member of a tribe who considered vengeance as sacred as the rest of the code of *pakhto*, Ismail had a lot of respect for Richard Camellion, ever since he had seen the Death Merchant in action against the mine-laying Soviet patrol. Why the American was so brave he might have been an Afghan!

"You heard me. I said charge them. Why should we wait for those Russian swine to come to us?" Camellion laid it on thick, appealing to Ismail's sense of manhood, to his radical sense of pride in being an Afghan. "What kind of men are we? Why should we lie here like frightened rabbits? We should go to them—kill them before they even have a chance to regroup."

Ismail considered for a moment. "Torak might not like the idea. He is getting old and does not think fast."

"You are the son of *Malik* Khair *khel* Ghazi. He is the leader. Do you not have the right to make the decision in his absence?"

A canny look jumped into Ismail's ebony eyes. "You are trying to talk me into something, my American friend. Is that not so?"

Touché! "Yes, I am!" Camellion admitted. "I'm trying to save as many of our lives and kill as many of the enemy as possible. We'll lose less men in a charge than waiting here for them to lob grenades at us. . . ."

"I will think about it. . . ."

Several minutes crawled by. No one spoke. There was only the brisk and scorching *siah bad* and the unnatural quiet, for the terrible crashing sound of the bursting 125mm shells had terrified the birds and other animals into silence— and had killed many. Only five feet ahead of the Death Merchant lay a rust brown marmot killed by concussion. Dozens of ibex had roamed through the hills, but not a single one was in sight.

The first Russian troops appeared, scores in light brown uniforms and helmets and boots, each one armed with an AKM, spare ammo and four RGD-5 grenades hanging from chest straps.

The Death Merchant wriggled closer to Ismail and whispered, "Listen! If those animals get close enough to use grenades, we'll be in trouble. After we kill the first wave we have to charge and get close enough to stop the rest of them from using their grenades."

Ismail didn't answer.

Like bedbugs seeking a meal in the dark, more Soviet troops appeared . . . running singly, in pairs, and in small groups . . . first to the left, then to the right, ducking first one way and then another, but always forward.

Walking right into it! American soldiers wouldn't have been that stupid. Americans, seeing the tumbled masses of basalt large enough to conceal an enemy, would have been suspicious. American fighting men would have charged full speed ahead and have used grenades. *Not these brainwashed Russian goofs!* Indeed not. They had been told by their officers not to use grenades unless it was absolutely necessary. So far they hadn't even seen an Afghan!

They soon did! Torak Adjar cut loose with his old fashioned Soviet PPSh-4 SMG when the nearest Russian to him was twenty-nine feet away, the ugly snarling of the automatic weapon shattering the stillness with the force of a hammer smashing an egg shell.

Adjar's 7.62mm X 25 'P slugs stabbed into two Russians, both corpses not quite reaching the ground as scores of other Afghans, up and down the crooked line, cut loose with their SMGs, assault rifles, and semiautomatic rifles. In only ten seconds 131 pig farmers were cut down and lying sprawled out on the rocks.

Ismail Ghazi waited until the roaring of the weapons was echoing. He then yelled, *"Sunmji! Sunmji! Sunmji!"* at the top of his lungs—*"Charge! Charge! Charge!"* He followed with, *"Tuziz'q Allāh yi!"*—*All for the Glory of God.*

Shocked, Torak Adjar turned to Ismail who was getting to his feet. However, Adjar didn't have time to demand an explanation. All around him, to the left and the right, men were triggering off short bursts, jumping to their feet and yelling *"Allāh Akbār"* ("God is Great!").

Adjar wasn't one-tenth as shocked as Major Vladislav Gregorevitch who was in the second line from the rim, a hundred and fifty feet from the hillside. It was a catastrophe. With the realization that his force had moved into the mouth of a trap, he dove for cover behind a pile of slate close to a shell crater, three regulars and Captain Boris Zigorny taking a dive with him.

"My God! Where did they come from?" panted Zigorny. Only recently commissioned, he had only been in Afghanistan a month. "Comrade Major Gregorevitch, we must make an assault before we're wiped out."

Reaching for his walkie-talkie, a grim-faced Vladislav Gregorevitch didn't answer. . . .

During that single minute a lot more Russians died as the *mujahideen,* ducking and weaving and firing short steady bursts, stormed forward. By now, however, the well-trained Soviet assault troops had recovered from their initial surprise and were returning the fire, some reaching for RGD grenades. Twenty-six Afghans were ripped into bloody shreds by 7.62 AKM projectiles; another two died and a third was severely injured by a grenade. With both sides rushing toward each other, the Afghans and the Russians quickly found themselves eyeball to eyeball, staring—the Russians in disbelief—at each other.

The "anti-communist rebels" had the edge. This was their land, their sky, their earth, their water. Added to this intense patriotism was the conviction that they were following the will of Allah: killing the worst kind of infidel. All non-Muslims were infidels. But the Russians were more than nonbelievers. They were total evil. They didn't believe in any kind of god. Worst, they were against people who believed in a Supreme Being. Yes, the Russians were truly children of *Shaitin*.[2] The *Qur'an*[3] contained the words which proclaimed that truth. *La ilāh illa Allāh; Muhammad rasūl Allāh. . . .*[4]

Training was the only thing that the Russians had going for them. On the minus scale was their fear of the Afghans, whom they considered being only a step above animals. Coupled with this disadvantage was the shock of having walked into a trap.

Yelling and screaming, the Afghans and the Russians smashed together in hand-to-hand combat, everything, to each combatant, taking on a preternatural unreality. Past and future became equidistant, and there was only the hell of the blood present, with each cry, each moan, each scream a constant indictment of one's own determination to stay alive and a torturing reminder that the next bullet might mean the end of all hopes and dreams . . . the end of one's own world.

Hate-filled, frightened faces in front of him, the Death Merchant, very fluid in motion, kept low, constantly moving, every muscle tensed for instant action. He suddenly recalled that he had forgotten to tell Kinsey to take off his silly looking tweed hat. The hat marked him as a target. No time to worry about that now. He fired two more short bursts with the Port Said submachine gun, the slugs blowing up two more Russians who jerked, danced a final jig, and died. Then the SMG was empty.

Ducking to the left, Camellion tossed away the useless SMG and, with lightning quick motions, pulled the two Steyr GB auto pistols from their holsters, thumbed the safety levers to "F," and killed two more pig farmers coming at him with empty AKMs. From the corners of his eyes, Camellion saw that Hooppole and Ismail Ghazi were fighting like maniacs. But where was Kinsey? Rod and Ismail were on their own; Camellion had his own problem—and it was just about as bad

---

[2]The Muslim devil, the same as the Christian Satan. *Iblis*, a contraction of *Diabolos*, is another name for Old Nick.
[3]The true spelling of the "Koran."
[4]"There is no God but Allah; and Muhammad is the prophet of Allah."

as it could get. Three of the *Raydoviki* were charging him from the right, empty AKMs in their hands. The Soviet troops were in the same fix as the Afghans. They had exhausted their ammo in the AKMs and had not had the time to reload; and only Soviet officers carried sidearms.

Bronislav Khrenov, managing to grab Camellion's right wrist, tried to use the AKM barrel as a knife, to stab Camellion in the stomach. Camellion shot him with the left Steyr, the FMJ slug striking Khrenov in the chest. Just in time Camellion ducked the AKM swung by Yuri Dropiv, the barrel whizzing in an arc over his head. Dropiv had swung with such force that he was carried off balance by the miss, his own momentum half-spinning him around to his left so that he was half-turned to Guerguen Agayn, the third man coming at Camellion not with an empty Kalashnikov assault rifle but with an AKM bayonet. Dropiv's spin also exposed his right side to the Death Merchant who was not one to waste precious ammunition, especially since he had only two boxes of cartridges for the two GBs—and suppose another airdrop from Delhi did not come about?

Camellion moved in faster than cockroaches taking over an apartment in the ghetto. He let Dropiv have a powerfully-delivered *Sokuto Geri* sword-foot kick in the lower right side, the cannon ball slam snapping three of the man's ribs and knocking him into Agayn who went down on his right knee, cursing. Dropiv had stumbled and was half draped over Agayn who was now finding it difficult to keep from falling backward and sitting down on the ground.

Damn pig farmers! They dropped out of first grade—when they were thirty! Neither Dropiv nor Agayn had a chance to recover. Dropiv couldn't and Agayn was still trying to push Dropiv from him. The Death Merchant finished off Dropiv with a downward *Kekomi* kick, the heel of his left boot crashing into the fifth and the sixth thoracic vertebrae, squarely in the center of the back, about the level of the lower ends of the shoulder blades. Dropiv's spine cracked. The cord broke. The Russian died, his dead weight pushing against a frantic Guerguen Agayn. Agayn didn't remain frenzied with fear for very long. Camellion scrambled his brains with a 9mm GB slug, popping the Ruskie low in the forehead, just below the rim of his combat helmet.

Spinning around, Camellion holstered the two Steyr auto-pistols and started to pull the Oda-Mar knife. His fingers were going around the handle when he spotted three more Russians headed his way. Two were armed with AKM bayonets. The third, an officer, had a Vitmorkin machine pistol in his right hand—and he was raising the weapon straight at the Death Merchant.

Thinking he was as good as dead, Camellion had only one thought—*He's going with me into oblivion!* But how to take the pig farmer? There was no way he could pull the Oda-Mar from its holster and throw it as fast as the Vitmorkin could fire.

Camellion, however, wasn't stitched with slugs made in mother Russia. He wasn't because Lieutenant Kaarlo Balkin, the Soviet officer, didn't fire. He couldn't, finding it impossible to do so with three Carl Gustav SMG slugs in his body. Jerking like a puppet whose string controls had become tangled, he sagged to the ground, mouth open, eyes wide.

The Death Merchant hadn't seen who had fired the Carl Gustav SMG. Weapons were firing all over the place, and, amid all the shouts and yells, it was impossible to even halfway pinpoint the location. He had only heard the SMG fire and knew that whoever had pulled the trigger was behind him and to his right. He didn't have time to turn around and look either. He was too busy with the other two pig farmers coming at him. Nor did he have time to pull one of the GB pistols. Georgi Ter-Sarkisov, the taller of the two ivans and slightly ahead of Uri Yukapak, feinted with a straight-in jab then darted to Camellion's right. He intended to bore in from the side while Yukapak attacked from the front. Neither man suspected that they were dealing with certain death, with a kill-machine who had killed dozens of dummies with his bare hands.[5] They instantly found out.

Expertly tossing the Oda-Mar to his left hand, Camellion stabbed out to his left and at the same time jumped a foot off the ground, turning slightly to his left as he did so. His left-handed thrust caused Ter-Sarkisov to jump back to a position that placed him exactly where Camellion wanted

[5]Richard Camellion has written three books on bare-handed kills. Two are not available to the public. The third is: *Assassination: Theory & Practice.* Paladin Press, P.O. Box 1307, Boulder, Colorado 80306.

him. Camellion executed a high left-legged *Yoko Geri Kibuki* thunder kick, his heel like a ten-ton battering ram crashing into Ter-Sarkisov's Oriental-looking face. Never had the Russian been hit with such force. The blow shattered his front teeth, broke his nose, cracked his upper jaw, and broke his lower jaw in two places. In a universe of agony, Ter-Sarkisov staggered back, the world blurring around him, the sounds coming from him resembling a puppy's whining.

By now, seeing how Camellion had whacked out his comrade, Yuri Yukapak was having second thoughts; yet he was coming in too fast to back down, not that he wanted to. Yukapak was many things; a coward wasn't one of them. Fast, he attacked with a right-handed straight thrust which Camellion easily evaded by backstepping and sidestepping the AKM bayonet.

Simultaneously, the Death Merchant switched the Oda-Mar to his right hand, then blocked with the seven-inch stainless steel blade another thrust by Yukapak, and, by feinting with the Oda-Mar, redirected the Russian's right hand so that the pig farmer stabbed in toward him, to the right, a thrust that brought the tip of the AKM bayonet only inches from Camellion's stomach. A simple trick—*And the dummy fell for it.*

With his empty left hand, Camellion could not have done what he was about to do. Suddenly, however, his *right* hand was also empty; he had opened his fingers and let the Oda-Mar fall to the ground. Realization dawned in Yukapak's eyes. It was too late. The Death Merchant had him. He grabbed Yukapak's right wrist with both hands, twisted the arm viciously, and smiled when the AKM slipped from the man's hand. He then jerked and pulled Yukapak's arm in an upward and outward motion, so fast that Yukapak couldn't make any moves of retaliation. Chain-lightning fast, the Death Merchant spun and shot in under the elbow. Rotating and locking the elbow, his back now toward Yukapak, Camellion squatted into position to execute a shoulder throw, pulling heavily on the Russian's arm. Camellion, thrusting his body upward, then broke the arm at the elbow and dislocated the shoulder a micro-moment before he tossed the doomed man over his own head and shoulders and threw him to his back on the rocks. A short left snap kick to the side of Yukapak's neck started the Russian on his way to eternity.

Camellion picked up the Oda-Mar, looked to his right and, just in the nick of time, jerked back, the stream of 9mm Vitmorkin M.P. projectiles passing only several feet in front of him. *Double Damn!*

Once Rod Hooppole had exhausted the ammo in his AKM, he pulled his two Safari Arms MatchMaster auto-pistols and began blasting away, calmly and deliberately, each .45 ACP bullet ending the life of a Soviet trooper. It was to the good fortune of the ivans in the vicinity that Hooppole fired only four rounds before he was forced to stop. Afghans were between him and the Russians. The second reason was that two of the enemy were coming at him from both the left and the right, Gennadi Pivvy grabbing his left wrist with both hands, Oleg Zhayen-Kov coming in from the right. Aleksei Gorshokin, ten feet to the right, was also coming in fast.

Hooppole used his left foot to stomp on the right instep of Gennadi Pivvy, the goon who had his left wrist in a firm grip and had already forced him to drop the MatchMaster. Pivvy howled in agony, his fingers relaxing around Hooppole's wrist. Determined to see that day's sunset with all its sickening colors, Hooppole used his right MatchMaster on Oleg Zhayen-Kov as the big Russian made a grab for his right wrist. The MatchMaster roared, the bullet travelling only 22.6 inches to Zhayen-Kov's face, entering just below the nose. Teeth flew. Then the big bullet zipped through the Ruskie's mouth and dug a bloody tunnel through the back of his neck, his dying heart pumping blood out of his mouth.

Hooppole, however, wasn't fast enough to avoid Aleksei Gorshokin, a third piece of trash who reached out, wrapped one big hand around Hooppole's right wrist and twisted. With his left hand the Russian tried a straight *Sambo*[6] strike to the side of Hooppole's neck.

Jerking to one side, the British merc avoided the deadly stab, but he was still far from happy. First of all, Pivvy, even with his broken foot, was making a grab for him. In the second place, two more troopers, to his left, were rushing in his direction. Twisting slightly, Hooppole slammed Pivvy in the groin with a left-footed side thrust kick. A split second later, he pulled on Aleksei Gorshokin's right arm, jerking the

[6]The Russian version of karate.

Russian toward him, and smashing him in the solar plexus with a powerful left elbow *Hiji* that knocked the wind out of the man, paralyzed his diaphragm, and left him wide open for another blow. He got it. Hooppole powed him with a left-handed *Ura Ken* back fist that slammed into Gorshokin's mouth, or, technically, into his philtrum, the upper lip just above the gum line, about a quarter of an inch below the nose. A sharp blow here will result in broken teeth, possibly some wreckage of the nasal bones, and concussion to the brain since the upper jaw bones, or maxilla, are firmly anchored to the brain case. Hooppole didn't want to break teeth or cause concussion. He intended to kill the Russian airhead. He intended to break the *dens*, a small finger of bone that helps hold the skull in place on top of the vertebral column. That's exactly what Hooppole did with the back fist blow. He broke the *dens*, the terrific shock to the brain causing death as fast as Gorshokin could blink. A long sigh slid from Gorshokin, and he dropped, falling flat on his face and not moving. . . .

Hooppole wasn't concerned about Pivvy. The kick in the groin had mashed Pivvy's intestines and were making the sensory nerves leading to the scrotum scream in agony. The slob had sunk to his knees, then had fallen over on his left side, clutching his belly and moaning.

Hooppole had time only to stoop and pick up the Match-Master that Gorshokin had twisted from his right hand. Yet he wouldn't need the pistol as far as the two ivans rushing at him from the left were concerned. Valentin Pripoltysev and Dmitri Stivbun were not destined to reach Hooppole. Both had come to the attention of Reza Jahaubin and Ismail Ghazi, both of whom had just killed two pig farmers with Afghan *Hazkas*, knives with heavy 14-inch curved blades.

The two Russians headed for Hooppole were moving on a course that would take them right by Ghazi and Jahaubin. In their fury they didn't notice the two Afghans. Stivbun and Pripoltysev had singled out Hooppole because they had seen him whack out Aleksei Gorshokin and Gennadi Pivvy, both of whom had been their good friends. Stivbun and Pripoltysev intended to avenge them.

Pripoltysev was the first to have his plans wrecked—by Reza Jahaubin who was a tall, rather thin man, but three times stronger than he looked. Very fast, he reached out, grabbed the front rim of Pripoltysev's helmet, pulled on it and jerked back the man's head. Down came Jahaubin's right arm, the sharp blade of his *Hazka* cutting Pripoltysev's throat from ear to ear. Jugular veins severed, blood began gushing a foot from the doomed Russian's throat. Gurgling, he started to sink, his life fading in proportion to the blood jumping from the hideously "grinning mouth" in his throat.

Dmitri Stivbun was trapped as quickly by Ismail Ghazi who stuck out his right foot and tripped the man. Ismail could have killed him with one blow from the *Hazka*, but that would have been too merciful. He wanted the Russian piece of trash to *know* he was dying, to *feel* every second of it. As the surprised Stivbun started to fall forward, Ismail struck him at the base of the skull with the butt cap, or pommel, of the *Hazka*, just hard enough to stun the Russian. With a terrible look of hatred on his face, Ismail shoved the *Hazka* into his waistband, jumped in front of Stivbun, who was sagging, and grabbed the man's chin with both hands, palms inward, the heels of his hands against the chin. Ismail pulled Stivbun erect and smashed him in the stomach with a powerful left first. Before the Soviet trooper could double over, Ismail jumped behind him, wrapped his left arm underneath the man's chin, across his throat, pulled, and lifted Stivbun off his feet; very quickly—releasing his left arm at the same time—he hooked the finger of his right hand under Stivbun's chin, then the fingers of his left hand. Now, having Stivbun in a reverse neck pull, he twisted the man's head back and forth, employing the same method used to execute Afghan women who were proven adultresses.[7] Ismail couldn't complete the kill job, it being impossible to snap Stivbun's neck in this manner. Instead, he released the ivan and let him fall heavily to his back. Drawing his *Hazka*, Ismail hacked down across the Russian's left collarbone, the blade cutting through muscles, bone, veins and arteries. Stivbun would be a corpse within minutes. And so would Captain Robert Aksento who was considered an expert in *Sambo* and who had tried every trick he knew on Jugen Wesslin.

Breathing heavily, Aksento attempted a left one-finger spear stab to the German's throat and a right ridge-hand to

---

[7]The woman is securely bound to a chair and a metal band tightened around her head. There are two handles on the metal band. The woman's head is then twisted off.

Wesslin's left temple. The West German blocked both intended strikes, feinted with a left kneelift, which Aksento avoided, then came in very fast with a four-finger spear thrust aimed at the Russian's liver—or the "Seventh Intercostal Space." Aksento was a bit too slow in blocking the strike, although he did succeed, with his left forearm, in reducing much of its power. Nonetheless, he was staggered and hurt, his costal cartilages of the lower ribs in agony. On the left side of the body the costal cartilages overlap the stomach and spleen, and these two organs were also full of pain. Trying to keep from vomiting, Aksento staggered back. Wesslin would have killed him with the next three or four blows if Aksento hadn't stumbled within reach of Elrod Kinsey who was lying between two slabs of shale. Kinsey reached out with his Port Said SMG and thrust the barrel between the Russian's ankles, tripping him so that he fell forward.

Wesslin had him. A roundhouse kick to Aksento's solar plexus finished him off, the savage slam causing instant internal bleeding and extreme shock to the thoracic ganglia.

Kinsey should have continued to play dead. His intervention had made him and Wesslin a target of Lieutenant Kusan Efendovitch. The only thing wrong was that Efendovitch had not seen Richard Camellion, thirty feet to his right and fifty feet from Wesslin and Kinsey. However, the Death Merchant couldn't see Kinsey who was hidden from him by one of the slabs of shale, but he didn't have any diffculty seeing Lieutenant Efendovitch who, crouched, raised his Vitmorkin machine pistol. He didn't get to pull the trigger. "Baby" streaked through the air, the blade of the ice pick burying itself in the right side of Efendovitch's neck. The Soviet officer jumped and let out a loud gurgle. The Vitmorkin roared, but the muzzle was pointed downward and the stream of slugs zipped into the ground, most of them ricocheting.

The Death Merchant and Wesslin dropped and looked around the area. They were surprised to see that almost all of the men were Afghans and that those who were dying were uniformed *Raydoviki*. What could have been a hundred pig farmers were retreating to the northwest, heading for the rim and the slopes, *mujahideen*, screaming "*Allāh Akbār!*," chasing after them. Some of the Russians to the rear were even caught and with equal speed dispatched to their forefathers, either stabbed with

Hazkas or clubbed to death with empty AKMs and other weapons.

Camellion felt good. The Afghans had done it. They had repulsed the attack. They had kicked Russian ass and had won.

Just in case there were strays still alive and feeling stupid but treacherous, Camellion pulled one of his Steyrs, saw Wesslin getting to his feet, and across the way, saw Hooppole approaching Ismail Ghazi and three other Afghans who were searching Russian corpses. Then, just ahead, he saw Kinsey rear up and look fearfully around him. Seeing that the battle was over, Kinsey crawled from between the two slabs of shale, got to his feet, saw Camellion, and waved.

The Death Merchant went over to Kinsey, stepping over rocks and several Russian cold cuts.

"I see you made it in good shape," Camellion said, glancing at Wesslin who was also headed toward him and Kinsey. "But a little while ago you and Wesslin almost got it."

Kinsey didn't say anything, and Camellion sensed that something was troubling the CIA man.

"You mean the Russian?" said Wesslin. "I saw him raise the machine pistol but I was too far away to do anything about it." He turned and looked down at the dead Lieutenant Efendovitch and the black handle of "Baby" protruding from the side of his neck. "*Ach!* What did you use on the swine?"

"I was in the same fix earlier," remarked the Death Merchant. "Some pig farmer had a machine pistol on me. He was about fifteen feet away, about to shoot, and there wasn't anything I could do about it. The next thing I knew someone scratched him. It sounded like a Port Said. I can't be sure."

"I shot him," Kinsey spoke up. "I saw what the Russian was going to do, so I let him have it, with this." He held out the empty Port Said SMG. "It was the last of my ammo."

Camellion did a double take. "I owe you one. You saved my bacon."

Oddly enough, Kinsey looked more than embarrassed. *He seems worried about something. What? Or is he just having a case of the jitters?*

"You've already repaid him," Wesslin said with a half-laugh. "You saved his life and mine—remember. I'm in your debt, Herr Camellion."

The Death Merchant was watching Ismail Ghazi who, with

a group, was moving toward him, Kinsey and Wesslin. "We're going to have to get back to the caves. The Russians could start up with those 125s any moment. By now the chief officer of the mountain force has contacted the armored column below."

The Soviets didn't resume shelling the mountains. Afghans who remained at the rim reported that the surviving Soviet soldiers hurriedly retreated to their BTR-70 armored personnel carriers and BRDM-1 armored cars. Carrier and cars then roared back to the main column which turned and moved northwest.

The jubilant *mujahideen* collected weapons, ammo magazines, grenades and other materiél and counted the dead . . . theirs and the Russians.' Of the 375 *Raydoviki* who had come up the slopes, 203 were dead. On the debit side, 105 of the Afghans had been killed. It was bitterly ironic, pointed out an angry Torak Adjar. Arms and ammunition were always in short supply, but no longer.

"There are now only eighty-seven of us in this group," Adjar said, glaring at Ismail Ghazi. "We have more weapons that we can carry. Our men were killed without good reason, killed needlessly. Because of you, Ismail! Because you had to call out to the men to charge. Your father will hear of this."

"It was necessary that we charge the Russian pigs," Ismail said angrily. "The enemy would have retreated and we would not have been able to kill so many. More likely they would have thrown grenades into our positions. We would have been butchered."

Shallow-minded Adjar was not in the mood for reason. "You did not have the right to give the order," he raged. "A son does not disobey his father. Your father put me in charge of the defense."

"*Kuvii* Torak Adjar. It was I who advised Ismail that an attack was necessary. I advised him to give the order," the Death Merchant said, staring deeply into Adjar's eyes.

Baffled consternation fell over Adjar's dark face. He didn't know what he had glimpsed in the bright blue pools of Camellion's eyes; yet for some reason he felt a vague uneasiness bordering on fear.

"*You* advised him!" he said tightly to Camellion. "By what right? You are a guest in our camp. *Kuvii* Wesslin is our military adviser. *Kuvii* Wesslin, was an attack necessary? If so, why did you not advise us of the tactic?''

"Camellion is right." Wesslin's voice was cold, flat and practical. "If we hadn't attacked the Russians, we would have pinned them down. They would have advanced using grenades, or have brought up mortars. Either way, they would have won. *Ja,* few of us would be alive.''

"If that is so, why did you not tell us during the meeting?'' demanded Adjar, more angry than ever.

"Twice previously I advised that we attack," Wesslin said unsympathetically. "I advised 'attack' at the Kabinak Pass. The second time was in the mountains near Subiljique. I advised then to attack when they least expected it. Both times I was voted down. I would have been voted down this time, Torak, and you know it. Your voice would have been the loudest. I think Khair Ghazi will agree with me when I say that Ismail did right, and so did Camellion in advising him.''

Reluctantly, Khair Ghazi did agree, an hour later in the main cave.

"What is done cannot be changed," Khair Ghazi said solemnly. "It is always necessary to assume, not that the old ways are necessarily wrong, but that there may be a better way. I believe that in this case an attack saved lives and helped us to win the battle. Therefore, the attack was good.''

"It was also good psychologically," the Death Merchant said. "A good scare teaches far more than good advice, so the prophet has said. (*He didn't say anything of the kind, but I don't think that any of them know that he didn't!*) The Russians have to be scared.''

Ismail grinned. "This is the first time we have ever forced an entire Soviet armored column to retreat!''

"We are still in danger," Wesslin said. "The Russians know we won't remain here in these caves. If they know of the impending attack on Kabul, they will asssume we'll move northwest, at first in a roundabout way. Who knows where they might be waiting with an ambush?''

"We'll have scouts," said Ismail Ghazi. "An armored column isn't easy to hide.''

"I was only telling you the possibilities," Wesslin said. "And we can't discount planes finding and attacking us.''

"A hundred and ninety kilometers is a long way to go," muttered Hooppole in a tired voice, "especially since most of it will be through the Kush." He looked around uncertainly, and pulled at one end of his long handlebar mustache. Everywhere *mujahideen* were busy packing weapons and supplies for the journey that would take them within nineteen klicks of Kabul.

Khair Ghazi said, "We will go fourteen kilometers south to fool the Russians. By the time they return to their base and regroup, who knows? We might lose them." He unpinned the *taweez*[8] from his shoulder. "I am sure that some of the men from Bashawal will join us, now that we have ample weapons and supplies, that is, ammunition. Three hundred and fifteen magazines for AKMs is a godsend."

"That's only a drop in the bucket," Wesslin said, his eyes hard. "One extended battle with Russian swine and we'd use every round."

Kinsey and several Afghans came over to the group, Kinsey carrying a black metal case in each hand, each one slightly larger than a portable typewriter. The cases contained the special shortwave radio, the decoder and the dual scrambler.

One of the Afghans reported to Khair Ghazi that part of the ancient tomb of Hadji Mukib Naqaswar had collapsed, possibly from the severe concussion of Soviet 125mm shells, or from rockets and missiles from the Russian gunships.

"Another black mark against the Soviet demons," Khair Ghazi said savagely. "Our day will come. With the help of Allah we will drive the invaders from our country."

With the help of the CIA, old man! The Death Merchant disliked loose ends, unknowns, and trust in myths accepted as reality.

Double-ditto to Kinsey. He's the joker who said we'd be safe in Bashawal. Right then and there Camellion decided that the mission was a bust. He made up his mind about something else, too. He was not going to go into Kabul and commit suicide.

Grojean can go fly a milk bottle!

"It is time we start the journey," Khair Ghazi said and got to his feet. . . .

---

[8]A small silver box in which are sacred writings; are carried to ward off death and disease. It is a talisman similar to a Catholic religious medal.

CHAPTER SEVEN

Southeast moved the force that now numbered 108, 31 people from burned out Bashawal having joined Khair Ghazi's group. "Only 103," insisted Ismail Ghazi to Camellion, several days later after the Death Merchant happened to remark that it was difficult for so many people to move undetected through the mountains. "Five are women," Ismail said. "We cannot count them." The fact that two of the women from Bashawal were nurses did not impress Ismail whose own wife and nine children were in Pakistan. Neither did the fact that six of the eighty-seven survivors were women, young women whose husbands had died fighting the Russians. Muslim to the core, Ismail was convinced that while women should be protected and loved, they were still women whose place was in bed and in the kitchen.

Southeast, then straight north for twenty-four kilometers, then northwest—the direction of Kabul—moving mostly at night and hiding/sleeping by day, a dozen scouts always ahead, on each flank and to the rear. The worst was not the hard march, the ruggedness of the Kush, the danger in moving around rugged gorges or through steep forested valleys: it was the days when fires were not possible and everyone had to drink cold tea, eat dried goat and *nan* (chunks of dry bread). Intolerable to Richard Camellion and Rod Hooppole, both of whom were hot coffee drinkers.

Everyone was grateful when the terrain permitted the force to camp in a large cave or caves where the odors of burning wood and food could be trapped. This arrangement often had its drawbacks, unless the cave was very large. As Jugen Wesslin expressed it: "I don't know which is worse: cold food and clean air, or hot food, hot coffee and smoke?"

The only compensation—at least for the Death Merchant—was the raw beauty of the mountains. Peaks, thickly frosted with snow, were always present . . . stately, silent, aloof, giving the impression that they were only tolerating the presence of the force, that they were totally removed from the silly affairs of barbaric human beings. The mountains *were* removed, for like the wind nobody could own them; no one could conquer and possess them and hold them in bondage. Not even the Soviet Union.

"Never climb higher than you'd like to fall," Khair Ghazi remarked to Camellion one day. The force was always high in the craggy reaches, always suspended between sky and sunlight, between sky and moonlight. There was a reason for high movement. It was the safest route. The Russians stayed away from heights the way cats feared string and tin cans, ever since the *mujahideen* had ambushed three hundred crack Soviet paratroopers in the Nujikik Pass.

Always the force stayed far below the snow line. The guerrillas had to. The force had neither the clothing nor equipment to move through deep snow, traverse icy crevasses, and trek over entire massifs imprisoned by bitter cold. Already, even in the lowest reaches, there was a noticeable change in the air, a chilliness, especially after sunset, a frigidness that was a direct warning that within a few short months it would be impossible to travel the route the *mujahideen* were presently using. A modern army could fight winter campaigns.[1] The Nazi armies fought their best campaigns against Soviet partisans in the depths of the Russian winter. The Soviet army itself held out during weather in which the temperature would dip to thirty below zero.

To the Afghans, not having the logistic support of a western-style army, winter was also a deadly enemy. The cold and deep snow reduced their ability to move quickly cross-country, and Afghan camps and villages became more vulnerable, thus limiting the aid that women, old people, and even children could give to the freedom fighters. Far worse, snow and ice limited the *mujahideen*'s ability to counter attacks and avoid encirclement.

It was just the opposite with the Soviet forces that had half-tracks and helicopters, as well as other cold weather equipment. In fact, Soviet tacticians emphasized winter

[1]The American army won some of its best battles against the Indians in winter.

campaigns in anti-rebel operations. In short, the Soviets had the equipment. The Afghans did not.

Helicopters were especially valuable to the Russians, such as the huge Mi-6 HOOK that provided heavy-lift capability, and the multi-purpose Mi-8 HIP that was extensively employed as a main troop carrier and for aerial minelaying—an excellent way to reinforce a defensive perimeter quickly.

The HINDs were the work horses, however. They provided close air support for ground troops and made air strikes against villages; they also flew recon missions to detect and attack rebel groups, missions that were made easy by snow— when they could follow tracks and the number of alternative routes for Afghan movements was limited.

As Elrod Kinsey had explained, right after Camellion had come to Afghanistan, numerous roads were narrow and twisted through valleys overlooked by mountains—perfect for ambushes as the Soviets had learned the hard way. And so it was that whenever a Soviet force, a column or a supply party moved in enemy territory, it was always accompanied by HIND gunships.

Almost every day the *mujahideen* spotted HINDs and other Soviet helicopters, sometimes overhead, but more often in the distance. There were also fixed-wing aircraft, usually high flying fighter jets, but occasionally a transport-cargo craft. When a plane was heard the force would hide in the rocks or among trees. Whether any of the planes detected the rebels was a moot question. The altitude of any plane wouldn't make any difference, not with infrared photography, heat sensing devices, and other modern detection methods.

During the afternoon of the day after the battle on the mountaintop, Camellion, who had memorized callup signals and wave frequencies, stretched out the hundred foot wire antenna—Kinsey assisting—and contacted *Redwing* in New Delhi. He told the CIA man at the other end that "This mission is no longer feasible," that the conclusion of his analysis was that Khair Ghazi's attack against the Russians in Kabul was doomed to fail and that "I don't intend to be one of the victims. When and where are you going to make the arms drop?"

Came back the reply, cold and crisp: "Why do you want to know?"

"Because one of those choppers will lift me out of here."

"I don't have the authority to release you from your contract," the words came through the headphones. "I'll have to contact the higher authorities. Let me speak to *Sugarcane*."

"Sugarcane" didn't learn anything of real value. *Redwing* wanted to know why *Mockingbird* wanted to dump the mission. Kinsey told him: The odds of rescuing Fritz Werholtz and Stewart Hemschire were nil.

Redwing then wanted to know if *Sugarcane* could talk *Mockingbird* into changing his mind.

A thin smile of amusement crossed the Death Merchant's face. Didn't *Redwing* know the transmitter had two mikes and two pairs of headphones and that he was listening in? Camellion didn't interrupt. To do so would have been counterproductive. *Redwing* was only a "mouthpiece"; he had no authority of his own.

Kinsey, expecting Camellion to say something, glanced in his direction. The Death Merchant shook his head.

Again *Redwing* asked if *Sugarcane* thought he could somehow make *Mockingbird* change his mind.

Kinsey told him: do elephants fly—and at what locale in the mountains would the Company drop the thousands of assault rifles, ammo and grenades—and when?

The matter was still under discussion by higher authorities—and try to get *Mockingbird* to change his mind. Call back in four days unless an emergency developed. Out. . . .

Kinsey switched off the shortwave and took off the headphones.

"Sorry, Camellion. All we can do is wait," he said as the Death Merchant handed him the headphones he had been wearing. "You know how it is trying to get information from a main contact station—I suppose you do."

"Yes, I know."

Kinsey closed the panel of the transmitter and lowered his voice.

"Just for the record, I want you to know that I don't blame you for not going into Kabul." He paused and looked around to make sure that none of the Afghans were within hearing range. None were. "The attack hasn't a chance of succeeding. The combined power of the *mujahideen* will make a big splash, but when the surf rolls out the *mujahideen* will be with it and the Ruskies will retain control of the city."

"I suppose we can excuse Khair Ghazi on the grounds of ignorance and patriotism," Camellion said, a crooked smile on his face. "We have to give him credit. The attack on Kabul, even if it fails—and it will—will unite the Afghans even more and renew their determination. The true blockheads are the Company—and learned blockheads are greater blockheads than ignorant ones. Then again, the Company doesn't really give a damn about the Afghans. It can't. If four or five thousand die and their deaths cause the Soviets trouble, then it's well and good. And practical."

The force had stopped on the Vilikom Chokim, a mile-high plateau, and was eating supper while the setting sun washed the high peaks with a deep red. Even in the twilight, Camellion could see that Kinsey was edgy, as if something were troubling him. Then again, who wasn't under a strain?

Kinsey closed the second case, then turned and looked directly at the Death Merchant. "Listen, there is something I must tell you." He sounded hesitant and labored, as though he were forcing himself to speak.

"I'm listening."

"It's about the other day on the mountain. I . . . I froze. Once I got out there, I was so damned scared I couldn't think. All I wanted to do was run back to the caves. That's why I was lying there when you saw me. I couldn't run; my pride wouldn't let me. But I couldn't fight either. All I could do was lie there. But I know I killed a dozen of them with my pistol and subgun."

"And saved my life," Camellion said congenially. "Quit punishing yourself. There isn't a man alive who hasn't frozen at sometime or other in his life."

"You, too?"

"Me, too," lied the Death Merchant.

"Then you don't think I'm a coward?" Kinsey looked hopeful.

"You went out there and didn't run. You didn't 'freeze' either or you wouldn't have been able to fire your weapons. No, you're not a coward, and that's the truth. Now tell me something about Kabul?"

"If I can . . ."

"How far is the Central Prison from the Soviet main base in Kabul?"

*　　*　　*

94

In a few more days the force was scouting a village of seventy-one houses perched precariously on the side of a mountain, the weathered-wood structures propped up by hundreds of long poles. Khair Ghazi and his men were in the region of the Nuristanis, in Nuristan, a mountainous region some five thousand square miles in extent, a land of forests with deep ravines separated by high mountains.

The Nuristanis were a proud people, and although they were hospitable and friendly, they were also very aggressive and quick to avenge any injury. They were also great warriors, explained Ismail Ghazi to the Death Merchant as they waited for two recon men to return to the group from the village.

For almost a thousand years the Nuristanis held out against the tide of Islam that had spread eastward across Asia from Arabia. They raided Muslim settlements and passing caravans in the various valleys, including the Kabul valley. These raids became so common that they became institutionalized; a successful warrior being rewarded according to the number of men he killed. In this manner he could achieve rank and improve his status at home.

The Death Merchant put away his binoculars, but continued to observe the houses a half mile ahead, wondering why a stiff wind didn't topple them down the side of the mountain. The numerous poles—none larger than a man's arm—didn't look all that sturdy.

"Ismail, have the Russians ever tried to lay a trap in one of these out of the way villages?" he asked. "Have they ever moved in by surprise and tried to make everything look normal in the hope that *mujahideen* would come strolling in?"

"Several times they tried, years ago," answered Ismail. "Their traps never succeeded. There are certain signs that tell us when the Russians are in a village. It is not likely that the Russians are in Failiyi, the village below. They would have had to land troops by helicopter. The choppers would then have to leave and that would mean the troops would be isolated. That is not the way the Russians like to do things."

"Failiyi is important to you and your father, isn't it?" Jugen Wesslin said to Ismail. . . .

"Yes, *kuvii* Wesslin, it is," was all Ismail said. The West German did not press for more information. He only glanced at Camellion, who also sensed that the village was very important to Khair Ghazi and his *mujahideen*. More than once Ghazi had mentioned Failiyi, often saying that the force was only so many kilometers from Failiya. That was not too unusual in itself; Ghazi's constant reference to Failiya was. It was as though the village was the center around which some secret plan revolved. The Death Merchant suspected it was. Wesslin, Hooppole and Kinsey were of the same opinion— and just as irritated as Camellion over the extreme secrecy of the Afghans.

Several hours later, all four found that their suspicion was correct. Failiya was a communications center, a "post office" for messages. This became apparent soon after Khair Ghazi introduced them to Wakil Jil Aldubbah, the head man of Failiya, a wrinkled piece of humanity in his eighties, dressed in dark robes and turban and smoking a waterpipe. Three Timex watches were on his right wrist.

With Wakil Jil Aldubbah was a heavy-faced mustached individual wearing western-type clothing and a turban. Bearded, he appeared to be in his middle thirties. A Colt .45 in a canvas holster was belted around his waist.

Wakil Jil Aldubbah introduced the man as Kar Ali Shitoh. A member of the Chahar Aimaq,[2] Kar Ali Shitoh was a representative of Abdullah Saljoonque.

Khair Ghazi and Kar Ali Shitoh greeted each other warmly in the Afghan manner, each man putting out his right arm and grasping the other's forearm. Shitoh spoke rapidly, speaking surprisingly good English (later the Death Merchant and the other Westerners would learn that Shitoh had studied engineering in the United States and was from a wealthy family in Maimana.

Kar Ali Shitoh explained that Abdullah Saljoonque and 1,940 of his men were scattered throughout the suburbs of Kabul and were waiting for Mohammad Malikyar and his *mujahideen*. The rest of Khair Ghazi's force, some 2,400 men, were hiding in the mountains northeast of Kabul. They were under the command of Amud Mojidi.

"Has *Malik* Abdullah Saljoonque received any word from

---

[2]Four tribes, the Kati, Waigali, Paruni, and Ashkuni. They have been classified as Dardic languages and belong to the Indo-Iranian family.

Malik Mohammad Malikyar?'' asked Khair Ghazi. "How far from Kabul is Malikyar and his group?''

Khair Ghazi was seated across the small table from Wakil Jil Aldubbah. To the Death Merchant and the other men from the west, it was pleasant to sit off the floor again. In most Afghan homes the only furnishings were carpets, but the Nuristanis used simple chairs and tables. Wakil Jil Aldubbah's collection dated from pre-Islamic times and was elaborately carved.

Shitoh said, "When I started the journey to Failiya—that was eight days ago—*Malik* Mohammad Malikyar was only nineteen kilometers from Kabul and was being harassed by Soviet gunships. The Russians haven't sent any troops against him because they don't dare weaken their base in Kabul, not with Saljoonque and his men, and your force, *Malik* Khair Ghazi, so close to the city. The Russians know an attack is coming but they don't know when.''

"What about messages from carrier pigeons?'' inquired Torak Adjar.

"There haven't been any, not since I've been here,'' Kar Ali Shitoh said and glanced at Wakil Jil Aldubbah who slowly shook his head.

"It doesn't matter,'' Khair Ghazi said quietly. "Saljoonque and his people are in place, and Malikyar is on the way. The rest of our own force is waiting for us. Once we are close to Kabul, we will merge into one army and attack.''

"That is why *Malik* Saljoonque sent me to meet you,'' said Kar Ali Shitoh, "to let you know that all was in readiness. But we must have the arms from our friends in the west.''

"Tomorrow we'll make radio contact with the people responsible for the arms,'' interrupted Elrod Kinsey. "I can tell you now that the drop will take place close to Kabul so that distribution to the three groups will not be hampered by distance.''

Interjected the Death Merchant, "The people in the West might still be undecided as to the best way to deliver the arms. There's no guarantee that we'll know tomorrow when and where the arms will be dropped.''

"Yes . . . that's so,'' Kinsey agreed.

"They have promised weapons; I am sure they will keep their word,'' Khair Ghazi said. His eyes went to Wakil Jil

Aldubbah. "It would be of great help if some of your people joined us in our cause, in our fight against the invaders."

"*Doulat i Jumhouri ye Afghanistan*[3] is your nation as well as ours; it is only right that you should help," Ismail Ghazi said briskly, a deep frown on his face.

Wakil Jil Aldubbah's voice became as hard as his eyes. "Our country is Nuristan, these mountains for many miles. Our cattle, everything we need is in these mountains. The Russians have not bothered us. We will not bother them."

Sebghatullah Mahlik spoke up angrily from across the room.

"You know why the Russians haven't interfered with your way of life! They don't want thousands of Nuristanis fighting them. If the Russians firmly controlled this land, they would come at you with everything they have."

Snapped Ismail, "Wakil Jil Aldubbah, you are the senior member of the Council. The other members would follow your lead if you recommended assistance to our cause in the form of men." He watched Aldubbah intently for a reaction.

"We are assisting your cause," Aldubbah said slyly, no anger in his voice. "Do we not receive your carrier pigeons? Do we not arrange for messages to be passed back and forth? We receive messengers. Is not Kar Ali Shitoh sitting before you? But I will not try to influence the Council to lend our young men to your cause."

"But it's—" began Ismail, his tone more angry than previously.

"Silence, Ismail!" Khair Ghazi glared at his son and held up a hand. "You know better than to insult a man in his own house. It is not our way. I would prefer that he help, and in his way he is helping. His decision not to send men is his. We must respect that decision."

Grim-faced, Ismail remained silent.

Acting as if none of his guests had spoken harsh words, Wakil Jil Aldubbah put down the long stem of his water pipe and smiled at Khair Ghazi. "You and your people are welcome to spend this night in Failiya, most welcome."

"Thank you, Wakil Jil Aldubbah," Khair Ghazi said politely. "We will move out in a short time. There is a full moon tonight and we will be able to move many kilometers before sunrise. The closer we get to the Kabul valley the greater

[3]The full name of Afghanistan.

becomes the danger of our being attacked by the Russians. This is especially true of air attacks. Every second is precious and it is best that we do not linger."

Another annoying feature of the move northwest was being unable to take a bath or shave. The water the force carried had to be used for drinking and, when fires were permitted, for cooking. Besides, when the force stopped for the night—the "night" usually being the day—every man was so exhausted that no one thought of shaving, much less taking a bath, even if the force had been camped under Niagara Falls.

The Death Merchant had seen a lot of fantastic things in his missions throughout the world. Nonetheless, he was amazed at the sustained pace made by the Afghans. Movement was automatically slowed by dangerous terrain, especially when going around, or climbing down into, steep gorges. During such times the men would rope themselves together, a tactic that wasn't necessary the night that Khair Ghazi met with Wakil Jil Aldubbah. That night the force moved rapidly down the mountain trail and pushed onward across a forested plateau, again reaching the mountainous region shortly after 07.00 the next morning. By 07.44 every man was high in the mountains and looking at the fog-filled valley below, at the silent clouds of pale white drifting through the trees that, in entire areas, were invisible.

The Death Merchant and the other Westerners watched Khair Ghazi and his aides pore over a large map, their sanctuary for a moment a large depression in the side of the mountain. A flaw had developed, and Ghazi and his men were trying to decide whether to rest during the day or push on and rest that night. If they moved during the day, they would also have to stop that night, due to the Aknib Limok, a tremendous gorge through which the force would have to move. Not that it had to. It could take an alternate route. But if it did it would lose several days. The gorge was the problem. Going through it in daylight would be tricky. To try it at night would be a step close to suicide.

"But look at the terrain," said Torak Adjar who was down on his knees next to Torak Adjar. He moved a long finger along a crooked line on the dirty paper map. "This is the narrow trail on the face of the mountain. For most of the day we would be strung out on that trail. Furthermore, there is no indication on the map of caves or overhangs where we could hide and be safe from Soviet gunships if they attacked."

Khair Ghazi thought for a moment. "Then, Torak, you are in favor of remaining in this vicinity and proceeding along the face trail at night?"

"What's the point?" butted in Ismail. "We would still have to stop tonight when we came to the gorge! And to risk the entire force, to expose it to Soviet aircraft, does not make sense. One does not lock his house against thieves for thirty days, then leave the door unlocked and the windows open on the thirty-first day. We should wait here and negotiate the mountain trail tonight."

"I agree with Ismail," Sebghatullah Mahlik said evenly. "We should not expose ourselves needlessly to Soviet helicopters. With rockets and missiles they could kill every one of us on that open trail."

I feel we should move over the face trail only at night," Torak Adjar said, frowning in annoyance at Ismail. The boy was not respectful of his elders. "But the decision must be yours, Khair Ghazi. You are our leader."

Khair Ghazi looked over at a silent Jugen Wesslin who was opening a pack of British *Players* cigarettes. "Let's get the opinion of our military adviser and the other men from the West who are helping us."

"You seldom listen to my advice," said Wesslin, taking a cigarette from the box. "But, for what it's worth, I'm convinced we should remain here for the day and not move out until darkness. *Kuvii* Mahlik and Ismail are right. The HINDs could use missiles and rockets and bring down the mountain on us."

"We should move out tonight," said Rod Hooppole, giving his opinion.

"The same here," Kinsey said promptly. "Remain here for now."

"One often has to take a calculated risk," Camellion stated, "but never one of this magnitude. We have to stay here until darkness. Soviet choppers would wipe us out, right down to the last man—and woman."

"Oh yes, I do agree," Khair Ghazi said, sounding pleased. "We shall spend the day here and move out tonight."

"I will tell the others," Torak Adjar said, pushing himself

up. "None of them wanted to move over that trail in the sunshine."

Getting to his feet, Camellion touched Kinsey on the shoulder. "Let's set up the short wave, old buddy."

Kinsey nodded. "We might as well."

"I'll help," Wesslin offered.

The task required the better part of an hour, it taking that long to stretch the antenna where it would not be obstructed by rock. Wesslin, who was very agile, had to climb a seventy-foot pinnacle and loop the end of the wire around a small boulder, after which Kinsey and Camellion pulled the wire out to its full length of two hundred fifty feet while Wesslin returned to the ground.

"I'll make the initial contact, if it's all right with you," Kinsey said to Camellion who was putting on headphones.

"Be my guest." The Death Merchant picked up one of the microphones. "Find out about the drop. If *Redwing* stalls tell him that Ghazi is beginning to have second thoughts."

"You sound as if you might have changed your mind about going into Kabul," Kinsey mused, putting on headphones.

"It's possible," Camellion drawled, "depending on what *Redwing* has to say."

Kinsey flipped the "ON" switches of the transmitter, the decoder, and the dual scrambler, and checked to make sure the dial was set to the correct frequency—*it was!*—and that the signal strength was in the green.

Kinsey began calling—"*Sugarcane* calling *Redwing*. *Sugarcane* calling *Redwing*. *Sugarcane* calling *Redwing*. . . ."

The CIA station in New Delhi, India, replied within a few minutes. Camellion and Kinsey knew at once that it was a different operator than the one they had talked to previously. One hundred percent different. This operator was a woman—and with a sexy voice.

Kinsey made his progress report, stating that Khair Ghazi and his *mujahideen* should be in the Kabul sector in nine days and—"in the suburbs of Kabul in eleven." What about the shipment of arms? When would they be dropped and where—"We have to know. Khair Ghazi is becoming nervous and is starting to doubt our word. Over."

Redwing came directly to the point. "The arms will be dropped in the Zaranj section of the Kabul valley," the woman said. "The precise coordinates will be worked out after you arrive in the area and report that the area is safe and free from enemy interference. Over and acknowledge please."

Kinsey and the Death Merchant locked eyes for a second. The Zaranj section was only eleven klicks—or seven miles—from the eastern outskirts of Kabul!

"What about a cover operation?" Kinsey spoke into the mike. "You must have one, or Russian jets will shoot those cargo planes out of the sky. Over."

"There is such a plan. We shall give you the details during the next radio contact. You will report once you are in the Kabul valley and make contact with the other rebel leaders. Acknowledge. Over."

"You're 'acknowledged,' damn it!" Kinsey said crossly. Again he glanced at the Death Merchant. Only seven miles from Kabul! It was madness!

"Is *Mockingbird* available?" asked *Redwing*. "Over."

"I'm here and listening to every word," Camellion said in a lazy manner. "I assume you have a message for me—or should I have said an offer? Over."

There was a brief pause at the other end. *Redwing* then said, the woman's voice all business, "The Higher Authority has authorized me to tell you that your fee will be doubled if you undertake the operation in Kabul. What is your answer? Over."

"Agreed. (*But not because of any two hundred grand.*) Over."

"Let me speak to *Sugarcane*. Over."

"This is *Sugarcane*," Kinsey said. "Over."

"Do you have any questions? Over."

"No. Over."

"Out."

Kinsey switched off the transmitter and its two attachments, disgust on his face. "Someone in the Company has lost his mind. Dropping the stuff in the Zaranj section doesn't make sense. Naturally the drop must be close to where all the *mujahideen* have assembled, but that close to Kabul is really asking for trouble."

"The airdrop will never work, not in the Zaranj section— nein, never!" Wesslin put his hands on his hips and glanced up at the top of the pinnacle where the antenna was attached. "It doesn't make any difference what kind of decoy operation the CIA has. The Soviet high command is aware that Kabul is going to be attacked. They'll have radar all over the place.

Mein Gott! The cargo planes will never reach the Kabul area.''

"We're making a hasty evaluation," Camellion observed mildly. "We don't know what kind of ruse the Company has cooked up. I'm sure The Center is aware of Russian radar. I don't think D.C. is going to spend ten million bucks in arms only to have them shot down by the Russians."

"You're probably right, but it's still shaving too close to the skin for comfort." Kinsey closed the panel on the second case, stood up, looked after Wesslin walking toward the pinnacle rock, then frowned. "Oh shit!" he said. "I forgot to disconnect the antenna from the transmitter." Abruptly then he looked at Camellion. "By the way, what made you change your mind about going into the Kabul? I know it wasn't the money. You'd be just as dead if they tripled your contract fee. Of course, it's none of my business."

"An idea is only as good as its execution," Camellion said, "although there's no such thing as too much money. The Central Prison in Kabul is almost a mile from Soviet headquarters. Hopefully the Russians will have only a token force at the prison. With a small force . . . Well, you know the old saying about casting your bread upon the waters. . . ."

"Sure I do. But a dozen wet loaves of bread isn't going to help us free Hemschire and Werholtz." Giving Camellion a skeptical look, Kinsey got down on one knee and began to remove the end of the antenna from the transmitter.

The Death Merchant disliked having a person say only half of what was on his mind. It was as irritating as saying a woman was "half-pregnant."

Camellion said, "You were there the other day when Khair Ghazi said he'd receive word from his contact in Kabul once we reached the Kabul valley. Once we know exactly where Werholtz and Hemschire are, that's half the battle."

Kinsey let the wire fall to the ground and began screwing on the terminal caps in the rear of the shortwave.

"There's no question that Ghazi will help," he said, starting to disconnect the transmitter from the case containing the dual scrambler and the decoder.[4] "Let's say we find Werholtz

---

[4]Pulsed transmission. Decoder and dual scramblers work with a speed of microseconds, much too fast for enemy finders to zero in and pick up. Even if they could, the transmissions could not be deciphered.

and Hemschire and manage to get them out of the prison. Getting them out of Kabul and into the mountains is a different matter. You know the odds.''

''They're slightly in our favor.'' Camellion said what he considered to be the truth. ''And what do you mean by 'we?' ''

''Us. You and I. Wesslin and Hooppole and say fifty of our friends who wear checkered tablecloths around their heads. I'm going with you and the others!'' He looked up and stared hard at the Death Merchant. ''Don't try to talk me out of it.''

''You don't have to prove anything to me or any of the others,'' Camellion said in a kindly voice. ''You don't owe us anything.''

''That's right, I don't. I do owe it to myself.'' Kinsey stood up. ''We'd better hold the wire for Wesslin. He's a third of the way to the top.''

That night the slow crawl along the trail on the face of the mountain went as scheduled, with a lot of trepidation. As a rule, Soviet gunships didn't fly at night and especially in the mountains. That didn't mean they couldn't. If HINDs did show up, the darkness would not be total protection. All Soviet gunships carried infrared night vision devices. Soviet gunships did not appear. The force did make it across the face of the mountain and by dawn had reached the Aknib Limok, one of the deepest gorges in Afghanistan. Rough-cut volcanic walls reared straight up a thousand feet, the west rim bathed in bright sunshine, the west side filled with light at the top, the brightness turning gray, then changing to darkness as the walls moved downward toward the gorge's floor that was cut up with miniature ravines that were treacherous because wheatgrass and *durga* bushes grew thickly around and in them so that, in the twilight, an unwary person could walk straight into them. Columns of basalt stood crookedly like silent sentinels, some rising from the very floor of the ravines, others from the bottom of the gorge itself. In some regions there were boulders so large that one had to crawl over them one by one. In other areas the rocks ranged from the size of a house to a grain of sand, much of the smaller rocks mingling with broken slate and shale to form a dangerous scree, several feet deep.

It took the force all day to navigate through the gorge, to

wade through the scree, avoid the ravines—the most shallow one was seventy-five feet, and climb over boulders. By the time the sun had dropped and total darkness was over the area, the entire force was in the highlands, each member ready to drop from exhaustion, including the Death Merchant. All night and all day it had moved, with only a ten minute rest every few hours and a two hour break at dawn.

During the days that followed, Khair Ghazi and the *mujahideen* closed in on the Kabul valley as rapidly as possible, the twisting route going along mountain trails, through forested valleys, and around mountains "growing" out of mountains.

Sixty-four kilometers from the Kabul valley, they came to a large encampment of Kuchis, Afghan nomads who seldom stayed in one place more than several months. There were dozens of black goat-hair tents, some horses, hundreds of sheep, and scores of yaks—the latter, ridiculous shaggy beasts, used for heavy baggage.

The Kuchis were not warriors, and Ibrahim Punjib, the headman, was not happy to see Khair Ghazi and his heavily armed *mujahideen*. However, custom had to prevail. Punjib nervously invited Ghazi and his aides and Camellion and the other Westerners into his tent and courteously invited them to sit down. To one side women were baking bread in a stone oven. Other women brought tea in tin cups while Ibrahim Punjib and his two sons explained that runners from Abdullah Saljoonque and Mohammad Malikyar were seeking Khair Ghazi.

"Only yesterday a messenger and the four men with him passed this way. He was seeking you, wanting to know if we had seen you," Punjib said, Opening a small box, he took out a pinch of snuff and sniffed it into his hand.

Had the Kuchis seen any Russians? Yes. Three days earlier a Soviet armored column had passed close by.

"Now please go, Malik Khair Ghazi," urged Punjib. "Your being here is a danger, for us and for you. . . ."

A week after the *mujahideen* had moved through the Aknib Limok, they came to the ruins of Shahr-i-Chulghula, an ochre-colored citadel sitting on a hill in the center of the plain. This was the "Fort of Noise," the name recalling the screams of thirty-one thousand people who were massacred seven hundred and fifty years ago by Genghis Khan in his fury over losing his favorite grandson in battle nearby.

It was at Shahr-i-Chulghula that they found the five men sent by Mohammad Malikyar and Abdullah Saljoonque.

"They and many of their men are waiting close to the Jam Minaret," Fawin Ja-Kusi, the messenger, informed Khair Ghazi. Tall and broad-shouldered, he was less than thirty in years, and had a very pointy chin. "We"—he waved a hand at the other four men—"assumed that since you were headed in this direction, you would stop at Shahr-i-Chulghula. We knew that the coward Ibrahim Punjib would tell you that we had passed through his camp."

"Allah was merciful," Khair Ghazi said. "Give me a report on what has taken place since we left the caves near Bashawal."

Elrod Kinsey leaned close to the Death Merchant and whispered, "The Jam Minaret is in the Zaranj section of the Kabul valley. That's a lucky break for us."

Camellion nodded slowly. To the northeast he could see the snows of Karl Marx peak in Soviet Russia; to the east rose the higher peaks of the Kush. Beneath the distant clouds, ninety-two miles away, to the east, lay Communist China.

A lucky break? It would take more than "luck" to get them into Kabul, much less into the Central Prison, then out of the city and back into the mountains.

And miracles no longer happen. They went out with the Middle Ages.

Fudge. . . .

CHAPER EIGHT

15.00 hours. Three days after meeting Fawin Ja-Kusi at Shahr-i-Chulghula:

After Khair Ghazi, Abdullah Saljoonque and Mohammad Malikyar had exchanged "*Lesta sha*(s)" and "*Kor yenji, kaa unji*(s)," Khair Ghazi introduced Richard Camellion, Kinsey, Wesslin, and Hooppole to the two leaders of the two other groups of *mujahideen*, informing them that the four men from the West had fought well and brave against the murderers from the land of the hammer and the sickle.

"*Staray ma-shi*," Abdullah Saljoonque said solemnly, his eyes moving over the Death Merchant and the other men, keen eyes that probed and analyzed.

Mohammad Malikyar greeted Camellion and the others with another traditional phrase, saying, "*Nosi baruui nib quji'il*" ("May all the days of your life be sweet."). Then in English without the least trace of an accent, "I'm glad that you men are with us. We need experts who are familiar with Soviet methods of killing."

"We are more than happy to be here, *Malik* Mohammad Malikyar and *Malik* Abdullah Saljoonque. We will help you all we can," Kinsey said heartily. As the CIA officer, he was technically the spokesmen for the group of four, even though *Redwing* had informed Kinsey that it was the Death Merchant who would make all final decisions.

Sitting on the rug, toward the rear of the large camp, Camellion let his gaze wander through the opening of the tent to the outside. Saljoonque and Malikyar and the several hundred Afghan fighters with them had chosen the campsite with care, having pitched tents under a gigantic ledge that, like some monstrous tongue, stretched out for several hundred feet and was more than a hundred feet in thickness. It was impossible for Soviet helicopters to spot the *mujahideen* camped under the ledge. Even if the Russians had known the location of the freedom fighters, missiles could never have penetrated the long, thick overhang that jutted out from one of the mountains at the very edge of the Kush.

Looking west, the Death Merchant could see the hazy outline of the Jam Minaret in the distance. A sacred landmark to Afghans, the minaret—twenty-two stories above the ground—was a monument to ancient history, the entire tower lavishly decorated with flower patterns and graceful Arabic script. Scattered around the beautiful tower was the ruins of an ancient city of stone that had been part of the Ghorid dynasty.

During the middle of the twelfth century, the Ghorid dynasty had arisen from these valleys and, from its capital at Firoz Koh, Turquoise Mountain, had swept across Afghanistan and India as far as Bengal. Bold in battle, the Ghorids were also patrons of art, but they made the mistake of spreading their empire too thin. Within a few hundred years they were overthrown and forgotten, except to history.

There wasn't anything ancient about Abdullah Saljoonque, Mohammad Malikyar and their men, in spite of there seeming to be "centuries" between Saljoonque and Malikyar.

Wearing wool O.D. pants, a khaki shirt, Canadian "bush jacket" and Russian officer's boots, Malikyar was smooth-faced, his features pleasant and healthy-looking. Only thirty-three years old, he was six feet two inches tall and was not a man who knew the world from only the narrow viewpoint of an Afghan who had never been beyond the borders of his native country. A dentist who had practiced in Kabul, Malikyar had studied in Turkey and had spent time in England, Greece and Egypt.

Malikyar and Saljoonque had been discussed often during the move north, and it had not come as a surprise to the Death Merchant that Malikyar was educated and far removed from "It-is-the-will-of-Allah" Afghan tribesman. That was still another misconception of uninformed people: that the *mujahideen* were ignorant, superstitious hill people. Many were. Great numbers were not. Forty percent of the Afghan fighters were educated, were from the professions, or had been white collar workers. The remainder were farmers and herdsmen. What they all had in common was their deep hatred of the Soviet

Union and their determination to kill every Russian invader they could get their hands on.

Abdullah Saljoonque was also educated, but only by the standards if Islam. By Western standards he was a moron. Saljoonque was a *mullah*, or religious leader, and as such viewed the world through the eyes of a man whose bubble brain was dominated by the "Teachings of the Prophet." It had been Saljoonque who had been reluctant to form an alliance with Malikyar and Ghazi, firmly convinced that to accept aid from the West, from non-Muslims, from infidels, would be a horrible sin against Allah; but like all religious crackpots who can easily rationalize what God wants or doesn't want, Saljoonque changed his mind when he say that secret aid from the "infidels" in the CIA was invaluable. His slogan then became, *"Allah works in mysterious ways."*

Wearing the small, white turban of a *mullah*, Saljoonque was tall, thin, and dressed in *la'jus*, the dark cotton robe of an Afghan hillman. A hennaed beard brightened his otherwise long and serious face. His voice was equally serious as he gave the news of Soviet activity to Khair Ghazi and the other men sitting on the rug.

"The Russians know we are coming to attack," he said, his voice excited, "and they have done many things to prepare for us. They are too wise to spread their forces thin, and so they have abandoned the outlying area around Kabul and are concentrating their forces around the airbase and their headquarters."

"*Mullah* Saljoonque." The Death Merchant spoke. "Do you have any information on the number of troops guarding the Central Prison?"

Saljoonque's old but crafty eyes evaluated Camellion for some seconds. "Why do you want to know? What is so important about the Central Prison?"

Kinsey had assured Camellion that Khair Ghazi had given his word that he had not informed either Saljoonque or Malikyar about Fritz Werholtz and Stewart Hemschire. There wasn't any way of knowing who might be an informer, either among Malikyar or Saljoonque's *mujahideen*, or, for that matter, among Khair Ghazi's guerrillas. Saljoonque's question proved that Khair Ghazi had kept his word.

The Death Merchant had his answer prepared. "To free the prisoners and blow up the Central Prison would be an inspiration to every Afghan in the nation and a severe blow to the Soviets. Do you not agree?''

Saljoonque licked thin lips. ''That is very good reasoning, *kuvii* Richard Camellion. We are very concerned with the poor victims inside that hole of hell. Our main worry is that the savages from the north will execute them in a fit of bloodlust.''

''That kind of massacre isn't likely,'' Malikyar's deep voice insinuated itself into the conversation. ''The Russians are butchers, but they're not stupid. General Mozzhechkov knows that such a slaughter would unite all of Afghanistan against them.''

Malikyar stood an even six foot three, and his medium-full, well-trimmed mustache complemented his raven eyes and thick black hair. The Death Merchant sized him up as a man who knew how to carry out actions in a goal-oriented, purposeful way.

''It is possible that the KGB guards at the prison might slaughter the inmates at the last moment, when we attack?'' offered Hassan Shahdidri. One of Saljoonque's lieutenants, he was squat and blind in his left eye, the result of a piece of shrapnel. Over the blind eye was a green patch.

''It's a risk we'll have to take,'' Camellion said quickly. ''I ask all of you: how would it look if we didn't try to free those poor souls in the Central Prison? Everyone knows how prisoners are tortured hideously in Unit-K!''

''I agree, *kuvii* Camellion,'' Khair Ghazi said firmly.

''You're right; I don't doubt it.'' Looking at the Death Merchant, Mohammad Malikyar reached into the left top pocket of his bush jacket and took out a pack of *Golden Crescent* Turkish cigarettes. ''But such an attack won't be easy.''

The Death Merchant was on instant alert. What was going on that he didn't know about?

Admitted Abdullah Saljoonque, ''I am in agreement with all of you. ''We must attack the Central Prison. Allah would not forgive us if we didn't. The attack will be costly. The Soviets have almost a thousand men around the prison. Those devils have guessed that we might attack the prison as a symbolic blow to freedom and have acted accordingly.''

The Death Merchant felt as if he had been kicked in the

stomach by a mule. *A thousand troops! Great gobs of goosegrease and gumbo!*

Rod Hooppole cleared his throat uncomfortably. Elrod Kinsey, sitting across the rug from Camellion, caught his eye, Kinsey's look clearly saying—*Impossible!*

Grab the damned bulls by the horns and see what happens. There's no other route for me to go.

"I am willing to lead the attack against the Central Prison, if you will give me the men." Camellion quickly tacked on, "Naturally, with some of your lieutenants accompanying me."

Komi al-Badmor, one of Malikyar's aides, said in a practical manner, "The men will not follow an infidel." He turned his sun beaten face toward Camellion. "I mean no disrespect; yet you are not of our faith."

"I realize that." Camellion was polite. "However, they would follow one of you. I would be willing to plan the assault. Would that not be agreeable?"

"How many men would you require?" Abdullah Saljoonque's face was emphasized by a narrow fringe of closely trimmed beard that ended in a point at his chin.

"At least a thousand."

"I truly think that one thousand five hundred would be a better number," said Saljoonque, his tone, like his eyes, thoughtful. "Half that number will die by machine guns. They will die for a good cause. As you have said though, *kuvii* Richard Camellion"—his gaze swung first to Khair Ghazi, then to Mohammad Malikyar—"it is a question of manpower."

"We do not have the men," Khair Ghazi said reluctantly, his voice said, "not for a separate force to be used solely against the prison. We have almost 7,000 men. It will require from 3,000 to 4,000 to attack the airport. That leaves only 3,000 to storm the headquarters of the Russians which is very heavily guarded. Yet somehow an effort must be made to free the prisoners in the Central Prison. The *Ummah*[1] would never forgive us."

"What has the *Ummah* ever done for us?" grumbled Torak Adjar. "Except for the Egyptians, we are receiving no

[1]The universal brotherhood of Islam. It must be remembered that Islam is more than a religion; it is also a complete and systematic political ideology.

aid from our brothers. The Americans are doing more for us, and they are infidels!''

"One should not slur our brothers of the *Ummah*,'' Saljoonque said in admonishment. "We are all of the one true faith.''

"It is the truth, *Mullah* Saljoonque.'' Adjar stuck grimly to his guns. "Allah does not want us to put our heads in the sand and pretend things are not as they really are.''

"As the plan of attack now stands,'' went on Khair Ghazi, "one group, the largest, will come in from the north, the south, and the west. The smaller group will attack—''

"I will be in charge of the column coming in from the west!'' interjected Ismail Ghazi loudly, cutting off his father. "I and several hundred men will attack Central Prison. There, the matter is settled!''

"It sure is!'' snapped Jugen Wesslin, giving a sneering little laugh. "You and those men will be cut down like ripe wheat before a sharp blade.''

The other men in the circle regarded Ismail, now glaring at Wesslin, with mournful looking eyes.

The Death Merchant had had enough of Ismail, whom he considered a positive danger—*Now is as good a time as any I suppose. . . .*

"*Malik* Khair *khel* Bahauddin Ghazi. I must speak plainly. I must speak the truth.''

His eyes widening slightly, Khair Ghazi nodded. "Please do, *kuvii* Camellion.''

"It would be a grave mistake to let Ismail lead the men,'' stated the Death Merchant, knowing he was making an enemy of Ismail for life. "He is brave, but he does not have the training; and he is too rash in his judgments. We will lose many many men under the best of leadership. However, I don't see any reason why hundreds should die because of Ismail's rash actions.''

Ismail Ghazi was stunned, so amazed by Camellion's words that all he could do was sit there and stare disbelievingly at the Death Merchant, his mouth half-open, the veins in his neck pulsating faster and faster. Full realization struck him like a thunderbolt and he exploded, jumping to his feet.

"You damned infidel!'' he shouted, his voice dripping hatred. "How dare you accuse me of stupid actions! It was I who decided to attack the mine-laying patrol not far from Kabul. It was I—"

"And it was Camellion who took the most chances," spoke up Rod Hooppole angrily, "and stopped the Russians in the armored car from blowing all of us into little pieces. Your nutty plan cost Mului Imu his life and us priceless information, or haven't you ever heard of tactical intelligence?"

"Enough!" The word came from Khair Ghazi with the finality of a rifle shot. "Enough from the three of you! I will not tolerate such bickering. We are not children here."

"But you heard them!" snarled Ismail, a maniacal look on his face. "You heard them lie and insult me. I demand—"

"Ismail, shut up! When will you learn that to handle yourself you must use your head, and that to handle others you must use your heart. Seldom do you use your head, and you replace your heart with temper. Sit down!"

His features pure devilish rage, Ismail dropped to the rug. Khair Ghazi removed the "monocle" from his eye and half-smiled at the Death Merchant who regarded him with calm, unswerving eyes.

"It is twice as difficult to crush a half-truth as a whole lie," he said. "You have done neither. All you have done is state the truth. I know that you have. I know because you told me what I have known for a long time."

"My father!" began a shocked Ismail, the words choked.

"Be quiet!" Khair Ghazi raised his left hand but did not look at his son. "Some day you may learn that a man who enjoys responsibility usually gets it, but that a man who merely exercises authority always loses it." His gaze rested on the Death Merchant. "Ismail will not lead any of the men, *kuvii* Camellion. I had never intended him to."

Mohammad Malikyar, a chain smoker, lighted another *Golden Crescent* and exhaled noisily. He spoke rapidly, "Listen, all of you. We will have those extra thousand men— from the people in the suburbs around Kabul. I am sure of it."

"I do not understand," Khair Ghazi said, leaning forward, interest on his wrinkled face.

"Much has happened since you moved into the Kush and onto Bashawal and back to this area," said Malikyar. "As we explained, the Soviets have abandoned the suburbs around Kabul. Before they pulled back, they did attack suspected pockets of resistance. Almost always they were repulsed, not only by the *mujahideen*, but by the people. Even women and children attacked tanks and other vehicles with Molotov cocktails, as your own Amud Mojidi will verify. That is why he is not with us. He is keeping order in the suburbs.''

Khair Ghazi sat up straight. ''Mojidi has moved out of the mountains!'' he exclaimed with some surprise.

''But he did not have orders from you, Khair Ghazi!'' Sebghatullah Mahlik said sternly. ''He should have remained in the Kush with the men.''

''We had not received word from Mojidi,'' Khair Ghazi said to Malikyar. ''We had assumed that you and Mullah Saljoonque had made contact with him and the rest of my forces. But why? Why did he and the force not remain in the mountains?''

''He had to come down, *Malik* Khair Ghazi,'' said Malikyar. ''The Russians were becoming totally ruthless, shooting indiscriminately, killing even women and children. It was at the approach of Amud Mojidi, combined with the approach of my men and *Mullah* Saljoonque's *mujahideen*, that forced the Soviet forces to abandon the suburbs.''

''The last report we had was that they were concentrating their sweeps on the outer edge of Kabul, but still well within the city limits,'' said Komi al-Badmor.

''They are using their usual tactics,'' commented Jasim Luory, one of Malikyar's men. ''They will attack very quickly. Troops will land by helicopter or road to form a cordon surrounding the objective. The cordon—''

''The cordon is almost always established one day in advance from the objective!'' inserted Yasir Haduim, who was a lieutenant of Abdullah Saljoonque.

The Death Merchant was well aware how the Soviet forces operated. The cordon would secure naturally strategic terrain and dig in, with each sub-unit in visual contact with those on its flanks, creating total encirclement of the objective; mobile detachments would be held in reserve behind the cordon to pursue any *mujahideen* who might break through.

Outside the city, in open country, it would be different. When columns moved on the open roads, the HINDs would be overhead, *half* of the HINDs. They would watch for Afghan activity. The other HINDs would land troops on crests ahead of the column. In addition to its powerful armament, each HIND could carry eight to sixteen troops. These troops, belonging to standard motorized rifle units rather than special airmobile units, would secure any ambush positions and provide flank security until the column had passed.

"Even women and children!" exclaimed Khair Ghazi. He looked excitedly at Mohammad Malikyar. "Fighting Soviet armor?"

"It is true, all of it," Malikyar said, crushing out his cigarette. "Even the old ones—men and women—went after the Russians."

"I will tell you a true story," Abdullah Saljoonque said ceremoniously. "A few weeks ago it was the talk of everyone in Kabul. An old man—he was eighty-four years old—was a gatekeeper at a small children's school. One morning before the little ones arrived, the old one entered a classroom where a teacher was preparing the day's lessons. He told the teacher that his sons and daughters and other relatives had fled to Pakistan and, because of his age, he was certain that he would never see them again. 'I will die here in Kabul,' he said. He also told the teacher he had prayed that morning and promised Allah he would kill four Russians before the sun set. The teacher looked at him in amazement, then laughed. You see, he thought the old one was not right in the head. The old man left the school and walked to a bazaar. In its center was a Soviet tank. The crew had gotten out and were sitting nearby, drinking hot tea and smoking cigarettes. The old man walked up behind the Russians and, using a *Hazka*, decapitated two of the dogs before they knew what was happening. The other Russians started to run to their tank. The old man ran after them. He caught up with one of the Russians and buried the blade in the man's skull. The other Russians, by this time, regained the safety of their tank. The old man fled the bazaar, but was soon caught and taken to the turncoat governor, who quickly convened a court. The pig of a governor—you know he had been installed by the Russians— asked the old man why he had done such a terrible thing. The old man replied that he would tell, but first every person present must recite the *Shahadah*[2] to prove they were all

[2]In Arabic: "There is no God but Allah, and Mohammed is the messenger of Allah."

115

Muslims. The court agreed, and all present recited the *Shahadah*. The old man told them he now believed they were all Muslims. He said that he had prayed to Allah that morning and promised to kill four Russians before the end of the day, and if they would please excuse him for ten minutes, he would like to find the fourth and kill him.''

Pausing, Mullah Abdullah Saljoonque studied the circle of faces. ''I tell you the story as an indicator of how the people in Kabul feel. They will fight the Soviet dogs with their bare hands if necessary.''

Mohammad Malikyar seemed to be enjoying himself as he said, ''Already in some of the suburbs those traitors who willingly helped the Russians are paying for their crimes. We estimate that so far several hundred of these Judases have been shot and executed in other ways by patriotic citizens.''

Malikyar then reiterated. ''We'll have those extra thousand fighters. I am sure. But they can't fight with their bare hands. Mr. Kinsey, can we be assured of weapons coming from your organization?''

''Yes, you can,'' responded Kinsey, who proceeded to give a report of the arrangements made by *Redwing*. He finished with, ''We still have to work out the exact coordinates.''

Nothing more was said, the group being interrupted by several veiled women who stepped between Hassan Shahdidri and Yasir Haduim and placed large trays inside the circle, trays filled with chicken, mutton, bread, grapes, and yogurt.

''The Zaranj area is free of the enemy at the present time,'' said Saljoonque, after the women left and the men began eating. His hand, holding a strip of mutton, paused in front of him, as if he had remembered something important. ''We can't be sure that the section will remain that way.''

''Soviet interference from the air is not really a problem,'' the Death Merchant interposed. ''We'll be in contact with our people while the planes are in flight. Should Soviet aircraft suddenly appear, our planes will have to turn back and another attempt will have to be made.''

Camellion resumed eating, pretending to enjoy the mutton, which he didn't. The chicken would have been delicious without the thick brown sauce dripping from each piece. Camellion couldn't decide whether the sauce tasted like burnt rubber or whiskey flavored with molasses. He had decided that the Afghans were as crazy-brave as the CIA was ruthless, the former because it was their way and they didn't know any better, the latter because the Agency did what it had to do to contain the organized gangsterism called Communism.

"Speaking of the drop of weapons," began Jugen Wesslin, addressing the entire group, "in my opinion the cargo planes will be shot down before they even get to Zaranj region."

"You can't be that certain," Rod Hooppole said.

"Your military adviser is pessimistic about the operation, Malik Khair Ghazi." Abdullah Saljoonque's soft voice was curious and probing. "I find thar rather odd that a military adviser from the West should be against the plan."

"He speaks what he feels it is his duty to speak," answered Khair Ghazi. "We do not always agree with him, but we do respect his honesty."

"Tell me, *kuvii* Wesslin, why do you think the drop will not succeed?" pursued Saljoonque, using the end of a knife blade to dip into a bowl of yogurt.

Camellion interposed in a quick voice, "It's only 170 kilometers from the Pakistan border to Kabul. That's only a hop around the block for aircraft." Such an argument was weak and Camellion knew it. For fast fighter jets 170 klicks was a skip around the house! At the time, it was the best he could do.

"Even so, the Russians aren't stupid," Wesslin countered. "Their radar will pick up the transports the instant they cross the border—and how long will it take fighters from the Kabul airbase to intercept them? Fifteen minutes at the most!"

"The Company knows what it's doing!" snapped Kinsey in an angry tone as he reached out and picked up a chicken leg from one of the brass trays. "I'm positive that the experts planning the drop are not going to send in planes only to have them shot down."

"We'll see," Wesslin retorted.

"Soviet aircraft avoids the mountains and mountainous areas," commented Mohammad Malikyar. He continued to chew as he spoke, making loud noises. "They're afraid of our ground-to-air missiles. They think we have ten times the number Grails and Stingers that we actually have." He chuckled for several moments. "We have six Stingers and ten Grails with us, scattered up above, all round this camp, and that's all we have. Tell me, Mr. Kinsey, will your people be dropping more missiles or just ground weapons?"

117

"I won't know until after I talk with them the next time," Kinsey explained. "I can only tell you I'm certain the drop is going to be made."

"And when will you contact your people by radio?" asked Torak Adjar, who began to stuff yogurt into his mouth. "I would assume"—he stopped to swallow—"it will be as soon as we decide on the best location in the Zaranj section."

"All we need to know is the 'where,' " said Kinsey.

The darkness was not a problem. Some of the *mujahideen* had carried the long antenna up to high rocks before sunset and the wire was in place by the time Elrod Kinsey turned on the shortwave, made contact with *Redwing* and gave the station the coordinates for the airdrop. Four times he repeated the longitude and the latitude, then asked for and received double confirmation.

Redwing: How soon do you want us to deliver the goods, and what time?

This time the operator was a man with a high-pitched voice.

Time of delivery had also been discussed by the group. "Four days from now, at 15.00," Kinsey spoke into the mike. "Our Russian friends don't care for the early morning hours. Over."

Redwing: "Four days? Couldn't the time be shortened to two?"

"No it can't! It will take two days to get to the drop area and another day to recon the Russians. At this point we don't know that they won't be in the area. As I told you earlier, I'll contact you so that you can be sure the area is safe. Confirm. Over."

The drop of supplies and arms would take place only 6.436 kilometers, or four land miles northeast of Dukimor, in a suburb of Kabul. After a good deal of discussion, it had been decided that the best available locale was the Sirq Plain that, on the north, the south and the east, was ringed by mountains riddled with caves—a natural fortress in that missiles from gunships would not be able to reach the *mujahideen*. It was also unlikely that the Russians would land either regular troops or commandos on the plain and expose them to triple crossfire. An armored force from Kabul? Negative. There was too much danger of an ambush in going through the

118

streets of Dukimor. To bypass the city would require too much time.

"Even if it weren't for the mountains the Soviets wouldn't dare send troops past Dukimor," Mohammed Malikyar had said.

For a change, Jugen Wesslin had been in agreement. "*Ja*, the Russians always play it safe. They wouldn't want to take strength from their garrisons at the airbase and at their headquarters in Kabul."

Redwing: "Very well. We'll deliver on your coordinates, four days from this day at 15.00. Over."

Kinsey shifted the wad of tobacco in his mouth, spit a stream of juice on the ground and requested that *Redwing* give information regarding the method and/or methods that would be employed to insure the safety of the delivery planes.

"There will be twelve modified Fairchilds[3] accompanied by fifteen H-56 fighters,"[4] said *Redwing*. "We assure you that those twenty-seven planes will get the job done. Over."

Stunned, Kinsey almost swallowed his wad of tobacco. In contrast, a self-satisfied smile crept over the Death Merchant's tanned face. Twenty-seven planes were an armada! What did the Company intend to drop—tanks? Several Fairchilds could easily carry three to four thousand automatic rifles! Another thing: why would the Pakistan government permit such a large number of aircraft to leave its soil and fly into Afghanistan? The Paks were frightened frigid of the Russians! *Unless the Agency has proved to the Paks that the Soviet Union won't invade Pakistan! There has to be more. The Russians can send up a hundred SU-17 and SU-20s from the base in Kabul. They'd zap those twenty-seven planes out of the blue in nothing flat!*

"That's it?" Kinsey almost snarled into the mike. "Quit insulting my intelligence and give me the rest of it damned fast. Twenty-seven planes would have less chance of getting through than a snowball in the center of the sun! What's the gimmick? And why we're at it, why so many planes? Over, God damn it!"

"This is *Mockingbird*," cut in the Death Merchant, hold-

---

[3]Fairchild C-119 Packet. The C-119 to -119K Boxcar and AC-119 Shadow.

[4]The Hawker Siddeley Hunter—Hunter 1 to 79.

ing the small, square mike close to his mouth. "We have to give the Afghans a reasonable explanation. Wesslin has already told them the plan will fail—and that kraut is your own man whom you sent months ago. We can't tell the Afghans that twenty-seven planes are coming in without some kind of special protection. They'd think we were out of our skulls. Don't stall on this. Either give us the information or I'll be forced to tell them the drop has been scratched. I'll tell you something else. If I have to do that, you can tell the 'Higher Authority' to take the two hundred grand and ram it up a camel's butt. Now let's have some facts."

There was a long pause at the other end of the transmission, some 830 miles away. Kinsey glanced worriedly at Camellion. Neither man spoke. At length the reply came in:

"Each aircraft, including the Fairchilds, will carry a new type of missile. Technically, it's the B-L-X Medusa. For security reasons, we can't give you information about the missile. We can assure you they will protect the aircraft. Over."

"The Russians can send up a hundred fighters from Kabul!" Kinsey said coldly. "Or don't numbers make a difference?"

"We said that the missiles will protect the aircraft," came back the reply. "We can tell you this: each Medusa is actually twelve missiles. Over."

"Hold on a moment," Camellion barked into the mike. He took his finger off the button and motioned to Kinsey, indicating that he should also deactivate the mike in his hand.

Kinsey did so and regarded Camellion expectantly. "We're not going to get any more out of them about the missile," he whispered, even though the nearest Afghan was a hundred feet away. They had moved the transmitter away from the ledges and the overhangs and were out in the open, in the sight of only God and the stars (and possibly a U.S. or Soviet satellite or two).

"Tell them to give you a list of the arms they're going to drop," whispered Camellion. Twelve Fairchilds could supply a small army."

"I was thinking the same thing." Kinsey pressed the button on the mike.

The list of weapons was awesome—4,000 assault rifles and 6 mags for each weapon; 5,000 frag grenades; 1,000 shoulder-fired Stinger missiles; 5 heavy machine guns and 20,000 rounds of .50-caliber ammo; ten 3-in. mortars, and 50 rounds for each weapon; 1,000 MAS anti-tank free-flight disposable missiles.

". . . Over," finished *Redwing*.

"We have it," Kinsey said in a kind of awed voice. "Out."

"The Afghans aren't going to believe this," Kinsey said, removing the antenna from the rear terminals of the transmitter. "I'm trying to decide whether or not I do."

The Death Merchant didn't comment. The world was one big variable married to a lot of "ifs" and "maybes." He was positive of one thing:

If there's any way of killing evil, it's not by killing men!

CHAPTER NINE

"A barber learns to shave on an orphan's face, and a wise man always knows his friends," *Mullah* Abdullah Saljoonque said to Camellion and Kinsey after they gave the good news to the group of *mujahideen*. "In the United States we have found a true friend. Surely your nation is favored by Allah."

Even if we are infidels! Camellion mused to himself. But the Death Merchant only nodded with Kinsey and thanked the *Mullah*, after which Kinsey gave Saljoonque and the rest of the Afghans a lot of garbage about how the U.S. Government wanted to preserve freedom throughout the world and would do all it could, not only to contain Communism but to eventually smash it.

Destroy Communism? The Death Merchant was pessimistic, his dim view based on solid evidence. The United States would be lucky if it could stave off its own internal collapse. Serious energy problems were right around the corner, and unless something was done quickly by 1990 the American transportation system would collapse. Aliens from Asia, from Mexico and Latin American had already ruined many major cities. The demise of their economy and the free enterprise system was staring the American people in the face, while lawlessness was increasing, due to Kennedy-type liberalism.[1]

The decline and fall of America, like ancient Rome. . . .

Foolish little men! Everyone knows he is right. And the dimwits in government are convinced they are right. But KNOWING is one thing and BELIEVING quite another. None of us KNOWS very much about anything. We've only convinced ourselves that we do. The truth is that we just BELIEVE. Real knowing involves divine awareness, divine cosmic consciousness, and none of us has any of that. If we did, we would not be on this little three-dimensional globe. If I had any sense I wouldn't be in this damned country!

The entire group moved out the next morning at dawn and headed west. Progress was slow. It had to be, not only because of the number of the *mujahideen*—almost a thousand— but because they could not move with total freedom in open country. Out of necessity, the march had to be restricted to areas that offered measures of protection from possible Soviet aircraft. No one actually expected HINDs or any other kind of planes. But who could be sure? Where was the man who could say he was *positive* the Soviets wouldn't attack?

That afternoon they crossed the asphalt highway that connected Kabul with Kandahar, 380 miles to the southwest. The road, built by the U.S. Agency for International Development, intersected another road—this one of concrete—that had been built by the Soviet Union. The pig farmer road stretched north and connected with another road that led to the Soviet Union.

Toward dusk they came to the small town of Wakhan, a village of four hundred houses on the long slope of a steep hill. The houses were built of wood—squared logs chinked with mud and stones—and on the flat roofs corn, walnuts, beans, mulberries, and apricots had been spread out to dry.

The village council and a large crowd of happy people came out to meet the fighters, Alja Khan, the *Jukiabkr,* or leader of the council, almost weeping for joy as he explained that the small Soviet force had pulled out ten days ago.

''The sons of diseased dogs left during the dark hours of

---

[1] All this was foreseen by a recent symposium with both U.S. mayors and scientists in attendance.

the night," said Alja Khan, who was as thin as a rifle and a foot taller than a broomstick. "A hundred of Allah's cursed they were. The police didn't know they had left until the next morning. Those ten policemen were from our own people. They were traitors. We hanged them the same morning. You honored men will see them hanging there when we go into the town. They will hang there until they rot."

The force didn't see the ten corpses swinging from branches of trees in the hot and brisk *siah bad*. It didn't because it didn't go into Wakhan. It moved on and camped in the hills. Again the *mujahideen* moved on at dawn, scores of guards, with walkie-talkies, posted on each flank, to the rear and several miles in front of the main groups.

At 10.00 four *mujahideen* brought two young men, hardly out of their teens, to Khair Ghazi and explained that they had met the two four and a half klicks to the west and that one of them claimed to be a messenger from Amud Mojidi, the man in charge of Khair Ghazi's main force.

"It is this one, *Malik* Khair Ghazi," one of the guerrillas said. "His name is Amanullah Gotume."

Khair Ghazi studied the round faced youth who was dressed in Western clothes. "*Staray ma-shi,*" he said to Gotume. "Give me the message."

"*Kor yenji, kaa unji,* oh, *Malik* Khair Ghazi," replied Gotume nervously. "Amid Mojidi said—"

"Enough!" Khair Ghazi spoke sharply. "You are not a messenger from Amud Mojidi." He motioned to one of his men. "Cut his throat."

One of the *mujahideen* instantly pulled his *Hazka* from the tight sash around his waist and made a grab for the terrified Amanullah Gotume, who let out a gurgling squawk and fell to his knees, thinking that he would soon be facing Allah. Another of Ghazi's men wrapped an arm around the neck of the other man and pulled his *Hazka*.

"Wait!" commanded Ghazi. "Do not kill him, not yet." He then said to Gotume. "If Amud Mojidi sent to to me, did he not instruct you to tell me something before you gave the message?"

"Y-Yes. I-I f-forgot," gasped Amanullah Gotume, shaking like a leaf in a hard breeze. "He said to first tell you that 'the grapes are still green.' "

"Release him. He is from Mojidi," said Khair Ghazi. "Give me the message."

"He said to tell you that he is waiting for you in Mitokin. He said to tell you that your *mujahideen* and the *mujahideen* of *Malik* Abdullah Saljoonque and *Malik* Mohammad Malikyar have surrounded Kabul and are awaiting your arrival and the arrival of *Malik* Abdullah Saljoonque and *Malik* Mohammad Malikyar."

"What of Soviet activity in the area?" demanded Khair Ghazi.

"They are bombing from the air, attacking Mitokin, Pitask, Limgokar and other outlying areas. Many innocent people are dying. The soviet dogs are turning everything into a hell, oh, *Malik* Khair Ghazi."

"The area ahead . . . is it free of Russians?" Ismail Ghazi glared at Gotume. "Did you see any on your way to us?"

"No, we did not. . . ."

The march toward Dukimor continued, but not without incident. Ten miles east of where the airdrop was scheduled to take place, eight Soviet Mi-24 HINDs attacked. However, the force had been warned by advance scouts, now six miles ahead of the small army, and was safely concealed in rocks and the men with the Stinger and the Grail missiles were ready by the time the gunships were seen.

"The Mi-24s have three vulnerable points that are impossible to armor," the Death Merchant mentioned to Rod Hooppole and Mohammad Malikyar, both of whom were lying with him underneath a large outcropping of basalt surrounded by large boulders. "The turbine air intake, the tail rotor assembly and the oil tank. Heh-heh! That oil tank is conveniently located beneath the red star on the fuselage."

Malikyar flipped away his *Golden Crescent*. "It doesn't make any difference," he said in his clipped voice. "Once the Stingers and the Grails sight the target, it's all over. Even if the gunships stay high, they still have to come low enough to get within range of the missiles."

"Yeah and the fighters don't fare so well either in these parts." Hooppole almost had to shout, for by now the enemy gunships were very close. "With their thin skin they're vulnerable to ground fire. Then there's their flight limitations at low altitudes, especially low atmospheric density. Oh-oh! Here they come.''

The HINDs came in at five hundred feet, all eight spread out in a line, not more than several hundred feet apart—a tipoff of the *mujahideen* below that the Soviet gunships intended to make only one quick run, in the hope that their rockets and missiles could do the job in one quick swoop. . . .

The HINDs did their best; they fired off their ''Spiral'' missiles and 57mm rockets from the pylons on their stubby wings, the several hundred violent explosions shaking the rocks and destroying scores of linden and poplar trees, the tremendous bursts throwing up tons of blasted rock and killing five of the *mujahideen* with Stinger missiles.

The other freedom fighter with the American Stinger and ten men with the Soviet Grails fired . . . eleven quick whooshes and eleven tail streams. The missiles were on their way.

The Soviet pilots did their best again, now to avoid and/or outrun the missiles, putting their choppers through every maneuver possible.

None worked.

BLAAAAMMMM-BLAAAAMMMM-BLAAAAMMMM-BLAAAA-MMMM! There were very brief but bright balls of flame and booming concussion, and four of the Mi-24 HINDs exploded together. In less time than it took Mohammad Malikyar to light another *Golden Crescent*, the four other HINDs exploded, filling the dreary and smoky sky with pieces and parts of machines, and even smaller pieces and parts of what had been men, the whole mass—much of it burning—raining down to plink and plunk on the rocks.

The Soviet gunships had caused damage, a quick count revealing that eighty-seven *mujahideen* had been killed, some by falling rock, others by concussion from exploding Soviet missiles and rockets. Two men had been turned into corpses by falling debris from the blown apart choppers.

Hours later, after the force had reorganized, burned the dead under loose rock, and resumed movement, Jugen Werner Wesslin remarked to Camellion and Elrod Kinsey, ''You can't blame the educated Afghans for despising the United States, in spite of what Saljoonque said. Most of the tribesmen have never heard of your Uncle Sam. It's different with the white collar and the professional classes. They can't under-

125

stand official U.S. reluctance to provide weapons for a struggle which is, by any definition, clearly a fight for freedom. This is particularly repulsive to educated Afghans in view of the common Soviet policy of supplying massive aid to enemies of the United States. For example, the amounts of Soviet aid to the Vietnamese communists. Surface-to-air missiles, anti-tank weapons, light and heavy weapons, radar-controlled anti-aircraft—you name it and the Russians gave it to the gooks to use to kill Americans.[2] Washington knew where the stuff was coming from. The whole world knew. But it was business as usual. No one even hinted at going to war with the Soviet Union.''

"Look my German friend," said Kinsey, "you can't expect the U.S. to risk a nuclear war with the Soviet Union in any effort to aid the Afghans. And where in hell do you think the arms in the Fairchilds are coming from? From the same people who are paying your fee as a military adviser— the great American taxpayer.''

"*Ja*, but it's the first massive aid attempt your country has made," Wesslin said. "If I know the Paks, it cost your government plenty. The Paks are like your *Amerikaner* businessmen— they'd sell their souls for money, if the price is right.''

"You have a lot to learn about politics, Wesslin," the Death Merchant said. "Like killing, politics is a malleable art, acquiescent and philosophically flexible. . . .''

04.00 hours. The section of the Zaranj plain, where the airdrop would be made, was at least reached. Looking around with the other men, the Death Merchant saw that the area was perfect, not only for the drop but for the protection of the *mujahideen*, that is, before they moved into the suburbs.

Steep brick-red hills were on each side of the Sirq Plain which was, at its widest, a thousand yards. The plain narrowed to a mere five hundred feet to the east where there were more red mountains, these larger than the hills on the north and the south. These mountains were also covered with flaming yellow poplars and, here and there were small clumps of wild apricot trees.

There was a flaw. Should Soviet helicopter gunships appear after the drop, while the Afghans were out on the plain

[2]57,500 Americans were killed. 300,000 others were wounded.

carrying the crates, catastrophe would become reality. The *mujahideen* would be shot apart.

"*Herr* Camellion, what is your opinion?" Jugen Wesslin looked up at the dreary sky. For days the clouds had thickened until, this day, there were blue-black clouds tumbling all over the sky.

"It's a matter of luck," Camellion replied. "It will take an hour or more to carry the crates to the caves. That's a lot of time. But there isn't any way we can condense it."

"Why not make the drop over the hills?" suggested Wesslin, who then answered himself. "I suppose the trees exclude that possibility."

"Plus carrying down heavy crates downward over rocks," finished the Death Merchant.

Hooppole spoke up. "Since the women from Dukimor brought all that water, I'm not going to wait any longer. I'm going to shave and take a bath."

"It's a good idea," said Wesslin, who looked again at the sky.

At the approach of the guerrillas, the people of Dukimor, only 3.9 miles to the west, had rushed out to meet them, offering help and bringing more than food and water and the use of their homes . . . those houses that hadn't been burned out. They also brought reports of Soviet activity in Kabul. The Russian forces had abandoned Dukimor and, as far as any of the people knew, the other suburbs.

"Return to your houses," Khair Ghazi had told the crowd of happy people. "For the present, that is the best way you can help us fight the evil dung from the north."

The Death Merchant had quickly whispered into the Afghan leader's ear, who then added, "We can use a hundred strong men tomorrow morning to help us move arms and other weapons. Be here at one o'clock tomorrow morning."

Representatives had also come from Amud Mojidi, Abdullah Saljoonque, and Mohammad Malikyar, arriving in nine captured GOR-4 Soviet army trucks. Mojidi and Khair Ghazi's men were in Pestiwar, a town south of Kabul. Saljoonque's force was in Lashkar to the north. Malikyar's fighters were scattered out in Kemdash, to the west. To the east, six hundred men from all three forces were in Saljug, the suburb that controlled the highways to the east. Any Soviet ground

127

force attacking the Sirq Plain would have to move through Saljug.

A conference had been held and it was decided that the representatives would remain with the force. After the drop, the arms would be taken into Dukimor and from there taken by truck to the three forces. The three leaders would go with the weapons; with the three leaders would go the battle plans for the attacks on the Soviet airbase, the Soviet headquarters and . . . the Central Prison in Kabul.

There was a problem, one that was strictly Richard Camellion's. That problem was Ismail Mohammed Ghazi. Mohammad Malikyar had warned the Death Merchant, "Ismail will never forgive you for speaking out against him in front of the others. He has a hill-type mentality and is dominated by the revenger part of the *Pakhto* code. Watch your back, night and day, my American friend."

Camellion had thanked the Afghan leader, adding, "I've been doing that." Thinking of how Ismail had been avoiding him, he didn't add what he felt was a certainty: that he would be forced to kill Ismail Ghazi.

Should the Russians not do the job for me. . . .

Elrod Kinsey contacted *Redwing* at 07.00 and again reported that, according to all available reports, the area was free of Soviet ground forces.

Was the drop still scheduled for 15.00 hours?

Affirmative, replied *Redwing*.

Would darkness be a problem?

Haven't you heard of night sight devices? Call us back at 14.00.

At 10:34 P.M. it began to drizzle, a fine, steady drizzle.

"It's almost a certainty that Soviet choppers will attack us before they attack the Fairchilds and their escorts," offered Rod Hooppole who was in a cave, south of the plain, with Camellion, Kinsey, Torak Adjar and forty of the *mujahideen belonging to Mullah* Saljoonque. The entrance of the cave had been partially blocked with stones to hide the glow of burning candles. The men who had blocked the opening had been very careful that none of the stones touched the antenna of Kinsey's shortwave.

"It is a very real possibility," conceded the Death Merchant.

128

"The force is safe in these caves, unless a missile explodes in front of the mouth or the Russians use clustered thermite."

"Clustered thermite?" Torak Adjar became alert. The dozens of candles had generated hundreds of shadows, many of which, flickering over Adjar, made him look like something out of the *Arabian Nights*. "What is this clustered thermite?"

"A hundred times worse than *Voska* 'Dragon Fire,' " explained the Death Merchant. "The thermite is made into packets and exploded by a central charge. The individual packages then explode on contact. I doubt if the Russians use CT. It would be ineffective against us in these caves. But CT would be ideal after the arms were dropped and the crates were lying out there on the plain, depending on how the gunships attacked and how they dispersed the CT."

"Why did you not mention this before now?" Adjar stared at Camellion, his tone both angry and worried. "For the love of Allah, all the arms could be destroyed by this CT as you call it!"

"Why add to the worries the leaders already have," Camellion said. "CT or not, there wasn't anything we could do about it; there still isn't. All we can do is hope that everything goes well."

Nodding, Adjar smiled at Camellion. "Allah has given you wisdom, *kuvii* Camellion. If begging should ever be your unfortunate lot, I know you will knock only at the large gates."

Hooppole got slowly to his feet, stretched, then sat down again on the blanket. "Well, laddies, all I can say is that those—what's the name of those new missiles?"

"The B-L-X Medusa," Kinsey said, glancing at the "computer" chronograph on his right wrist.

"Those Medusas had better work. Frankly, I don't believe the planes will get through. I think the instant those Fairchilds are inside Afghanistan the Russians will blow them out of the sky." Hooppole looked from face to face, as if expecting someone to violently disagree with him.

Camellion did, but mildly. "I think the Soviet planes will stay at a distance and keep our birds in sight on radar. The Soviet fighters won't attack until our birds get here."

Hooppole stared thoughtfully at the end of his glowing cigarette.

"I think you're wrong. Why should the Russians wait?"

129

"To see where the drop is going to take place."

"You could be right; I don't think you are. The Russians have to know we're in this area. Ipso facto, it follows that the Soviets would deduce these caves and these mountains. They're a natural defense. The plain in the middle is perfect for a drop."

The Death Merchant shrugged. "We'll see. . . ."

At 13.00 more than two hundred men from Dukimor arrived and were led through the drizzle and the darkness to the safety of the caves.

At 14.00 Kinsey again contacted *Redwing*. Zero hour. The Fairchilds were taking off from an airfield outside of Peshawar that was only forty-two miles from the Afghan border. The Hunter-56 fighters would follow and join the Fairchilds shortly before the cargo planes entered Afghanistan.

Kinsey shut off the shortwave and removed the headphones. "The show is on the road. . . ."

"All we can do is wait and have faith in Allah," Torak Adjar said. He then recited the Muslim *Shahadah*.

The Death Merchant put on his Canadian field cap and got to his feet. He had put on clean, black all-purpose coveralls, and had two Steyr GB pistols strapped around his waist. A walkie-talkie, in its leather case, was also on his belt.

"I'm going outside," he said and turned to go.

"I'll go with you," Hooppole said and got up. "We can always run back inside if we hear Soviet choppers."

"Count me in." Kinsey pushed himself up from the blanket.

They stood twenty feet from the entrance to the cave and looked up at the blackness that was the sky—not that they expected to hear the engines of the Fairchilds and the Hunter fighter escorts. It would be a while before the planes arrived. Soviet helicopter gunships could attack anytime.

Camellion squinted in the darkness. "There's no point in standing here in the open. Let's get over to that tree."

Their eyes slowly adjusting to the blackness, the three men walked to a poplar, sat down underneath the branches, on some rocks, and began the wait. Far to the west they could hear low rumblings, often four and five, right in a row. At other times there was only a single hollow reverberation. The sounds were explosions. As the representatives of the three forces of *mujahideen* had reported, the Russians were blowing up entire blocks of buildings in Kabul in an effort to create a buffer zone, a no man's land of rubble between themselves and the freedom fighters outside of the city.

The minutes dragged by, each second seeming to hold itself back as if to torture the men.

Hooppole said at length, "I say, have any of you ever wondered what it's like to be dead?"

"Wesslin would probably tell you it's like being in the Berlin of a hundred years ago," Kinsey said with a small laugh. "To him, that period was paradise."

"I think that dying is similar to drifting off to sleep in a soft rain," mused Camellion, "provided you die from natural causes. Those who die very suddenly, say from being shot or from a heart attack—I don't think they even know it. No doubt they're very confused to find themselves in another condition."

"Don't you mean 'another world?' " Hooppole said. He turned and looked at the Death Merchant who was sitting with his back against the trunk of the tree. " 'Condition' is a strange word to use for being dead."

"I don't see why. We're alive in the physical world, existing in time and space. 'Life' after death has to be out of time and space. It's a condition, a condition that's mental."

Hooppole shook his head. "Minds without bodies. The thought is weird. I can't even conceive of not being aware of my body."

"I don't mean it in the sense that you're implying," Camellion explained. "A mind existing in another continuum would have to be bodiless. And as far as not being aware of your body, are you aware of your actual physical body when you're asleep and having a vivid dream? No, you're not. Only the dream is real."

All three heard the sound, very faintly at first, almost non-existent among the rustling of the leaves in the strong breeze. Very quickly though the sound from the southeast grew louder so that within half a minute it became very obvious that Camellion, Kinsey, and Hooppole were hearing the engines of many airplanes, aircraft that was headed in their direction.

"By God, there they are!" Kinsey said excitedly, "and not a pig farmer in sight. Isn't that what you call the Russians, Camellion—pig farmers?"

"We can't see anything standing under this tree." Standing up, Hooppole sounded more excited than Kinsey. "Let's get out in the open. It will be two or three minutes before the planes get here."

"No way," Camellion said, moving out from underneath the branches of the poplar. "We'll be better off right in front of a cave, or do you want to risk having a crate of assault rifles crease your skull—if the planes get here."

"You have a point," muttered Hooppole, then to himself, "What I wouldn't give for an NVD." With another glance at the sky, he hurried after Camellion and Kinsey.

The sound of the planes were three times as loud by the time they reached the entrance to the cavern, a steady droning, increasing in volume, that was frightening.

More sounds, these rapidly increasing. Jet fighters! Coming in fast from the north—too far away to be a part of the armada from Pakistan. The sounds became very loud in three times the length of time it took Kinsey to spit out a brown stream of tobacco juice.

"Well, the fence has fallen down, the roof leaks, and the hail has wrecked the wheat," exclaimed Camellion. "We're not hearing Chinese lumberjacks cutting down trees with chop sticks! The pig farmers have arrived in force."

The "pig farmers" had indeed arrived, in the form of thirty-one SU-11 "Fishpot-C" fighters.[3] Each fighter plane carried four AA-1 "Alkali" missiles and had a top speed of Mach 0.95 or 1160 km/h (720 mph)—far from the best fighters the Soviets had, but more than efficient for use in Afghanistan. The SU-11s had radar-spotted the twelve Fairchilds and the fifteen Hunter fighters as soon as the twenty-seven planes had crossed the Pak/Afghan border and, like the H-56 Hunters, had been flying back and forth, "pacing" the air armada, waiting for the Fairchilds to parachute their cargoes.

The three men waited, staring intently at the black sky.

"I'd like to know why we're standing here like idiots!" Hooppole said in a loud voice. "We can't see a damn thing."

"We'll see plenty of those Ruskie fighters shoot down our birds," Kinsey said. "Should that happen, we can kiss Fritz Werholtz and Stewart Hemschire goodbye. We wouldn't get

[3]The Sukhoi—named for the designer, Pavel O. Sukhoi.

halfway to Central Prison with the weapons we now have—but try to tell that to Ghazi and Saljoonque!"

"I know. Malikyar has sense." Hooppole snorted. "The other two would try to get to the Russians with their bare hands."

"*Listen!*" yelled Camellion. "Hear it?"

All three heard the change in sound of the engines of the Fairchilds. The flying "boxcars" were only several klicks away from the Sirq Plain and the pilots, preparing to make the run for the drop, had changed the fuel mixture and were nosing down.

The Death Merchant, Kinsey and Hooppole couldn't see anything but blackness and the flashing red and white strobe lights on the wings and the noses of the Fairchilds as the twin-fuselaged cargo and troop transports dropped lower and lower and headed toward the plain. The pinpoints of light, darting back and forth at three times the speed of the Fairchilds, belonged to the H-56 Hunter fighters.

Camellion and his two companions had moved to the mouth of the cave and, joined by Torak Adjar and Mustif Lukmak, continued to watch with the calm fascination of men for whom violent death is only another incident.

Elated, the Soviet pilots were convinced that this would be an easy victory, that they had the invaders on the brink of total destruction. *Da!* The enemy had to be mad—to think that they could fly into Afghanistan and not be blasted from the sky!

The Fishpots zipped in very fast, ten from the north cutting toward the lumbering Fairchild boxcars. The other twenty-one Soviet fighters—these from the northeast—began shooting all over the sky to engage the H-56 Hunters.

Whoosh! Whoosh! Whoosh! Whoosh! The Soviet Fishpots shot off their Alkali missiles at the Hunters only microseconds before the Hunters fired theirs. The ten Soviet Fishpots, getting ready to destroy the Fairchild cargo planes, bored in at the targets, the pilots wanting to get closer, wanting to be sure. The pilots of all thirty-one SU-11 Fishpots gasped in disbelief when, through wide angle NVDs, they saw missiles streak from the top and the sides of the Fairchilds. Impossible! Cargo planes didn't carry missiles. Yet there they were.

Suddenly it was the 4th of July in the Afghan sky, although from the ground it was impossible to see what was taking place. What did happen is that each B-L-X Medusa missile, from both the Fairchilds and the Hunters, exploded. Only enormous *POPS*, like giant firecrackers, the explosions weren't of the ordinary kind; they weren't violent. The explosions were only the sounds of the "separators" turning each Medusa into thirteen separate missiles.

And every single one of them was streaking at either an Alkali missile or a SU-11 Fishpot!

The Russian pilots didn't have time to review their lives, pray, and indulge in all the rest of the unrealities that one reads about in books. They had time for only a few seconds of absolute horror.

There were 107 separate explosions, the majority of them sounding like one big *BERRRRRUMMMMMMMMM*, this crashing wall of sound followed by several more thunderous concussions. All Camellion and the others saw were giant flashes of bright red fire, blossoming and fading so fast that if any of the men had turned his head for a moment he would have missed them.

"I'll be damned!" muttered Hooppole in awe.

Mustif Lukmak began jabbering in *Pushto* and waving his hands all over the place.

"But who destroyed who?" shouted Torak Ædjar.

You mean "Who destroyed whom!" "Our guys blew up the pig farmers!" Camellion shouted back, "and we'll be the next to go if some of that pig farmer wreckage falls on us."

Camellion turned and was soon inside the cave, the others following. Adjar grabbed at Camellion's right arm and shouted to make himself heard above the roaring of the Fairchild boxcars, "How do you know, *kuvii* Camellion? How can you be sure it was the Russian dogs who were killed?"

The Death Merchant despised communists of any nationality, disarmament freaks, people who grabbed at him, cults, and green beans—and in that order. Keeping the lid on his boiling temper, he roughly pushed Adjar's hands aside and yelled back at the frantic Afghan, "The roaring outside is the cargo planes. That's how I know. Right now they're about to drop the arms."

The Fairchilds were doing just that. Flying at only 1,310 feet, the Boxcars zoomed over the dark plain, two at a time so as not to scatter the cargo over too wide of an area; and as they passed over, crates were pushed from the port and starboard cargo doors. Within minutes the sky was filled with drifting black parachutes, wooden crates swinging at the end of the shroud lines.

While the Hunter fighters zipped back and forth at five thousand feet, the first two Fairchilds roared upward, banked, turned, and prepared for another run.

In another thirteen minutes the task was completed and, while there were crates still floating downward, many many more were already on the ground. The Hunters and the Fairchilds were soon a memory, the sounds of their engines fading in the southeast.

"Let's go out and see what goodies Uncle Sugar brought us," Camellion suggested.

"This reminds me of a football field after the game, with all the lights turned out," Kinsey said, looking around at the hundreds of men, the *mujahideen* and the men from Dukimor, all of whom were carrying wooden crates, four, six or eight men to a crate, depending on its size. Other Afghans carried torches—sticks or broken branches around the ends of which were rags dipped in oil. However, there were many flashlights.

"This plain will become a morgue if Soviet fighters come back," Camellion said in a low voice. All around him he saw that the joyful Afghans were carrying not only crates but the parachutes as well. The silk could be made into shirts, and the tough nylon cords could be useful in many ways.

"Camellion—look! The planes brought more than arms." Hooppole sounded startled.

"*Redwing* didn't say anything about dropping two specialists," speculated Kinsey.

The Death Merchant turned around and saw a group of Afghans, Kar Ali Shitoh and Sebghatullah Mahlik among them, coming toward him and the others. With the Afghans were two men who had jumped from one of the Fairchilds. Both wore crash helmets, olive drab jungle fatigue pants and coat, U.S. Special Forces mountain boots and were weighed down with bags of equipment, the canvas straps of the bags crossing their chests and backs.

"Rod, did I ever tell you what you get when you cross a Mexican with an octopus?" Camellion said steadily. Coolly he watched the Afghans and the newcomers approach.

"This is the man named Camellion," said Sebghatullah

135

Mahlik happily when the Afghan and the two newcomers reached the Death Merchant.

"I'm John Smith," the larger of the two men said, taking off his Sierra ballistic helmet. Big-boned, he was muscular, at least six feet and had a strong but tough, clean-shaven face. He didn't offer his right hand.

Hooppole made a funny face and gave a low, quick laugh. " 'John Smith!' I say, your friend wouldn't be one of the 'Jones' boys, would he?"

"Listen, you! We didn't jump out of that bird to make jokes!" growled Smith, sounding as if he were trying to bite a marble in half and jabbing holes in the air with a finger as he spoke. "John Smith is my name—period."

"I'm Jason Bunker," the other man said in a voice as grim as a dirge. "Call me Jay—and no, I'm not related to Archie Bunker."

Several inches shorter than Smith, Bunker was also built like a concrete dry dock and had that same clean but hard look about him. His light brown hair was cut similar to Smith's, in a crew-cut. Only a few years past thirty-nine, both had the distinctive appearance of men who had led a very active life, out of doors in all kinds of weather.

"Don't mind Hooppole," Camellion said easily. "Half the lies his enemies tell about him are not true."

"Uh-huh, the British merc," Smith said, eyeing Hooppole.

"Former Sergeant-Major Hooppole of Her Majesty's Royal Marines," Hooppole said coldly.

Smith's gray eyes grabbed Kinsey. "You must be Elrod Kinsey, the spook?"

"That's what it says on my birth certificate." Kinsey thrust out his jaw and his tone became imperious. "And I'm a career employee of the United States Government. While we're at it, *Redwing* didn't tell me anything about you two. I should like to know your function, why you are here?"

"That's easy enough," Smith said. "We're weapons experts."

Jay Bunker hooked his hands over his A.L.E. belt. "We're here because some dimwit has the screwball idea that you birds can take Kabul from the ivans."

Sebghatullah Mahlik almost shouted in Bunker's face. "With the help of Allah, we will take Kabul from the Russian dogs. We will kill every single one of them!"

Realizing his mistake, Bunker proved himself a master at extracting his big foot from sensitive Afghan mouths. "And I believe you will do just that," he said earnestly. "With the help of Allah we'll cut the throat of every Russian in Kabul. That's why we're here. The United States government sent us to help."

"I assume *Redwing* told you that I make the final decisions?" said Camellion.

"Affirmative," Smith said. "But that doesn't mean you tell us when to crap and where to do it."

"No, it doesn't." Camellion looked straight at Smith. "It does mean that when it comes to the fighting, I'm the boss and that you two will listen with both ears wide open—or you'll wish you had. Got it?"

There was a second of silence, Smith and Bunker giving Camellion rapier-like looks. Finally Smith nodded. "Seems fair to me, Camellion."

"Yeah, sounds all right to me," Bunker said, then lighted a cigarette.

The Death Merchant got right down to the nitty-gritty. "Not to belittle your abilities, but why did *Redwing* feel we needed weapons specialists? We're not all that stupid in light and heavy stuff."

"*Redwing* didn't think you were," Smith said, sounding more friendly. "But you see, *Redwing* added some stuff that it didn't have time to tell you about over the shortwave. It came at the last moment from MICOM.[4] It's called RAW and means 'Rifleman's Assault Weapon.' It's an armor and masonry blockbuster that can be fired from a rifle. I'll tell you about it when we get away from this open area."

"Yeah, out here gives me the creeps," Bunker said, exhaling cigarette smoke. "If the ivans showed up they'd have a turkey shoot. Where are you guys holed up at?"

"Caves. In the mountains," Kinsey said.

"Let's get back to the caves," Camellion said. "We have a lot to discuss. *Kuvii* Mahlik, would you please take us to *Malik* Khair Ghazi and the two other leaders?"

They were halfway to the caves when Hooppole sidled up to Camellion and whispered, "You never did get to tell me. What do you get when you cross a Mexican with an octopus?"

"I don't know—but you should see it pick lettuce!"

[4] U.S. Army Missile Command.

CHAPTER TEN

"These Afghans are like dry reeds seeking the company of fire," John Smith remarked to the Death Merchant. Agreeing, Camellion nodded. "As the good prophet would have said, 'With them it's weapons ready and good sense absent.'"

Regardless of the impetuosity of the *mujahideen*, the assault rifles (West German G3A13s, Valmet M-M82 "Bullpups," and the new U.S. M16A1E1s), grenades, heavy .50 cal. Browning MGs, and other weapons were moved to Dukimor without incident. Included were five hundred RAWs. The crates had been moved in the nine GOR-4 Soviet army trucks, plus another six trucks that were brought from Dukimor.

In Dukimor the *mujahideens* took refuge in many of the stone and wooden houses in the southeast section of the city. The Death Merchant and the other men working for the CIA and the three Afghan leaders and their aides took over a large two story house built of sun-dried bricks, the former home of Ali Tu-Tobq, who had been a prosperous coffee merchant. He and his entire family had disappeared into KGB torture chambers.

Toward the street the bare walls of the house were broken only by a large wooden door, protruding pipes for waste and rainwater, and a niche from which sewage could be emptied. To a middle class American, the house was a slum dwelling. Down Moon Row Street, in front of the house, was an open ditch. In some of the other houses was an occasional beautifully carved window on a guest room; otherwise, all the houses were like Ali Tu-Tobq's: they were oriented toward the courtyards where women were busy working.

The main battle plan had been formulated with little effort—a surprise to the Death Merchant and the other Company men who had assumed that the Afghans would be reluctant to follow professional advice. But the Afghans had been very cooperative, and the attack plans had matured with amazing speed. Abdullah Saljoonque's forces would attack from Lashkar, a suburb north of Kabul; they would move south in three columns, one straight at the Soviet headquarters in Kabul, the other two side columns executing a pincer's movement. They would bore in from the east and the west at the same time that Mohammad Malikyar's small army headed east from Kemdash, his main group stabbing northeast, his objective the Chinarq Square group of fortified buildings that were Soviet headquarters. The two branches of Malikyar's force would link up with the pincer columns of Saljoonque's *mujahideen*.

Quartered mostly in Pestiwar, Khair Ghazi's men would move east and attack the Soviet airbase, in conjunction with the six hundred guerrillas from Saljug. They would move southwest against the airbase, under the leadership of Danibor Zam, one of Saljoonque's better men.

The only misunderstanding had been on the part of Jay Bunker who, for a time, could not understand what had happened to the seven hundred fighters in Chewakée, a large village northwest of Kabul. It was explained that a hundred of them had been killed in a battle with Soviet ground forces and that the rest of them were in Saljug and would, with Khair Ghazi's group, attack the Soviet airfield.

A special messenger had been waiting for Khair Ghazi in Dukimor, a woman, and for a long time the two had held a whispered conference, after which Ghazi walked over to Camellion and Kinsey and smiled.

"*Kuvii* Camellion, *kuvii* Kinsey," Khair Ghazi said. "The two men you wish to rescue are still alive. They are on the third floor of the prison, in cell 318. It is a large cell, and other unfortunates are with them."

Fine. But how? What was the best method that could be used to attack the Central Prison? Counting the men who had volunteered in Dukimor, the force would be 1,230 men.

"No matter how we attack, we won't move from Dukimor until 15.00," the Death Merchant said.

"Fifteen hundred?" echoed Saljoonque.

"Three o'clock in the morning," said Camellion, "three hours after the other three forces begin the attack. The Soviets will have forward observers all over the city. Should they see a column moving northwest from Dukimor, they might guess the prison is the objective of that force and rush men from the airbase and Soviet headquarters."

139

"Good thinking, Camellion," muttered John Smith, rubbing the end of his nose.

"Yes, *kuvii* Camellion. I understand your reasoning," agreed Abdullah Saljoonque.

"My informant reported that there is a contingent of only 1500 around the prison," Khar Ghazi said thoughtfully. He continued to polish his "monocle." "Some 250 of them are members of the regular Afghan Army. This proves that the Soviets are desperate, or they wouldn't be trusting our people."

"Then why are they?" Jay Bunker looked quickly from Camellion to Khair Ghazi. "I thought the Soviets had almost two hundred thousand men in this country?"

"They have," said Camellion, "but those troops are scattered all over Afghanistan, in and around other major cities. The entire nation would rise up in revolt if General Mozzhechkov pulled even a tenth of his occupation force toward Kabul."

After more discussion over how to attack the Central Prison, the Death Merchant finally raised his hands for attention.

"Gentlemen, gentlemen! We're looking for an answer that isn't there," he said in a loud, firm voice. "It's like trying to figure out why a person can't tickle himself. The only way to attack the Central Prison is to do it—to attack! A frontal assault all around the prison. That's the only way to do it."

"We'll have a hundred RAWs," John Smith said slowly, wiping small beads of perspiration from his high forehead. "We might, however, use half of them getting to the prison."

"So what? We'll also have fifty Stingers," Jay Bunker reminded him. "And I doubt if we're going to meet a hundred armored vehicles on the way in. That's for damned sure."

Every time the Death Merchant looked at or heard Smith and Bunker, he was reminded of the truism about bad first impressions. The two weapons experts were decent enough joes once one got to know them. Both had been officers in Special Forces in 'Nam and, since then, after finding civilian life dreary (*The calm was frustrating*! said Smith), had worked for the Company as individual contractors. Both men had seen action in South America, Africa, and parts of Asia. Smith had just come from Egypt, Bunker from Lebanon.

"There'll never be peace in the Middle East," Bunker had remarked to Camellion and Hooppole. He then pointed out the fallacy that the U.S. could solve the problem by withdraw-

140

ing arms support from Israel. The U.S. couldn't do any such thing because Israel was a nuclear power and possessed the will to use that power, even if it meant the end of Israel itself. Thus if the U.S. did exercise its full power against Israel, it would only lead to a nuclear holocaust in an area of vital importance to the world.

The United States was trapped!

"Most people fail to understand this," Bunker had explained. "Another fact, whether we like it or not, is that the ultimate superpower confrontation will take place in the Middle East. I'm convinced of it."

So was the Death Merchant. The Israelis believed that only by expansion and by preventive military strike could security be gained and kept. Conversely, the Arabs were convinced that only by the destruction of Israel could a home be found for the Palestinians; yet, for military reasons, Islam could not support the Palestinians. And there could be no compromise.

That left only the Soviet Union that was already supplying arms and aid to the Palestinians through the PLO. But the Soviet Union knows that sooner or later it will have to intervene directly in the Middle East. If the Western powers could convince the U.S.S.R. that such action on its part would lead to immediate retaliation, the Russians would think more than twice.

"But the Soviets are convinced that American pacifist groups will deter us for a sufficiently long time to make retaliation impossible," Bunker said. "We can see it happening now with all the fools who want a nuclear freeze in the U.S. They're too stupid and too misinformed to realize that even if such a freeze were possible on both sides, it would still mean the Soviets were way out in front."

"I'll buy that, Jay," John Smith agreed. "Some months ago, I was talking to the COS[1] of the station in New Delhi. He's convinced that World War III will begin in the Middle East, as a result of a single Russian miscalculation."[2]

---

[1]Chief of Station.
[2]That miscalculation will begin a short nuclear war, but not the final thermonuclear conflict. The Middle East war will be the beginning of the end not only of the Soviet Union but of the Vatican. The entire economy of the world will have to be reconstructed and vast changes will take place in the U.S. Due to the Middle East war, Red China will make its moves.

The Death Merchant didn't say anything. Why bother? Why tell Smith and Bunker that the short but deadly war in the Middle East would only be the prelude to World War III?

Communications between the groups would not be a problem. Constant contact would be maintained by hand-held Horizone transceivers. With a range of thirty-two klicks (twenty mi), the seven-watt C834-W-H was among the most powerful walkie-talkies in the world.

Mohammad Malikyar finished lighting a cigarette, then, exhaling, turned to Ghazi and Saljoonque. "All we have to do now is send messengers to Danibor Zam at Saljug. Zam is more or less isolated and will have to be given details of the plan, particularly about the part he'll play in attacking the airbase. The messengers can also take him several of the new walkie-talkies that came in the air drop."

After some thought, Khair Ghazi said, "Six messengers. They can leave half an hour apart from each other."

John Smith's eyes narrowed. "The messengers will carry the plans in code, I hope?"

Malikyar, with a thin smile, nodded. "Yes, a complex code, We use parts from the Koran."

The Death Merchant thought of the things that had been done. For example, the shortwave had been left in the cave. After the battle, he and the others would return to the cave, contact *Redwing* and make arrangements to be lifted out of Afghanistan. If they got killed in Kabul, it wouldn't matter.

The Afghans couldn't possibly take Kabul from the Soviet forces. The *mujahideen* would do a lot of damage and kill thousands of pig farmers, but conquer the city—no.

"It's a dumb stunt," Jay Bunker had said. "The ivans will smoke the Afghan faster than Social Security pays out money."[3]

Camellion had not argued. "I know."

"The Afghans know it, too," Kinsey had said bitterly. "To them it's a religious cause."

The Death Merchant, wearing .44 Alaskan Auto-Mags that had been in one of the bags carried by John Smith, stood up.

[3]$17,000.00 a minute, every single minute around the clock.

"Gentlemen, we have a lot to do and midnight is only six hours away," he said in a businesslike tone. "We still have a lot of coordinating to do."

"Yeah . . . and only one day left until tomorrow," Rod Hooppole muttered to no one in particular.

CHAPTER ELEVEN

If laughter is the shortest distance between two people, then the Russians and the Afghans in Kabul were light years apart. There wasn't any laughter on either side; there was only the iron-bound resolution to show no mercy and to kill as many of the enemy as possible.

From the beginning the attacks of the *mujahideen* got off to a poor start, in that the coordinated movement of the three forces—four, counting Danibor Zam and his six hundred in Saljug—was delayed. The movement of Abdullah Saljoonque's Force-D was much slower than had been anticipated, the loss of time due to Force-D's having captured six T-64 tanks whose Afghan crews were not familiar with the controls. At length, Jasim Luory, one of Saljoonque's lieutenants, called on a Horizone W-T and reported to Malikyar, Ghazi, and Zam that Saljoonque was ready to proceed.

The attack of the three forces began at 15.49. Zam's Force-Y would hold fast outside of Saljug until contacted by Khair Ghazi's Force-C and was told that Ghazi's men were ready to move against the Soviet airbase.

"At least you won't have to worry about Ismail shooting you in the back," commented Elrod Kinsey in a low voice so that the four Afghans in the room couldn't hear his words. "It was a smart move on Khair Ghazi's part, taking Ismail with him.

Impatient for his own force—Force-R(escue)—to spear into Kabul, the Death Merchant acknowledged with a slight bitter smile. "The real test of a man is to possess power without abusing it. Khair Ghazi may be 'backward' by educated standards, but he has a nobility of character that would make him a wise ruler."

Camellion looked around the enormous sitting room of Ali Tu-Tobq's house. Every fighter was ready and armed to the teeth, including the four English-speaking Afghans who would transmit orders from Camellion to the *mujahideen*.

Rod Hooppole walked across the room to the Death Merchant, an H/K assault rifle swinging in his left hand. Like the Death Merchant and the other men, he was a walking arsenal and a packhorse of equipment.

"It's 2:45," he said nervously. "We should get started. It will take an hour to get the force under way."

"Yeah, we might as well move out," Camellion said. "The schedule is shot to hell anyhow, not that it makes all that much of a difference. You did check with the Afghans? We don't want them wasting RAWs and Stingers."

"Kar Ali Shitoh is going to be with the men who have the Stingers, and Melih Yehen with the RAW boys," said Hooppole. "They assured me that they won't fire unless it's a genuine target that calls for a RAW or a Stinger."

Wiping his bald as a rock head, Kinsey sighed. "I don't think we'll meet any resistance until we're well into Kabul. But who knows. We will be able to get a lot of information from people on the way."

The Death Merchant sounded all business. "Let's get the show on the road."

There was order enough, the 1,230 guerrillas moving forward in orderly fashion, in small groups, seven scouts with walkie-talkies a block out in front . . . creeping along the sides of buildings and through deserted streets. Women and old people, children and the sick, were indoors, praying to Allah and hoping that somehow they would remain alive and continue to live when the battle was over. If the freedom forces lost the battle, would the Russians demand restitution? Would the dogs from the north make reprisals?

To make progress toward the Central Prison more difficult, the Russians had disabled the street lighting system, which had never been all that efficient. There was only the darkness and the stink of smoke from dying fires of buildings the

Soviets had demolished with explosives. Now and then little groups of people would call out from the darkness, then approach from the side and wish them good luck in the name of Allah. These people would explain that, as far as they knew, there were no Russians in the area.

The Death Merchant, all the Company men, Kamal Din Buhzid and Fazal Bhutto were with the first group, just behind the scouts. Camellion called a halt for a conference when two of the scouts reported over a walkie-talkie that they were within sight of the bridge that crossed the Kabul River.

Camellion told Fazal Bhutto, who was holding a Horizone W-T in his hand, to order the scouts to remain where they were. "Tell them that we'll join them in short order."

John Smith said quickly, "The bridge will be mined, no doubt with explosives that can be set off by observers with remote-control doodads."

"I don't think so," Jay Bunker disagreed. "The ivans never waste anything if they can help it. They know damn good and well that they would be seen and that people would inform any approaching force of the danger."

"*Kuvii* Bhutto, how deep is the Kabul River in this area?" Camellion asked the huge, bearded man who had just switched off the Horizone transceiver.

Bhutto's little black eyes became stationary with thought. "Where the bridge is the water is three to four meters deep. To the west, perhaps a third of a kilometer, the water is shallow and one can wade across. What will we do, *kuvii* Camellion?"

"Right now, let's have a look at the bridge," the Death Merchant said in an easy manner. "Once we're there have some of the men round up people in houses closest to the bridge. They—"

"If any of the houses are still standing!" thrust in Elrod Kinsey.

"They might be able to tell us something," Camellion finished. He turned to Kinsey. "Whether we find anyone or not, we're still not going to cross that bridge."

In only a little while the group was staring at the outline of the bridge in the darkness. It was a simple truss bridge one hundred fifty feet long underneath which flowed the dirty water of the Kabul River.

Shortly, some of the *mujahideen* had rounded up a dozen

men and women from houses facing the bridge, all of whom confirmed that the bridge had been mined.

"The godless ones worked half a day underneath the bridge," one old man excitedly said. "They put boxes under the bridge."

Jugen Wesslin made a long, sad face. "None of it makes sense. The Russians knew we'd assume the bridge is mined and find some of the Afghans who saw them mine it."

"You're giving those damned Ruskies too much credit," Hooppole said, frowning. "They couldn't be sure that anyone would be around to tell what they had done. For all they knew, these people could have fled to the countryside."

"Hooppole is right," Camellion said heavily and swung his gaze to Fazal Bhutto and Kamal Din Buhzid. "Pass the word to the entire force. Tell the men we're going to cross west of here, where we can wade across." He emphasized, "And no one is to cross until I give the word."

The wide section of water looked as bleak as the River Styx, every bit as ill omened as the flow under the bridge that the force had left an hour earlier. On this side of the river, for an area of several blocks facing the water, houses had been destroyed and were only piles of rubble.

Standing close to the shore, the Death Merchant and the other men studied the water, some of the men glancing impatiently at Camellion.

"What are we waiting for?" asked Hooppole morosely. "Here we are and there's the water! Let's cross."

Camellion straightened his Canadian field cap, his eyes mere slits.

"First, I want to make a test. Let's stand back about thirty feet."

"Why?" asked Smith with interest.

"Because I don't believe in taking unnecessary chances."

Once they had retreated to the requested distance, Camellion pulled a PRB-423 controlled frag grenade from one of his bags, jerked out the pin and threw the grenade so that it would hit the water a few feet from the shore.

BLAMMMMMMMM! The grenade exploded with a roar that could have been half a dozen grenades. At once, most of the men realized why: the river bed was mined.

"Those bloody Russian sons of bitches!" Hooppole bit off the words.

"And you were the one who said I was overrating the Russian swine!" Wesslin said happily in revenge.

Hooppole acted as if he hadn't heard the West German.

"A mine field! It figures," Smith said reasonably. "It should be easy enough to clear with grenades."

The Death Merchant spoke to Bhutto and Buhzid and told them what he wanted to do. Presently, thirty of the *mujahideen* were lined up, eight to ten feet apart. As instructed by Bhutto and Buhzid, the Afghans began to throw grenades, at first just beyond the shore. Moving closer, they began to throw farther out. The system was infallible. Throw. Move forward. Throw again.

BLAMMMMMM! BLAMMMMMMMM! BLAMMMMMMM! BLAMMMMMMMM! Grenades and mines exploded simultaneously, the roaring deafening, the sprays of water enormous. In twenty minutes a three hundred foot wide path had been cleared and the thirty men were knee deep in the middle of the water. They had completed the job. Their last thirty grenades had fallen on the opposite shore.

The Death Merchant gave the order for the force to advance across the river— ". . . And make sure you tell the men to keep within the three hundred foot area."

Kamal Din Buhzid and Fazal Bhutto stared at him, their expressions fearful, uncertain, hesitant.

Elrod Kinsey leaned toward the Death Merchant and whispered, "You're the leader. The *mujahideen* expect you to cross first—not only the rank and file but Bhutto and Buhzid. It's the custom."

Camellion glanced around at the other men, who were regarding him solemnly. "I could use a cover, assuming we reach the other side."

Wesslin gave a chilling little laugh. "And if we do not reach the other shore?"

"In that case it won't make any difference, will it?" Camellion said drily. "We will. The Afghans did a fine job with those grenades."

"What the hell! I'll go with you," offered John Smith. "I don't have anything better to do at the moment."

"Good enough. Stay ten feet behind me."

"Like hell I will. I'll walk beside you."

Lazily, carrying Ingram MAC-10 SMGs in their right hands, Camellion and Smith walked across the shore and were soon in water up to their ankles. The force had lost enough time and Camellion didn't slosh across the Kabul River as though he were trying to walk on eggshells without breaking any. Either the grenades had done their job or they hadn't. Just the same, the two men felt tiny stabs of uncertainty each time they put down a foot and felt something hard. Was it a rock or the pressure-red surface of an anti-personnel mine?

Nothing happened. There weren't any explosions. Ten minutes later, the Death Merchant and Smith were on the north shore. The rest of the force began wading across the river, until finally Force-R was within the city limits of Kabul. The river was the boundry line.

The Cosmic Lord of Death lay over Kabul, and every man, Afghan and Westerner alike, could feel his grim presence. So could the people huddled fearfully in their homes in this section of the city, the Tajik area. Sunni Muslims, the Tajiks were noted for their beautiful weaving, a talent expressed mainly in rugs.

Again people came out of the shadows to meet the ones they considered liberators, to wish the *mujahideen* well and to tell them that there weren't any enemy troops in the vicinity.

After moving steadily northeast for half an hour, the Death Merchant called a halt. He and a dozen members of the force went into a deserted house on a narrow, twisting street and held a conference, Camellion wanting to be certain that Force-R was on the right route.

Camellion unfolded the map that Mohammad Malikyar had drawn. Malikyar had printed names in both Afghan and English and had used colored pencils to mark important streets and avenues. Down on their knees, by the light of flashlights, the men studied the map.

The Death Merchant put his finger on a square across which was printed CENTRAL PRISON. South of the square was Haddam Street. North of the prison was Path of the Weary Way Street. To the east was a block of apartment buildings. A large parking area was to the west.

There was only one thing wrong with the map: Malikyar had drawn only the main thoroughfares.

"*Kuvii* Buhzid, here's our objective." Camellion tapped

the square on the map and looked at the man's shadowed face. "Have you any idea of our present location?"

Kamal Buhzid, who had lived in Kabul until the Soviet "liberation," leaned closer to the map. At length he said, "I cannot be positive of our location, not from what is marked here. I do think we are right at this position."

He put the end of his finger on the map, several inches to the left of a long blue line marked Huzkisar Way. The blue line moved from the southeast to the northwest. Camellion did know that Huzkisar Way was the long street with the most fashionable shops and stores in Kabul.

Staring at the map, Elrod Kinsey spoke up, "Camellion, if *kuvii* Buhzid is correct, we're less than a mile and a half from the prison."

"If we're that close, where's the Ruskies?" asked Rod Hooppole in a curious voice. "They don't have all that many troops in Kabul, but surely they have some roving patrols."

"I've been thinking the same thing," John Smith said. "After all, observers, watching the bridge, must have reported that we've crossed over. Unless the Russians are half asleep, they should have figured out by now that our objective is the Central Prison."

"I'm convinced the pig farmers are wide awake and waiting," Camellion said ruefully. "We'll find out, sooner or later."

They found out sooner, in another twenty minutes, when the scouts came to the Street of the Jars, where they were met by five Afghans in Western type clothes. All five were armed with Russian AKMs, Soviet grenades and sidearms. The four men said they were members of *Allah's United Muslims for Freedom of Afghanistan*, a recently formed group whose members were businessmen and professionals, from medicine and the arts and the sciences. The leader was Lamiz Junikiz, a thirty-two-year-old chemist employed by the Kabul Chemical Works in Lashkar, north of Kabul. In another twenty minutes, Junikiz and some of his men were standing before the Death Merchant and telling Camellion and the other amazed men how they had been creating havoc with Soviet armor for the past two days—. . . ever since the filthy Russian dogs began pulling back to their headquarters."

"How did you do it?" asked Camellion.

Mainly with homemade weapons, Junikiz, a thin boyish-looking individual, explained. The group had made its own mortar-howitzer "cannon"—the barrel was made from drainpipe, the carriage from gas and other plumbing, with provision for both direct and high-angle firing. "For the propellant we use an old sock filled with potassium chlorate. We then pour sulphuric acid gently into the touch hole. After a momentary delay the P-C explodes."

The "shell" was a Molotov cocktail with petrol and sulphuric acid mix wrapped in a chlorated envelope and fitted into a cut-off tin can.

Junikiz and his group also had their own brand of impact grenades and incendiaries. The impact grenades were ordinary Soviet RGD-5 grenades with the pins removed. The grenades were slipped into glass jars of a size that would not permit the handles to move outward and trigger the igniters. The space around the grenade was then filled with nails and petrol or oil. The tops of the jars were screwed on.

The impact incendiaries were made of thermite. Lamiz Junikiz grinned, revealing broken teeth. "It is not difficult to make thermite from iron oxide or iron rust, aluminum powder and potassium permanganate, or gunpowder," he explained.

The rest was easy. Thermite was poured into empty cola cans; at the top of the cans were placed small bags of sugar/chlorate into which was thrust a wick.

"Several dozens of the thermite cans will take care of any Soviet tank," Junikiz said, pride ringing in his voice. "The crew cannot stand the intense heat and has to come out. Once they are out of the tank, we kill the sons of low sows. . . ."

It was then that the Death Merchant decided to capture a Soviet tank, if he could, but not by dousing it with thermite. At the time, he didn't mention his intention to the group.

"*Kuvii* Lamiz Junikiz, you and your men are welcome to join us," Camellion offered. "Our destination is the Central Prison. We intend to free every prisoner."

Force-R crossed Huzkisar Way, the wide street that ran from one end of Kabul to the other, the eerie, expectant feeling intensified by the darkness, by the hundreds of "dead" neon signs hanging over shops and stores. It was difficult to believe that, until only a few days ago, this was one of the busiest streets in Kabul, with modern Kabulis in Western suits and lambskin hats mingling with turbaned Tajiks and

Pushtuns wearing Afghan knee-length shirts and baggy pantaloons. Here too one would have found Uzbeks and Turkomans from the north, in high black boots and long striped robes. One would have seen stocky Hazaras, swarthy Baluchis and tall Nuristanis. Horse carts, jeeps, and Russian taxis would have been moving slowly through crowds of people. Crowds would have been pressing into the teashops, all drawn by the sizzle of shish kebab and the blare of Islamic music from scratchy loudspeakers. Nearby, enterprising young boys would be renting water pipes, at a penny a puff. Bolts of cloth would be hung from stalls. Neon signs would be blazing with color.

No longer. Now there was only the darkness and the silence.

Four blocks west of Huzkisar Way, the scouts—three of Junikiz's men had joined them—saw the Soviet armor coming down the center of a cobblestone road—two T-64s, two BMP combat infantry carriers and five BTR-40 armored cars, the entire line of armor proceeding slowly in a southern direction.

"Men, I want one of those tanks intact," Camellion voiced his intention to capture one of the T-64s.

"And I have a friend who wants to be President of the United States," mocked Hooppole jovially. "I say, tell us another funny one."

"Damn it, Rod! Listen!" admonished Kinsey. "This is no time for joking!"

An angry expression spread over Hooppole's face, but he didn't say anything.

"Knocking out that armor is not a problem." Smith's hard eyes bored into Camellion. "Capturing a tank is another matter."

"We can knock out every vehicle with either RAWs or Stingers," Camellion said, "all except one tank, say the lead tank."

"And just like that you expect the crew of the last vehicle to surrender?" Wesslin said in exasperation. "They will never do it!"

"The crew will require some persuasion," Camellion said, speaking mechanically. "Once the other vehicles are knocked out, all I have to do is leap up on the tank from the rear and

151

give the three pig farmers a choice—either surrender or be burned to death by thermite. Who knows? It might work.''

Hooppole didn't hesitate. ''I think you're nuts, Camellion. That's too much of a risk.''

''Suppose the crew refuses the offer?'' Jay Bunker tossed away his cigarette butt.

''In that case I'll douse the front of the tank with one of Junikiz's do-it-yourself thermite grenades, jump off, and get to safety,'' Camellion said simply.

''Well, it could work,'' Smith said hopefully. ''All we have to do is wait until the armor is in the right place—and where will you hide? You have to be far enough away when the armor explodes.''

''All we can do for the moment is play it by ear,'' the Death Merchant said, sounding faintly amused. ''*Kuvii* Junikiz, have one of your men bring me several of your contact incendiaries.''

''At once!'' said Lamiz Junikiz and hurried off.

''*Kuvii* Bhutto, get on the walkie-talkie and tell either Kar Shitoh or Melih Yegen to send up ten men with Stinger missiles. They're more used to firing Stingers than RAWs. Tell them to make it fast. We need speed.''

Fazal Bhutto tugged at his black beard and blinked in confusion at the Death Merchant. ''But there are only nine vehicles?'' he said in a voice that sounded like pebbles being crushed.

''One of the Stingers could be a dud. Or two for that matter.'' Camellion told him. ''Why take the chance?''

While Bhutto was on the Horizone W-T, Jay Bunker sidled up to the Death Merchant and whispered, ''Look, how can we be sure there are nine pieces, of armor, or even four or five? It's so dark out there you'd have a hard time seeing a bonfire!''

Camellion turned to Kamal Din Buhzid who had taken the call, on the Horizone, from the scouts. Buhzid, who had heard part of what Bunker had whispered and had guessed the rest, gave the explanation. At first, the scouts had only seen the lights from the first tank. Two of the scouts had then run forward on another street and crossed over roofs to look down and count the pairs of lights. Nine pairs, nine vehicles. The space of the lights told them the type of vehicle.

''The scouts have had plenty of practice,'' Buhzid said,

smiling. "We've been identifying Russian vehicles in that manner ever since those dogs invaded our land."

It took eleven minutes for the ten *mujahideen* with the shoulder-fired Stinger missiles to reach the Death Merchant and his special group; another thirteen mintues for Camellion, the ten men with the missiles, Wesslin, Bunker, Kamal Din Buhzid, and Lamiz Junikiz to creep up the street to the scouts. They did so by ducking from storefront to storefront, the Death Merchant carefully noticing the fronts of the stores and shops on both sides of Good Pink Soil Avenue.[1]

Here, not far from the center of Kabul, the buildings and businesses were as different from the stalls and tiny shops of the bazaars as night is from day. All the shops and stores on Good Pink Soil Avenue were modern, many with huge plate glass windows. Some windows had already been broken by looters, the glass lying in millions of pieces on the concrete sidewalks.

By the time the Death Merchant and the other fourteen men had reached the scouts, concealed in an area fronting the double doors of a furniture store, the Soviet armor was only a block away. The Russians were not proceeding at a steady rate. Every now and then the vehicles would grind to a stop and the observers in the armored cars would swing their turrets for a slow look around; then again the column would move forward on Good Pink Soil Avenue, the wide street that intersected Huzkisar Way. Since the street was wide, far too wide for Afghan "terrorists" to throw Molotov cocktails as the "good" Soviet soldiers, Camellion was gambling that the Russians would continue forward, straight toward him and the others, and not turn off.

Kamal Din Buhzid looked around the inset at the approaching Soviet armor that had again stopped so that the observers could analyze the area. Neither he nor anyone else could see the actual vehicles, not even an outline of the lead T-64 main battle tank. All that could be seen were the beams of the small white lights mounted on plates over the track idling wheels.

"Where should I position the men?" Buhzid whispered to Camellion. "I would suggest that clothing store halfway down

[1]The names of all streets have been translated into English— their literal meaning.

the block, on this side of the street. The store does not have any display platforms. The main part of the store begins past the broken windows. It will be very easy for the men to slip inside and fire when the vehicles are in front of the windows."

"The clothing store is my choice too," said Camellion, taking off his heavy bags of PRB frag grenades and spare ammo mags for his MAC SMG. "Listen, make sure they understand that they are not to destroy the lead tank. That's the baby I want."

"May Allah help you," the Afghan said sadly. "When you go after that tank, you had better run with great speed, as if you had eggs in your shoes."

The Death Merchant handed Lamiz Junikiz the two shoulder bags and continued in an urgent tone, "Another thing, the instant the men fire off their Stingers get them out of the store fast, out through the back of the building. The head tank might open fire with its gun. You understand?"

Buhzid looked questioningly at the Death Merchant, who couldn't decide whether the man was puzzled or angry. "We are not amateurs at killing Russian dogs," Buhzid said stiffly. "Do not worry; the job will be done properly. I go now with the men."

Turning from Camellion, Buhzid motioned to the ten *mujahideen*.

The Death Merchant looked at Wesslin, Bunker, and Lamiz Junikiz. Wesslin and Bunker were both taking off their own bags of grenades and spare ammo.

"What do you think you're doing?" Camellion said sharply. "I want you three to go back down the street with Buhzid and the missile boys."

"We're going to cover you when you go after the tank," Jay Bunker said brusquely. He cocked his head at Camellion and added laconically, "We see no reason why you should have all the fun."

"I stay here too!" Junikiz said firmly in his heavy accent. "This is my country! I fight!"

"You're all crazy," Camellion growled, faking displeasure but secretly pleased. "I never saw so many men governed by a death wish!"

"*Gott in Himmel!*" mocked Wesslin. "You are going to jump on a tank and you're calling us not right in the head!"

"OK, so we're all candidates for a rubber room," said

Camellion, who was looking around the inset up the street. "Hear those engines? We'd better get inside the furniture store."

The four moved through the smashed door of the establishment and got down behind a group of overturned tables, ten feet from the smashed glass window.

The Russian armored column stopped, the engines of the vehicles idling. The Russians were taking another look-see. . . .

"Slow bastards, aren't they?" Bunker said crossly.

"Slow and cautious, my *Amerikaner* friend," Wesslin commented.

"*Kuvii* Camellion, how can we be sure that the surviving tank will not fire at us?" whispered Junikiz in a low, nervous voice.

"Not a chance, friend Junikiz." Bunker sounded very sincere. "Our Christian god protects drunks, little children, Democrats, and Americans."

The Death Merchant told Junikiz the truth. "They could and might. It's not likely they will. The clothing store is one hundred fifty feet—forty-five meters to you—down the street. The Russian commander in the tank won't think the missiles were fired from here; the angle is too steep. He'll either shell the clothing store or the area directly across the street from the tank."

"Listen! They've started up again," Wesslin whispered. "Let's get out there."

They four got up, made their way to the wrecked door, stepped through the glassless frame, and got down by the blue glass bricks of the inset. Straining their eyes, they stared after the vehicles that were strung out in a line, not six feet apart.

The Soviet column stopped again, when the lead T-64 was not more than twenty-five feet beyond the far side of the clothing store and the last vehicle, an armored car, was thirty feet past the furniture store.

"Back inside, all of you," ordered the Death Merchant. "If Buhzid doesn't have them fire within the next ten seconds, he'll have missed the best chance he could ever have, and there's going to be a lot of junk flying."

They turned and hurried back through the door, stumbling slightly in the darkness. They were getting down behind the tables when eight eyes sighted through infrared guidance systems and eight fingers squeezed eight triggers. Eight Stinger missiles streaked out from their disposable launchers and rocketed toward the targets.

The Death Merchant and his men didn't see the eight bright balls of fire as the Stingers struck one T-64, the two BMP troop carriers and the five BTR-40 armored cars. They did hear the crashing explosions, so close together as to be indistinguishable in time. The two carriers and the five armored cars flew apart with terrific violence and a concussion that pounded at the center of one's brain, much of the junk and debris falling to the sidewalks—turrets, armor plate, mangled bodies, etc.

A Stinger had exploded against the left side of the T-64, right above one of the top rollers of the track. Heavily armored, the tank didn't disintegrate. When the smoke cleared, there was a gaping hole in the tank, the smoking cavity revealing twisted metal and parts of the inside of the tank. Concussion had killed the crew.

Camellion and the three men rushed to the outside of the furniture store, got down in the inset and stared at the wreckage created by the deadly Stinger missiles. All that was left of the two carriers and the five armored cars were the chassis and big wheels, twisted metal protruding from the crooked and twisted frames. Engines, some twisted on their mountings, smoked, while wide areas around the demolished machines were covered with burning wreckage and pieces of bodies, a torso here, arms and legs there. The "dead" T-64 just sat there, its engine grumbling, black oily smoke drifting from the maw in its left side.

It was the first T-64 in which Camellion was interested, especially its turret that contained the deadly 125mm smoothbore gun. The turret was now turning slowly to the left.

"That mother is going to fire, just as sure as God makes little bunches of grapes." Bunker bit off his words.

"I don't think so—or the gunner would be lowering the barrel," whispered the Death Merchant. "Let's see what the pig farmer commander has in mind. If the turret quits moving, we'll jump back inside."

The turret didn't quit moving. Slowly it continued to move left. The long barrel, tilted upward, was facing the clothing store when the spotlight, right behind the barrel, was switched on and, controlled automatically from inside the tank, began to play its bright white beam over the front of the clothing store and the other buildings.

"Back inside—quick!" ordered the Death Merchant.

Turret and gun continued to turn, the bright beam moving all over the place, up, down, sideways, sweeping the area, for several seconds raking over the spot where the Death Merchant and the others had been crouching.

"Apparently he doesn't want to waste shells on an enemy he can't see," whispered Wesslin from behind the overturned tables. "*Ja*, that's it."

Finally turret and cannon had made a complete circle and once more the barrel was poked over and beyond the front of the tank. The water-cooled diesel throbbed with new power as the driver began to change gears. The left track started in motion, the wide, heavy links of the track clanking over the idling wheels, the top rollers, the road wheels, and through the sprocket wheel. With the right track remaining stationary, the tank turned completely around, to the left, and the driver started to move the vehicle forward, going to his right to avoid the wrecked T-64 and the smoking chassis of the other wrecked vehicles.

The Death Merchant waited until the heavy throbbing of the diesel told him that the T-64 was past the furniture store; then he and the other men raced to the outside and stared after the rolling fortress whose speed was increasing. It was clear that the commander was not a fool. Like any sensible man he was going to retreat as quickly as possible.

Wesslin said anxiously, "If we're going to do it, we'll never have a better chance."

"Only one of you can go," Camellion said. "The top of the turret isn't wide enough to hold three of us. If the tank spins and the third man was caught in front of it, they'd blow him up through the driver's slit."

"I'll go," Jay Bunker said.

A .44 Alaskan AMP[2] in his right hand, Camellion left the inset in front of the doorway and sprinted after the departing tank. Pounding the stones right behind him came Bunker, an Ingram MAC-10 machine pistol[3] in his left hand, and the canvas carrying strap over his left shoulder.

[2]Auto Mag pistol.
[3]Machine pistol or submachine gun, it's all the same.

Due to the flickering light of the burning wreckage, it wasn't difficult to keep the tank in sight. It wasn't easy to climb aboard the monster, once the two men had closed in, mainly because the rear of the long turret protruded over the rear of the tank.

Camellion was the first to make contact. Shoving the AMP into its long holster, he grabbed the lower frame of the external storage rack, behind the turret bustle, put his left foot on the rear towing hook, and pulled himself over the rear of the turret, the steel hard against his body. The middle part of his body was directly over the commander's cupola, wedged against the commander's machine gun, a light 7.62 ShKAS weapon.

The tank was grinding to a halt as Bunker pulled himself over the rear of the turret, wriggled beside the Death Merchant and grabbed the lower part of the machine gun mount with both big hands.

Camellion called out loudly in the Russian: "Attention, tank commander. We're Americans. We want to talk to you."

Talk? *Nyet!* The tank began to spin, first one way and then another. Then it started to spin completely around on its tracks. At the same time, the turret began to swing back and forth, Captain Vadim Pinkin hoping to throw the unwelcome guests off balance and dislodge them from his vehicle.

He didn't succeed. Bunker and Camellion held onto the machine gun mount as tightly as they could, knowing their lives depended on their grip. It was difficult. At times, when the tank spun and the turret jerked either to the left or the right, their bodies would shift so that their legs flew outward behind or to the side of the turret. But they didn't fall.

Finally the tank stopped its spinning.

"Watch it," Camellion warned Bunker. "He could be hoping to take us off guard and start all over again—and give me a match or a light."

"That Russian son of a bitch!" muttered Bunker.

Camellion yelled, "Tank commander! Do you want to talk or die by thermite or a missile. You can't escape! This tank is surrounded. I know you can hear me. If you want to listen, lower the barrel of your gun. Otherwise, fry and die."

There was a low whirring noise from inside the tank and the long barrel, with its fume extractors and muzzle brake, began to lower.

"It could be a trick," whispered Bunker, who continued to hold on to the machine gun mount. "Here's my cigarette lighter."

"We'll see," Camellion said, accepting the cigarette lighter. He then yelled down across the top of the turret and reached into a small bag on his hip, "World War III has started. We're Americans and we've invaded Afghanistan. Washington and Moscow have been destroyed by thermonuclear bombs. Come out now and live. We've saved you three for only one reason: we want the tank. If we can't have it, we'll destroy it and you with it. You have half a minute to decide. Look ahead of the tank and you'll see how you'll die if you don't surrender."

He pulled the cola can of thermite from the bag, opened the Zippo lighter, clicked it on, and touched the flame to the wick protruding from the top. He waited until all but an inch of the wick had burned down to the can and then he threw the bomb twenty feet in front of the tank.

The thermite exploded with the sound of an extra-loud whisper, spreading out intense white fire that stopped only a few feet from the front of the tank.

"I'm getting damned impatient with you pig farmers," Camellion yelled in Russian. "If you're going to surrender, raise the barrel. I warn you: any tricks like trying to throw us off and we'll burn you alive. Come out now or die. Through the commander's hatch—*NOW*!"

Again the low sound from inside the T-64. The gun barrel started to raise.

Jay Bunker made hee-hee-hee sounds. "If those peasants believe that crap about WW III, they're dumber than I think they are."

Standing now, the Death Merchant braced himself by holding onto the ShKAS machine gun, and looked down at the hatch. "Jay, watch that small hatch over the driver's compartment. All pig farmers are born liars. We can't trust these jokers."

"Yes you can—as long as you can see their hands! Holding the MAC-10 as one would hold an auto-pistol, Bunker kept his eyes on the square hatch above the driver's compartment.

Click! The hatch opened to its full extent, and a frightened face, topped by a thick leather tanker's helmet, looked up at the Death Merchant.

"Come on up, ivan," Camellion ordered. "Before you do, tell the other two down there in this metal coffin that they're not to come up until you're standing by the left side of the tank."

Captain Vadim Pinkin, a twenty-six year old, pudgy and of medium height, started to come through the hatch. The instant he stepped out onto the top hull of the turret, Bunker jumped off on the right side, ran around the rear of the tank and was confronting Pinkin by the time Pinkin had jumped off and was on the ground.

A few minutes more and Boris Orliv, the driver, and Porfiri Kupryanov, the gunner, were on the ground, standing beside Pinkin, their hands also high above their head.

"*Amerikanski*, in the war," croaked Pinkin, "our nations destroyed each other?"

"Hee-hee-hee . . . I was right," giggled Bunker. "They are dumber than I thought."

Once the *mujahideen* had gathered around, inside the furniture store, the Death Merchant started to question the three Soviet tankmen while a dozen men kept the beams of a dozen flashlights on the frightened captives.

Sitting on a table, dangling his feet back and forth, a .44 Alaskan held loosely in his right hand, the Death Merchant looked down at the three Russians sitting on the floor surrounded by a sea of hate-filled Afghan faces. The poor bastards. A little more and he would have felt sorry for them—until he remembered little Afghan boys and girls who had lost their hands and arms because of booby-trapped toys dropped by Soviet planes. Camellion and the other five men from the West didn't hate the three pig farmers on the floor. All six were only doing a job. The three captives were a part of that job. The three were simply there. They were objects, without faces or feelings, like bacteria on the slide of a microscope.

"Captain Pinkin, tell us how the defenses are set up around the Central Prison," Camellion said in perfect Russian, his tone mild and relaxed. "I advise you to talk. I tend to be an impatient fellow."

"And don't try to tell us you didn't come from the Central

Prison defenses,'' Elrod Kinsey said. "We know you did. Tell them that, Camellion.''

"Patience, old buddy. Patience.''

A shocked look jumped over Captain Vadim Pinkin's face. From the Kara-Kalpak region of the Soviet Union, there was an oriental cast to his dark features.

Boris Orliv and Porfiri Kupryanov stared at the Death Merchant, fear in their black eyes.

"We are prisoners of war,'' Pinkin said stiffly. "We are required to give only—''

"*Shut up!*'' Camellion's voice hit the Russian with the force of a shotgun blast. Still swinging his legs, Camellion raised the .44 Alaskan AMP, the muzzle of the long stainless steel barrel centered on Pinkin's chest. "I'm not interested in excuses. I said—*talk*. I meant it!''

He moved the AMP slightly to his left and pulled the trigger, the thunderous roar of the Auto Mag crashing throughout the large room. The large flat-nosed slug slammed into the upper stomach of Porfiri Kupryanov at a steep angle, zipped out by his tail bone and bored into the floor. Kupryanov jumped—as if a dozen springs in his butt had been released— fell forward, twitched several times, and lay still.

"Jesus!'' mumbled Hooppole, his mouth remaining half-open.

Horrified, Pinkin and Orliv gaped in horrified disbelief at the Death Merchant.

"B-But you—you guaranteed our l-lives!'' stammered Pinkin. "You said that if we surrendered—''

"I lied,'' Camellion said. "Besides, my word can only be good with human beings. You're Russians. That makes you lower than lice or Rance Galloways. Here's how it is. I need only one of you to talk and to tell me how to operate the tank. Which one of you is it going to be? Keep stalling and it will be neither one of you. You'll both be dead within the next five minutes.''

The two Russian tankmen talked, quickly answering every question put to them by the Death Merchant.

The interrogation completed, the Death Merchant got down from the table, motioned for the two Russians to get to their feet and snapped at Captain Pinkin, "We're going back to your tank, cockroach. You're going to show me how to run the damn thing.''

He turned to Kamal Din Buhzid. "*Kuvii* Buhzid, tell a couple of dozen of the *mujahideen* to come with me. They can stand guard around the tank."

"What do you want us to do with the other Russian dog, *kuvii* Camellion?" Buhzid asked, a sly, sinister tone in his voice.

"I don't need him," Camellion replied, grabbing the back of Captain Pinkin's uniform collar. "What you do with him is your business."

Hooppole spoke up, "See here. What good is the tank? We can't use it to fight other tanks at the prison. They'd blow us away before we could get off the second round!"

"I know that, Rod!" Camellion didn't seem concerned. "I don't intend to use the T-64 to fight other tanks. Don't worry about it now. What I want you and the others to do is contact the other forces and see what progress they've made. . . ."

"Good enough," Hooppole concurred. "I hope they've made more speed than we have."

He and the other men watched Camellion leave the furniture store with Captain Pinkin and fourteen of the *mujahideen*.

"Do you ever get the feeling that you're a dead man with only temporary use of your arms and legs," said Hooppole.

"*Ja*, especially when Camellion's around," Wesslin said in a low voice.

CHAPTER TWELVE

Hell lay a block and a half to the north, and it was brightly lighted with large emergency spotlights mounted on thirty foot steel poles, a brace of five lights on each pole. A pole was at each corner of the twenty-one foot high wall surrounding Kabul Central Prison. Another pole with five bright spots was at the entrance, the two wide steel doors in the center of the south wall.

Standing on the roof of a five-story apartment house, the

Death Merchant and the others could see a lot more as they studied the large penitentiary complex through binoculars. Four T-64 tanks were in front of the south wall. On the roof of the prison building were Soviet infantrymen grouped around *Playma* grenade launchers and ZPU-2 heavy machine guns. By the southeast corner of the prison wall was a 122mm self-propelled howitzer.

"It looks damned impregnable to me," Hooppole said emptily, his face as drained of enthusiasm as his voice. "We can't even approach the front of the prison without being mowed down by machine guns. Damn it. It's half a block from the rubble to the front of the prison."

No one added to his prediction of doom and disaster. The Russians had destroyed the buildings on Haddam Street that had faced the prison. Where the structures had stood was now rubble, debris and mounds of stones.

Camellion, slowly scanning the area beyond the prison walls and beyond the prison building, had to admit that the combined attacks were going well. Reports over the Horizone walkie-talkies were all bad. Abdullah Saljoonque's Force-D. and Mohammad Malikyar's Force-A. had already suffered an estimated thirty percent casualties. Even so, the two forces had destroyed twenty-six Soviet tanks with Stinger missiles and RAWs and were now preparing a direct assault against the Soviet headquarters complex. Khair Ghazi's Force-C. and Danibor Zam's six hundred men were attacking the airbase and so far had lost four hundred men.

"There's a way to do it," Camellion said, putting the binoculars into their case. "Let's wait and see what the recon parties have to report."

"Hold on!" John Smith was on the defensive. "If you're thinking of sneaking up to all that rubble to knock out the tanks and the self-propelled deal—forget it. The Russians will have observers in that pile of ruins."

"We can't use Stingers and RAWs from here," Jugen Wesslin said cautiously. "The range is too far. The tanks are too small a target."

Camellion eyed them angrily. "I suggest all of you stop bumping your gums and listen to what I have to say before you start yelling failure," he said briskly. "We can zero in on the rubble . . . say from the third floor of this building.

Any observers in those ruins will retreat, those who aren't scratched.''

"So what? The tanks will immediately start blasting away at this building," Jay Bunker growled. "The Russians will instantly suspect we're going to make a frontal assault—and we still won't be able to get across the area. That puts us right back to where we are now, at square one."

The beep-beep-beep from Kamal Din Buhzid and Fazal Bhutto's walkie-talkies was a signal for silence as Bhutto answered the call and soon had a report from the recon parties. The scouts reported that north of the prison, just outside the outer wall, were thirteen BMP infantry combat vehicles and several machine gun nests behind barbed wire, rolled out concertina style. Behind the south wall of the parking lot, west of the prison, were twenty more BMP carriers and six BTR-40 armored cars. The apartment building to the east appeared to be deserted.

Bhutto made the "hold" signal on the walkie-talkie and looked over at the Death Merchant. "The scouts want to know whether they should return or remain where they are."

"Tell them to hold fast," Camellion said. "Tell them we'll join them in an hour or so."

Bunker, down on his haunches, sounded enthusiastic. "A four-sided attack makes more sense, but it doesn't tell us how to knock out those tanks and that damned howitzer."

"The main attack will come from here. It will be against the front of the prison," Camellion said as a statement of fact. In response to the you-must-be-kidding stares, he told the group how the attack would be made.

Stingers—fired from the third floor of this building—would undoubtedly draw fire from the four T-64s and the 122mm howitzer. The five big guns would saturate the entire forward area with fire, on the assumption that the rebels were going to attack from the south.

The force would be divided into four brigades, 324 men to a brigade. Three would attack from the north, the east, and the west. And the fourth? "That's us," Camellion said. "After the tanks stop the shelling, I and twenty men will sneak up to the ruins and wait until the other three brigades start attacking. We'll then destroy the tanks and the howitzer. The fourth brigade will then attack from the south."

"It's a good plan," commented Elrod Kinsey. "But what

will you do if those T-64s start firing while you're moving up to the ruins, or after you're in the rocks?''

"It's a chance we'll have to take," replied Camellion. He glanced up at the pitch black sky when thunder rumbled to the distant west. *That's all we need: rain!* "I'm hoping the Soviets will think our short shelling of the ruins was a ploy and that the real attack is coming from the west. You see, we'll have the west brigade attack first, say ten minutes ahead of the other groups. Those T-64s will no doubt turn and head west to shell what they think is the main body— I hope.''

Wesslin looked puzzled. "What about the captured tank we have?''

"First things first," Camellion said. "Let's get organized. *Kuvii* Buhzid, *kuvii* Bhutto, here's what I want you to do. . . .''

In the darkness it wasn't easy to divide the men into four brigades, although there wasn't any problem placing twenty-four men on the third floor of the apartment building— Camellion, Rod Hooppole and Jugen Wesslin being a part of the group because they wanted to try out RAWs which they had never fired. Kamal Din Buhzid was also present.

Lined up at the dark windows, the twenty-one Afghans lined up in their sights the stretch of ruins to the north and waited for Buhzid to order them to fire.

"Tell them to fire the instant we do," Camellion, squinting down the sight of an M16 A1E1 automatic rifle,[1] instructed Buhzid. Then to Hooppole and Wesslin, "You men ready?''

"Anytime," Wesslin said.

"One more thing," Camellion said to Buhzid. "Tell the men to get the hell out of here the moment they fire—downstairs and out the back way as fast as they can move. It will take the pig farmer tank men several minutes to elevate the barrels on those tanks and zero in. By the time they do, we had better be on the ground floor at minimum.''

Buhzid began jabbering to the Afghans.

The Death Merchant sighted down the updated M16, thinking about the RAW, the Rifleman's Assault Weapon that was

---

[1] The M16 A1E1 is an updated version of the M16. The M16 A1E1 is more modern, has a heavier barrel and can pierce helmets at eight hundred meters. It fires the 5.56 mm NATO round.

designed to give all riflemen the instant capability of defeating such obstacles as concrete bunkers, walls, and armored vehicles. The system required very little training to use; it was as easy as fixing a bayonet. The man firing attaches the unit to his rifle, pulls out the safety pin and fires an ordinary cartridge at any target, using standard sights. Within a quarter of a second, the RAW is propelled from its launch frame—attached to the barrel of the rifle—and flies straight to the target in less than two seconds with zero trajectory.

The RAW's launcher frame holds a tube which is free to rotate on bearings and which contains rear vents, as well as two side vents consisting of two curved tubes that are at opposing right angles to the axis of the main tube. The projectile—it resembles a round metal ball—fits into the main tube and up against part of the main launcher support. It is this portion of the support that has a hole drilled through it which connects with the muzzle sleeve. The removal of the safety pin unblocks a firing pin at the lower end of the hole where it meets the body of the projectile. When the bullet leaves the muzzle of the rifle, some of the expanding gas flows down the launcher-tube hole and through the bracket. With the safety pin removed, the gas is free to strike the firing pin, driving it into a primer in the rear of the projectile and starting the rocket motor that drives the five inch diameter ball-projectile. As gas is expelled from the rocket, it is directed through the two right-angled tubes, causing the main tube and the "ball" to spin sixty revolutions per second. At launch, the gases are directed through the rear vents and diverted away from the man pulling the trigger.

The RAW warhead is armed through a conventional thrust/pin mechanism. Upon contact, the front part flattens, giving a "squash head" effect for the thirty-four ounces of TNT that explodes. The RAW is rifle munition with artillery power.

Here goes nothing . . . halfway between tomorrow's dreams and today's nightmares! Camellion gently pulled the trigger, feeling the jar of the rifle's butt against his shoulder as the cartridge exploded and the 5.56mm round zipped from the muzzle of the barrel. *SSSHHHHHHHHHHHHHH.* The RAW ball-projectile rocketed on its way.

At once, Hooppole, Wesslin, and the twenty-one Afghans fired and twenty-three more RAWs shot toward the ruins to the north, the Death Merchant glad that he had changed his mind about using Stinger missiles. *I'm positive that Stingers will kill a tank. Why waste them on stones?*

BLAMMMM-BLAMMMM-BLAMMMM-BLAMMMM-BLAM-MMM! Flashes of fire to the north and thunderous explosions. Tons of rock being pulverized and tossed upward, the dozen screams of Soviet observers short, quick, and drowned out in the blasts.

No sooner had the men fired than they turned, and, by the dim light coming from the poles in front of the front walls of the prison, raced out of the room and to the stairs in the hall. With the aid of flashlights, they almost fell down the stairs to the second floor, then onto the first floor and the firedoor at the rear of the hall dividing the building.

Camellion and the tiny group was fleeing through the firedoor when the first HE shell from three of the tanks in front of the prison exploded with concussions that shook the building to its foundations. Two of the 12mm HE shells fell short, landed, and exploded on the Street of Red Knives in front of the building. The third shell exploded on the roof, the blast creating a twenty foot hole. Very quickly the Soviet gunners adjusted their laser computer sights, and the shells began slamming into the front of the apartment house, exploding on the second, third, fourth, and fifth floors.

BERRRROWWWOOMMMMMMMMMMMM! The fourth T-64 and the self-propelled 122mm howitzer began to toss high explosives shells on the ruins—and every shell was wasted. Two of the brigades were two blocks to the east, the two other brigades two blocks to the west.

By the time the sixth and seventh shells struck the front of the building, the Death Merchant and his small group were a block down the alley, running east to join the brigade that would attack the front of the prison. However, the shelling of the building had stopped by the time Camellion and his group reached the brigade. Camellion saw that Fazal Bhutto was on the walkie-talkie telling the impatient scouts to be patient.

Panting, the Death Merchant thought for a moment. The tank and the howitzer were still plastering the ruins with shells—*But those pig farmers aren't going to waste shells. The shelling will have quit by the time the men with the Stingers get there.*

"*Kuvii* Buhzid, get the three other groups started, one to the west, one to the east, one to the north," the Death

Merchant said. "You know what to tell them: to be cautious and do absolutely nothing until they get the word from either you or Bhutto."

Taking the walkie-talkie from its case on his belt, Buzhid nodded solemnly, shadows flickering over his face. "They will contact me or Fazal. I will contact you, *kuvii* Camellion, by the ruins—with this instrument." He held up the Horizone walkie-talkie.

"That's right. You will contact me. But I won't be at the ruins. I'll be with the tank we captured."

Instantly a lot of eyebrows raised. Smiling in the own private chambers of his mind, Camellion explained: "We'd lose too much time if I went to the ruins, then had to run back three blocks to the tank. The moment I receive word from the group by the ruins that the tanks and the self-propelled gun have been destroyed, I'll head straight for the prison with the tank. I have to blast those machine gunners and the *Plamya* boys off the roof, or they'll kill hundreds of us." He glanced at Bhutto and Buhzid. As usual, their faces were a fierce mask. "*Kuvii* Bhutto, *kuvii* Buhzid, understand that some of the prisoners on the top floor of the prison will no doubt be killed when I shell the roof. I am sorry. It can't be helped. I hope you understand and explain it to the *mujahideen?*"

The two Afghans nodded. Fazal Bhutto said, "*Kuvii* Camellion, a man who has never been sick cannot be a good physician. Prisoners will die. It will be a case of a few dying so that many may live."

Camellion looked around at the man who were being well paid by the CIA, the exception being Kinsey who was on a regular Case Officer's salary.

"All right. Who wants to lead the group that goes to the ruins to blow up the tanks and the howitzer?"

"I'll do it." All five spoke at the same time; Kinsey continuing, "I must tell you that I haven't had any experience at this sort of thing. But I'm willing to give it a try."

"Smith, you take charge of the group," Camellion said, privately feeling that of all the men present, Kinsey was one of the bravest—*It must have taken a terrific effort of will for that bald tobacco chewer to make the offer*.

Smith shrugged. "Glad to do it. I'm not here for a tea drinking party."

"Bhutto, choose some men who halfway understand

English,'' Camellion said. ''They can transmit Smith's orders to the other men.''

''No, *kuvii* Camellion. It is not possible what you suggest,'' Fazal Bhutto said. ''The men will not obey the orders of an infidel. I will go with the group and transmit the orders.''

''As you will. Allah will surely reward you,'' Camellion said gently. ''There is just one more thing. I—''

''The brigade to the west will still attack first?'' Smith sounded anxious, then very serious. ''Look, Camellion. Personally, I think it's a lot of crap to wait until the boys from the west open fire. Hell! We'll be using Stinger missiles. Those goddamn tanks don't have to move and present their sides for us to whack them out. The Stingers can blow 'em up if they zing in head-on. It's like this. You're the boss, but when I handle a specific job, I have to do what I think best. I'm going to have to scratch those tanks my way.''

The Death Merchant liked Smith's lay-it-on-the-line attitude.

''Do it your way,'' Camellion promptly said. ''Once you get up to the ruins, you're the boss.''

''What's the other thing?'' asked Jay Bunker.

''I want someone to go with me and drive the tank,'' Camellion said, his eyes going to Jugen Wesslin, who had been in the West German army, was familiar with tanks and had already test driven the captured T-64.

Wesslin smiled easily. ''I would assume you're really asking for me to drive the tank?''

''You got it. But I'm democratic. Anyone can go.''

''I'll do it.''

''Count me in with the men who go to the ruins,'' Rod Hooppole said. ''I get nervous if I'm not doing something, and I want to see those tanks explode.''

''John, be extremely careful up there,'' Camellion advised Smith.

''Listen!'' interjected Kinsey. ''The Ruskies have stopped shelling the ruins.''

''Yeah, but they'll be watching like hungry hawks,'' Bunker said.

''They'll be watching the ruins and the entire area through NVDs,''[2] Camellion said to Smith. ''No doubt they have

[2]Night Vision Devices.

169

observers stationed in the apartment building east of the prison. You and Bhutto will have to move in very slowly."

"Affirmative," Smith said brusquely.

"Let's get started," the Death Merchant said. "We know what to do and how to do it."

He felt the first drops of rain fall on his shoulders.

You're sure you know how to fire the gun?" Tucking his ponytail under the back of his OD fatigue cap, Wesslin looked up at Camellion who had just pushed himself up through the hatch of the commander's cupola.

Camellion leaned down and closed the hatch, then jumped from the tank.

"I'm positive," he replied. "Captain Pinkin told me everything I needed to know before the Afghans sent him to his ancestors. All you have to do is drive. I'll do the rest."

He sniffed the air, sweet smelling from the very short shower. As suddenly as it had come the rain had stopped, but the thundering in the west was louder.

"The steering is relatively easy," Wesslin said. "The gear ratio and the bogie units are similar to the West German Panther. I rather suspect that each track of the T-64 has a triple turn bearing system and is geared in to the sprocket wheels. You can tell when you hear a faint clicking sound as the tank turns."

The Death Merchant looked around. He had driven the tank into the courtyard of a large house and in the darkness could see the glowing tip of cigarettes in the mouths or hands of some of the twelve Afghans posted to guard the vehicle. The wait began, the passage of time moving with all the swiftness of a crippled snail trying to slide through sticky goo. An hour passed. The Death Merchant walked slowly back and forth by the side of the tank, Wesslin's tension revealed by the score of cigarette butts at his feet.

After ninety-three long minutes, the Death Merchant and Wesslin heard a series of thundercracking explosions to the north.

"Stingers!" The word jumped out of Wesslin's mouth. He pushed his head forward and dropped his half-smoked cigarette to the ground. "Smith got those tanks and the howitzer."

Camellion looked at the Horizone W-T in his hand. "We'll know in a moment."

A few minutes later the W-T buzzed. The voice on the other end of the line belonged to Kamal Din Buhzid, who had news that was three quarter good and one quarter terrible. Smith, Hooppole and the Afghans had destroyed the four T-64 tanks in front of the prison, but the self-propelled 122mm howitzer had not even been scratched. It hadn't been because it wasn't there.

Buhzid's agitated voice came out of the walkie-talkie: *"Kuvii* Brown reported that as he and the other men were getting into position in the rocks, the big gun mounted on its own wheels turned around and moved north, along the east side of the prison. What are your orders, *kuvii* Camellion?"

"Donnerwetter!" snarled Wesslin. "That damned howitzer might as well be another tank." He looked sharply at the Death Merchant. "We can't fight that gun with the T-64. We're too inexperienced."

The Death Merchant did some fast thinking. *"Kuvii* Buhzid, instruct the three brigades to attack," Camellion spoke into the W-T. "They'll have to knock out the howitzer with RAWs and Stingers when they hit the armored cars and the other stuff—over."

"Your orders for the fourth brigade?"

"Wesslin and I will be coming by in the tank in a short while," Camellion said firmly. "Have the fourth brigade move out fifteen minutes after we pass, and tell Brown to move back. The howitzer might begin shelling the ruins. Over."

"He is pulling back now, *kuvii* Camellion. Over."

"You had better speak to one of your boys back here around the tank," Camellion said. "They don't understand English, and they wouldn't follow my orders even if they did."

In another ten minutes, Camellion and Wesslin were in the tank and ready to clank north, Wesslin in the driver's seat, Camellion behind the breech of the gun in the commander's chair.

Wesslin turned on the engine and yelled back to the Death Merchant as he let the powerful diesel warm up. "You have to be crazy to go out there in this tank, especially with that howitzer on the loose.

"You're not exactly all there yourself, my kraut friend," the Death Merchant flung back with a quick little laugh. "You're going with me!"

CHAPTER THIRTEEN

One of the most worried men in Kabul, Major Andrew Pytyr Sogolov stared out the window of the prison headquarters building at the penitentiary, a hundred feet to the east. There were fifteen hundred men in that prison—and every single one of them would give his life to get his hands around Sogolov's neck. The prisoners were Sogolov's greatest fear. If the situation outside didn't reverse itself, they might get a chance to do it.

There was nothing but death and destruction around the prison complex. The rebels were attacking, the main headquarters building itself shaking from the constant explosions. All the reports were black. Already the damned rebels has used missiles and some other kind of mysterious weapon to destroy nine armored cars and ten BMP carriers. But the mortars were intact and firing and the 122mm self propelled-weapon was throwing out shell after shell. Even inside Kovalev's office the air with thick with blue-gray fumes.

Wearing a battle helmet, Sogolov turned from the window, pulled a handkerchief from his suit coat and wiped perspiration from his high forehead. How could he have been so wrong? He had been absolutely certain that the rebel murderers *wouldn't* attack the prison and had said so to General Pavel Mozzhechkov, stating flatly that he was convinced that the ignorant Afghans would concentrate their pitiful forces against Soviet headquarters and against the airbase.

That damned Colonel Voukelitch. The son of a bitch! During the meeting, Voukelitch had disagreed, calmly telling General Mozzhechkov that, according to his "psychological evaluation of the Afghan *burzhuy svet*,"[1] the Afghans would attack the prison.

[1] "Class enemies."

General Mozzhechkov had agreed with Colonel Voukelitch.

Intelligently, Sogolov realized his bitterness stemmed not only from his intense envy of Voukelitch, but from his realization that the GRU Colonel had been correct. If he hadn't been, the penitentiary would have been left defenseless. Worse was Sogolov's having to admit that he had been wrong and that soon the KGB home office would know it. Damn it! How could he have known that the Americans would make an enormous airdrop and use some new kind of bursting missile to shoot down Soviet interceptors? There wasn't any proof that it had been the Americans. But who else could have made the drop? And those four tanks guarding the prison! Destroyed in seconds!

Sogolov turned nervously to Evhen Kovalev, the warden of the prison who, like Sogolov and the two other men in the office, was wearing a helmet and sweating blood.

"Comrade Kovalev, you had better go to the radio room and see if General Mozzhechkov has answered yet," Sogolov said, against wiping his face. "We must have reinforcements."

"Comrade, we only put in the call five minutes ago," protested Kovalev, who had high cheekbones, a hawkbill nose, and a shaggy mustache. "They said they would call back as soon as they had conferred with General Mozzhechkov."

"What's the use?" screeched Konstantin Zaostrevt. "Comrade General Mozzhechkov's headquarters has already informed us that they do not have the men and the armor to send!"

Sogolov glared at his assistant, feeling stupid and knowing that Zaostrevt was right.

Kovalev, sensing that Sogolov would probably ask again about the defenses inside the penitentiary, Kovalev said, "I assure you, Comrade. There isn't any way the antisocial elements can escape. They are securely locked inside their cells. Even if some of them did manage to get loose—it's impossible that they could—Chogevenkok, Daltizeb, and all the guards have machine pistols. An uprising is simply not possible."

Sogolov's eyebrows shot up. "Daltizeb?" he spit out the word. "Isn't that an Afghan name?" His voice rose in disbelief. "My God! You have given a machine pistol to an Afghan?"

"Comrade Sogolov, Sahazaba Daltizeb is completely trustworthy." Evhen Kovalev sounded positive. "He is the one the inmates refer to as 'Lard-Butt.' Surely, Comrade, you have heard of him?''

A sly gleam stole into Sogolov's eyes. Indeed he had heard of Lard-Butt. "*Da!* We can trust that one," Sogolov said. "He hates his countrymen more than we do. Wasn't he the—''

Suddenly there was a monstrous crashing sound above the third story of the headquarters building. A shell had exploded. The building trembled. Light fixtures on the wall shook. Some bits of plaster fell from the ceiling.

"It's that goddamn captured tank!" shouted Anatoli Bok, putting his arms over his head.

Came another sound—a grinding, a ripping, a tearing of metal from metal, from concrete. Quickly the crunch and crump became a loud crash as the radio tower fell from the roof, the top part slamming to the ground.

CHAPTER FOURTEEN

"You got it!" Wesslin shouted excitedly to the Death Merchant, who, peering through the commander's periscope of the T-64, watched the green painted radio tower topple from the roof of the administration building.

"Stay where you are," Camellion yelled. "I'm going to start taking out the machine gunners and the *Plamya* boys on the roof. Watch for the howitzer through your slit and periscope. When you see it, put our plan into effect. It's the only chance we'll have."

Camellion took his eyes from the screen and pushed the button that controlled the automatic loader. There was the smooth sound of well-oiled machinery in motion, then a clanking sound as another 125mm HE shell was moved from the storage rack, shoved over by the arm to the feeder, moved upward and pushed into the breech of the gun. Circuits clicked. The Y-arm moved. The breech closed and locked.

Switching the sights to the roof and throwing the computer-adjust switch, Camellion was forced to admit that the T-64 was a first rate kill-machine.

The T-64 was somewhat larger and heavier than previous Soviet tanks,[1] its weight ranging from 42-48 metric tons. According to Wesslin, it had a hydropneumatic suspension system that allowed its commander to raise or lower the total silhouette of the tank. Imagine!

The engine was a V-12 turbo-charged diesel with 760 horsepower, giving the T-64 a power-to-weight ratio of 13.5 to 16 hp/t (metric ton). The armor was of a Soviet-designed laminate type construction with additional armor plates spaced above crucial vulnerable points, which included above the turret, to help defeat air-burst weapons. The turret was not cast iron, but welded like all modern NATO tank turrets. The result was a more square and longer profile to allow for ammo storage in the rear.

Then there was the improved 125mm smooth-bore cannon with its automatic loading device and ammunition with partially combustible cases for ease of ejection. The tank had a new target tracking device which locked onto the target by means of a computer that used a combination laser and infra-red system; this system was combined with a weapons stabilization arrangement that enabled the gunner to keep the cannon pointed at a moving target even when the T-64 was in motion.

The ammunition was basically the same, the HE and the APFSDS rounds consisting of a tungsten-uranium alloy core that enabled the shells to move with a velocity of seventeen hundred meters per second—the highest velocity tank rounds in the world.

What Uncle Sam needs is the neutron bomb! It scares the bejesus out of the pig farmers.

The Death Merchant soon was sighted in on the group of *Raydoviki* grouped around several *Plamyas* and a heavy MG toward the edge of the south side roof of the prison building. The Russians were throwing out grenades all over the place in an effort to keep the Afghans from closing in. They were succeeding, they and the others, with *Plamyas* and heavy MGs, on the east, the west, and the north roofs of the square penitentiary building. Grenades were exploding all over the

[1]The latest Soviet tank is the T-80.

place, some very close to the tank. There wasn't any way the *mujahideen* could race across the open spaces. The constant concussions didn't bother the Death Merchant and Wesslin, both of whom wore special ear inserts they had found in the tank. While very effective against concussion, the plugs had special diaphragms that made it possible for one to hear spoken speech.

Camellion again looked through the sight. The 125mm cannon was on target. He pressed the firing button. A roar, the tank jumped back slightly and the shell was on its way. He didn't even have time to blink before he saw the roof explode with fire and smoke. When the mess cleared, there was only a giant hole with ragged, smoking edges, part of it on the south side of the fourth floor. The Russians and their "toys" had disappeared.

The Death Merchant realized that in order to blow up the *Plamyas* and machine gun crews on the other roofs, Wesslin would have to take the T-64 all around the building. Even so—*I still won't be able to knock out the Plamyas. Their crew can move back to the center of the roofs. I won't be able to see them, but they'll still be able to lob grenades to the ground.*

The only answer was that the Afghans in the brigade attacking from the east would have to use Stingers and MAWs from the upper stories of the apartment house. With all the explosions around the tank, it was not possible for him to know what might be going on at the apartment house. To find out, he swung the electrically-controlled ranging periscope to the northeast. He was just in time to see *mujahideen* shoving a large red, black, green and gold Afghan flag, attached to a long pole out a fifth story window of the apartment house. *Good! The Aghans have taken the apartment house!*

Instantly hundreds of 14.5mm and 7.62mm projectiles, from ZPU2 and ShKAS machine guns, ripped into the fluttering cloth, tearing it into hundreds of ribbons. The Death Merchant couldn't be sure. There was a lot of smoke and haze. He was fairly certain he saw the tips of Stingers and a few RAW "balls" protruding from other windows. He had! As he watched he saw a dozen slim contrails shoot out from just as many windows. He couldn't swing the periscope fast enough to see where the Stingers landed—at least on the south roof, the only side he could see from the tank's present position. He did hear the violent explosions, a series of blasts that mingled with the occasional *flub-flub-flub-flub* of exploding mortar shells that the pig farmers were throwing from behind the walls that were the outer square of the Kabul Central Prison complex.

BLAMMMMM! BLAMMMMM! The two detonations were so shattering that, in that slice of a thin second, Camellion thought the tank had exploded. The tank had taken two direct hits. By what? He soon found out.

Wesslin yelled from the driver's seat, "Armored cars! Four of them to our left!"

BLAMMMMM! Once more a 64mm shell exploded on the left side of the tank, against the turret protected by 150mm armor. Again the wall of noise that bored into the center of one's brain, as if trying to tear Wesslin and Camellion apart.

Then three more tremendous bombinations—maybe several hundred feet left of the tank.

"*Mein Gott!* Did you see it?" yelled Wesslin excitedly. "Three of the cars were hit by either RAWs or Stingers!"

The Death Merchant, busy with the ranging periscope, hadn't seen the three BTR-40s explode. He had heard the big blasts. In turning the scope, he had spotted something else that made his spine crawl—the self-propelled howitzer. It wasn't a 122mm job either. Camellion judged the cannon to be a 185-mm weapon. The howitzer was just clearing the southeast corner of the prison's outer wall.

"To our right—the howitzer! Get going, damned fast!" yelled Camellion, calculating that he and Wesslin and the T-64 had about a minute to live—unless . . .

Wesslin "got!" The sounds of gears meshing. Right track in rapid motion. Left track stationary. The T-64 turned rapidly to the right. Wesslin geared in, fed fuel to the powerful engine, and the tank began rolling straight at the howitzer, the Afghan flag—riddled with shrapnel holes—waving from the radio antenna on the left rear of the turret.

For any practical purpose, a self-propelled gun is another kind of tank. There are differences. A self-propelled gun is always larger. It is self-propelled only for mobility of movement. It is not designed to go into battle. In the case of the 185mm howitzer versus Camellion and Wesslin's T-64, the howitzer on its Ganef chassis weighed 24.6 tons and had a top speed of 31 mph. With a speed of 50 mph and weighing

39.3 tons, the T-64 was much faster and far heavier. The T-64 had another advantage, in that its maneuverability was almost three times that of the howitzer.

Speed and maneuverability explained why Jugen Wesslin was able to reach the 185mm gun-vehicle before the gunner could even begin to zero in for a round.

The tactic that Camellion and Wesslin was using was the only one possible under the circumstances: to stay so close to the enemy vehicle that it wouldn't be possible for the other crew to fire at the T-64. Now that the *Plamyas* and the machine guns on the roof had been silenced and the *mujahideen* were closing in from all four directions, it would be only a very short time before the howitzer was "killed" by either a Stinger or a RAW.

Wesslin had slowed and he did brake heavily; yet he had miscalculated. The front of the T-64 slammed into the right front corner of the self-propelled gun at an angle, the crash crumbling the right mud guard of the tank and making Camellion and Wesslin feel that they had hit the side of a mountain. The two vehicles stopped, their engines idling.

The driver of the 185mm gun then tried to back up his vehicle. Wesslin, who, in the driver's seat, was a mere six and a half feet from the other vehicle, changed gears and followed. Again tons of metal came together as Wesslin again slammed the front of the tank into the side of the big cannon. Once more Wesslin and the enemy driver went into neutral and waited.

In the tank, Camellion was watching the enemy vehicle through the commander's ranging scope and Wesslin, having closed the vision slit in front of the driver's seat, was using the driver wide-angle scope.

A whirring sound came from the other vehicle, and they saw the turret begin to turn to its right, the long barrel of the 185mm cannon perfectly horizontal. The Death Merchant and Wesslin also saw that the hatch of the enemy turret had opened and that a black-helmeted pig farmer was rearing up, a 7.62 mm Dragunov machine gun in his hands.

"What does that idiot think he is going to do with a *machinepistole*?" shouted Wesslin, his eyes glued to the periscope, his hands on the gear levers. "He might as well throw rocks at us!"

"I think he's going to try to 'blind' us, shoot out our

scopes on the outside," Camellion replied. "We had better hope to God that he misses."

The Russian did miss but not because he was a poor shot. No sooner had he pushed himself up through the round opening than he jumped and jerked violently, as if he were standing on a steel plate in his bare feet and someone had sent a charge of electricity through it. The corpse slumped down through the hatch, his body riddled with Afghan slugs.

In the meanwhile the turret of the self-propelled howitzer had made its one-fourth turn and there was a loud, ringing *CLANG* as the right side of the 185mm barrel struck the right side of the T-64's turret.

"Well, pon my sweet, silent soul!" Camellion grinned. "The damned dummy is going to try to push us aside. He can't do it."

Jugen Wesslin knew why without being told. Although the barrel of the 185mm cannon weighed four times as much as the barrel of the tank's 125mm smoothbore, the T-64 out weighed the other vehicle by fifteen tons, or thirty thousand pounds. The enemy vehicle was similar to a midget trying to brush aside a three hundred pound wrestler.

CLANG! CLANG! CLANG! Again and again the big barrel banged against the side of the tank's turret. The enemy vehicle then tried literally to push over the tank with the barrel. Again . . . failure.

The Death Merchant began turning the ranging periscope to the left. Everywhere, in front of the prison, he could see the *mujahideen* charging north. On all sides were explosions, especially to the north. He turned the scope to the north wall and smiled in satisfaction when he saw that a sixty foot section, west of the gates, had been blown down by Stinger missiles and RAWs and that Afghans were charging toward the long gap, many of them being blown up by mortar shells and heavy machine guns firing from the administration building and the second floor of the penitentiary. To his left, wrecked armored cars were burning, the red flames eating hungrily, the black smoke climbing into the sky. The worst was the dead and the dying. The ground was covered with Afghans. . . .

Suddenly, there was a mighty explosion from the left rear side of the 185mm gun-vehicle and Camellion and Wesslin heard loud crashing sounds on top of the tank as chunks and pieces of metal struck the forward hull and the turret.

A Stinger missile had blown up the vehicle.

"The driver's periscope is wrecked," Wesslin yelled back. "But I can use the forward vision slot."

Wesslin and Camellion got another surprise when they heard a familiar voice call out to them behind the tank, on the right corner.

"Open up! It's me!"

"Tell him to make it fast," Wesslin said angrily. "We have to get out of here. The ammunition in the gun-vehicle might explode. The damn thing is burning."

Thinking that John Smith was either one of the bravest—*Or he's the dumbest dude I ever met!*—the Death Merchant pressed the button. The hatch silently swung open on its gronge hinge. Camellion then got out of the gunner's chair and, hunched over in the cramped space, watched Smith climb down the short ladder to the observation platform.

The big American weapons specialist stared at Camellion for a moment in the dim light of the four wire-guarded bulbs. He laughed slightly.

"You should see yourself, Camellion!" joked Smith. "You look like a coal miner!"

"It's the fumes from the gun," said Camellion, moving back to the gunner's chair. "Sit down in the radio operator's chair and tell us what's happening out there."

Smith became very serious. "They're dying all over the place. As far as I know—" He caught the arms of the metal bucket chair as the tank jerked and Wesslin began to back the T-64 from the burning self-propelled gun. Inside the tank, the three men could smell the smoke filled with the stink of rubber, metal, cloth and other materials. "As far as I know, all our people are OK. But if it were up to me, I'd order a retreat. A couple of hundred more Afghans will die before we secure the penitentiary. The objective is not worth the cost."

The Death Merchant, coughing slightly from the smoke, shook his head. "The Afghans wouldn't listen to me, not this close to the prison. Besides, I have to get inside the prison, to the third floor, to Cell 318."

He got the reaction he expected from Smith whose eyes narrowed suspiciously and whose face became curious. "Have to?"

The Death Merchant told him why.

Smith sighed heavily and leaned forward on his "Bullput"

assault rifle. "So that's how that fruitcake crumbles! Well, we might as well get on with it. What's our next move with this tank?"

"We'll destroy the administration building and make an opening in the prison," Camellion said. He yelled down at Wesslin. "Take us right through the gap in the wall."

"It's as good as done!" Wesslin called back from the driver's compartment.

Within half a minute the T-64 was rolling toward the north wall.

Behind them the burning self-propelled gun blew itself apart.

CHAPTER FIFTEEN

Crouched on the floor of the second story of the prison administration building, Andrew Sogolov looked fearfully around him. The building was being shot to pieces, and all hope was gone. *You're going to die,* a small voice screamed in the back of Sogolov's mind. *Your life is over.* Vladimor Grushi, the assistant warden, was already dead, torn apart by a missile's exploding. The four crews of the four heavy machine guns were almost out of ammunition.

Konstantin Zaostrevt crawled on his hands and knees, across the glass and paper littered floor, to Sogolov. "We can't hold them off much longer," he panted, "and we can't expect help from General Mozzhechkov. Comrade, what are we going to do?"

During the past ten minutes, a lot of wild thoughts had raced through the sadistic mind of Sogolov. He had even analyzed the possibility of surrender. *Nyet! Nyet! Nyet!* While surrender was very possible, living after surrender was not. More than cognizant that he was one of the more hated men in Afghanistan, Sogolov entertained no illusions as to his destiny should he throw up the white flag—and to the fate of his family back home. The Afghans would cut him apart. *Nyet!* They would formally shoot him after a show trial. Shot is shot and dead is dead. Better to die here as a "hero" for the "glorious" Soviet Union.

The sound of a thunderous explosion came from the end of the hall, the violent concussion shaking the building. Sogolov and Zaostrevt looked at each other. Another missile had exploded.

Across the room, by the useless shortwave set, Anatoli Bok shouted, "Comrades, we've got to get out of here!"

Their eyes turned to the door of the radio room. An infantryman had staggered down the hall, from the room where the RAW had exploded. His uniform was in tatters. His arm hung uselessly at his left side which was a mass of blood. Chips of glass had cut his face to ribbons and blood dripped from his cheeks.

"Sir," he began, looking at Sogolov. Without another word he dropped to the floor.

"Pass the word," Sogolov muttered to Zaostrevt. "We'll use the tunnel and go to the prison. There isn't anything else we can do."

Zaostrevt stared dumbly at Sogolov. The tunnel had been built to facilitate the transportation of prisoners from Unit-K to the administration building.

"B-But what good will that do?" demanded Zaostrevt. "The Afghans will storm the prison, and they must know about Unit-K?"

"Konstantin, we're going to die," Sogolov said hollowly. "By making a stand in Unit-K, we'll push dying back a little longer. Or we can remain here and die sooner. . . ."

CHAPTER SIXTEEN

Up a lazy river to the right kidney . . . I'm shivering and I'm shaking from my balls to my knees—sang the Death Merchant at the top of his lungs, much to the amazement of John Smith. Jugen Wesslin wasn't surprised. He had assumed much earlier that the tall, lean man who called himself Richard Camellion was more than slightly strange.

"This is one hell of a time to sing anything!" said Smith loudly.

"You know what the Bible says—'Make a joyful noise for the Lord!' That's from Isaiah. I forget the chapter and verse. Wesslin! Stop the tank. We're in position."

Wesslin brought the T-64 to a dead stop, but kept the engine running. Camellion started looking through the periscope in earnest. The tank was only a hundred feet in front of the wide gap in the outer wall. There was the prison administration building, its windows shot out, the green-painted concrete blocks pitted with thousands of craters made by ricochets. The large door of the main entrance had been blown in. The hammer and sickle flag of the Soviet Union, on its shattered pole, lay on the ground. There were giant holes in the front of the building, from RAW explosions, the edges of the holes ragged with splintered boards and chunks of masonry hanging on twisted reinforcing wire. To the northwest was the smoking wreck of an armored car and four BMP infantry combat carriers, the area around the burning junk littered with Russian dead. There were more dead men scattered around the administration building, all Afghans.

The Death Merchant slowly turned the periscope. Large groups of *mujahideen* were to the left and the right of the long gap in the outer wall, and he could see that Hooppole, Kinsey, Bunker, and Kamal Din Buhzid were among those in the first group to the left; they and many of the Afghans turned to the tank, watching and waiting for it to open fire on the administration building and then on the prison from which machine guns were still firing.

Camellion adjusted for range and began to lower the barrel of the 125mm smoothbore cannon. Estimated range: 91.44 meters (300 feet). Circuits clicked. The Y-arm moved. An HE shell was shoved into the breech. The breech closed and locked. The Death Merchant pressed the firing button. The big gun roared and a large part of the front of the administration building, on the first floor, went flying into the air. Six more times the Death Merchant sent high explosive shells into the bottom floor, finally achieving the desired result. With a loud crash and a lot of dust the entire building collapsed.

"Wesslin, take us inside," shouted Camellion, his ears

ringing in spite of the sonic inserts, "and we'll take apart the prison itself."

Gears engaged. Wesslin fed fuel to the powerful engine. The tank moved toward the large rupture in the wall and was soon inside the prison grounds. Camellion had Wesslin turn the T-64 to the northeast, toward the west side of the penitentiary several hundred feet ahead; then he went to work with the gun.

BLAMMMMMMM! The first 125mm HE round opened a fifteen-foot hole on the first floor. The second shell silenced the firing of a heavy 12.7mm DShK-38 machine gun on the second floor. The next three rounds lengthened the hole in the wall so that, when the smoke and fumes cleared, there was a 60–70 feet long breach, through which one could see part of the interior.

Now that a way to the inside of the prison was open, the Afghans of the south and the west brigades charged forward with wild yells and fanatical shouts of "*IN'SHALLAH ALLAH*" and "*ALLAH AKBAR!*" a mob bent on vengeance for the horrors suffered at the hands of the Russians.

There was a loud banging on the back of the tank. Someone was signalling with either a pistol or the barrel of a rifle.

"It's us!" The voice belonged to Rod Hooppole. "Come on out and let's get this mission over with."

Once Camellion, Wesslin, and Smith were out of the T-64, they saw that the tiny group was composed of Bunker, Kinsey, Hooppole, and a fierce-looking Afghan with a long chin and a mustache that drooped a few inches on each side of his mouth. The man's name was Alfar Eudizap and he explained to the Death Merchant that Fazal Bhutto and Kamal Din Buhzid were with the units attacking the prison and that he had remained with Bunker and the two other men because he spoke English.

Even above the shouts of victory from the guerrillas charging toward the prison, Camellion and the rest of them could hear Soviet machine guns firing from the east and the north sides of the prison. The intense firing was followed by five very violent explosions. The brigades from the north and the east had silenced the machine guns with RAWs. The Death Merchant was quick to see that there were large gaps in the west and the north walls through which *mujahideen* were running, waving weapons above their heads.

"Camellion, Bhutto said to tell you that he's ordered the men not to free the prisoners until the prison has been secured," Kinsey said in a weak voice. "He figured the inmates would just be in the way, running back and forth."

A MAC-10 in his left hand, the Death Merchant looked toward the west wall of the prison. From inside he could hear the firing of automatic weapons. The Soviets were still fighting.

With other Afghans, they ran to the west side of the building, moved inside, and saw that the HE rounds had opened the wall to a long corridor and the locker room of guards. Afghans were crouched against the walls of the corridor and were inside the locker room. Others were firing around the edge of a wide doorway whose thick steel door had been blown inward by grenades. In front of the locker room, Fazel Bhutto and Kamal Din Buhzid were on their knees with four other men, studying a first floor plan of Kabul Central Prison. The Death Merchant and the others hurried over to the six.

Kamal Din Buhzid glanced up as Camellion got down beside him. "The room east of the hall is a large day room for the swine guards," Buhzid told him. His grimy finger touched the dirty map. "Here is the day room."

Camellion saw at once that to the east of the day room was a security area in front of hundreds of cells. In the center of the long area was the stairs to the second floor. North of the day room was a much smaller security area, the front, to the south, a tiny room with a double door. One door opened to the day room. The second door, to the rear of the closet-sized area, opened to the section containing the steps to the basement that was completely under the entire first floor.

"These steps, *kuvii* Camellion"—Buhzid touched the map— "lead to Unit-K, the torture chambers."

Fazal Bhutto tapped the map with the razor sharp end of a *Hazka*.

"It is here, from the first door to the area that has the basement steps, that the snakes are firing and preventing us from having farther into the building, from entering the day room."

The Death Merchant turned and gave Bhutto a hard look. "What's the problem?" he asked, irritated. "Why haven't you used a RAW, or even a grenade?"

Bhutto and Buhzid let Camellion have a blank, we-don't-understand stare. "*Kuvii* Camellion, *Malik* Khair Ghazi instructed us to follow your orders. We gave him our word that we would," Kamal Din Buhzid said. He sounded surprised, as if he might be thinking the Death Merchant was a moron. "We gave him our word that we would. You are the leader. You have not ordered us to use an explosive device against the door in the day room."

The Death Merchant wanted to laugh. He didn't, and kept his face serious—*American businessmen could take a lesson from these "ignorant people!"*

"I see," Camellion said. "I'll do it. I'll blow that door with a RAW. One of you instruct one of your men to give me a rifle and a RAW."

Buhzid got up, turned and jabbered to one of the rank and file *mujahideen*. The man immediately handed his rifle and RAW attachment to Camellion, who strode down the hall to the doorway, Kinsey, Smith, and Hooppole following. Four Afghans were still wasting ammo by periodically leaning around the edge of the doorway and triggering off quick rounds at the steel door north of the guard room. The enemy returned the fire through three round firing ports in the wide door.

Camellion darted to the right side. He had to be on the right side in order to have the correct angle of fire. But he didn't fire. He didn't have a chance to fire. While he was checking the RAW mount on the M16 A1E1 assault rifle, the Soviet Dragunov and the PPS43 submachine guns ceased firing. There was a dead silence, not only from beyond the steel door in the day room, but over the entire area.

The inmates of Kabul Central Prison had not made a noise all during the battle. Long before the assault had begun, the inmates had decided that their only chance was to be absolutely silent and not anger the KGB and Afghan turncoat guards, who just might machine-gun them.

The guards had disappeared from all the floors, but who knew when they might return? The inmates were certain that the prison was still in Soviet hands and under KGB control. If not, why were they still locked up? Why had no one freed them?

The silence was terrifying.

Some of the Afghans by the doorway looked at each other and whispered in their native tongue.

Kinsey whispered to the Death Merchant, "They could be talking over surrender. . . ."

"Those bloody bastards will never surrender," Hooppole gave his opinion. "They're up to some kind of new trick, I should think."

"They could be moving down to the basement," Camellion speculated.

The burst of submachine gun fire from *behind* the steel door was totally unexpected, and with the roaring of the weapon were short, quick yells.

More silence.

The Death Merchant stuck his head around the side of the doorway and stared at the cream-colored steel door. Across from him, to the left, Smith and an Afghan were leaning out, looking past overturned tables and chairs and scrutinizing the door north of the day room.

All at once the steel door opened a few inches, just enough so that they could see a thin crack between the edge of the door and the molding of the frame.

"I wonder who shot who?" whispered Smith.

(*You mean WHOM?*) "Wait and don't do anything rash," ordered the Death Merchant, who had placed the M16 A1E1 rifle and its RAW attachment on the floor and was holding his Ingram MAC-10 in his left hand, its muzzle trained on the steel door.

From behind the door a voice called out loudly in *Pushto*. The Afghans around the hall door began to talk excitedly among themselves. By then, Kamal Din Buhzid, Fazal Bhutto and the rest of the group that had been in front of the locker room had come down the corridor and they, too, had heard the man call out from behind the steel door.

The voice called out again. This time, whatever the man said, he was taking a lot longer to say it than the first time—*Or else he's added to it!*

"It's one of the Afghan guards," Kamal Din Buhzid explained to the Death Merchant and the other non-Afghans. "He said he wants to surrender. He wants to make sure we won't cut him down when he comes out."

"Fine. He can tell us how many of the enemy are in the basement," Camellion said. "Make sure your men don't blow him up the instant he sticks his head out the door. You can cut his throat after he tells us what we want to know."

Buhzid rattled off orders in *Pushto* to the men grouped around the edges of the doorway, after which he spoke loudly to the guard behind the steel door.

"I told him to come out and advance with his hands above his head," Buhzid explained to the Death Merchant and the other CIA men.

Muammer Geris snarled, "We'll shoot the seditious pig after he gives us the information we need."

"Shooting is too good for such a man," Lamiz Junikiz said ruthlessly. "He should die very slowly and very painfully."

The steel door swung open, and a man in the dark brown uniform of a KGB guard walked out, his arms stretched above his head as high as was possible. Not over five feet seven, the man weighed in the neighborhood of 250 pounds and was so fat he waddled from side to side when he walked. As bald as Kinsey, the man had a heavy black mustache that drooped and merged into his short beard, so that it appeared he had a very wide black circle "painted" around his mouth.

Several of the Afghans shouted something in *Pushto*, their voices vibrating with rage and hate. Kinsey glanced at the Death Merchant, his glance conveying that he, too, was wondering why the Afghans should get so worked up over one guard.

Fazal Bhutto spoke sharply to the men and they lapsed into silence.

"That guard is Sahazaba Daltizeb!" spit out Lamiz Junikiz. "He's the sadist the prisoners call 'Mr. Lard Butt!' "

"Lard Butt" waddled across the day room to the corridor door, stopping just inside the doorway, only three feet from Kamal Din Buhzid, who turned to the men, called for attention and spoke rapidly, making a lot of motions with his hands. Some of the *mujahideen* shouted a lot of jibber-jabber at Buhzid, and he, joined by Fazal Bhutto, shouted back. While the Death Merchant and the other men being paid by the CIA didn't know the exact nature of the discussion, they did know the controversy centered around "Mr. Lard-Butt." The only question in their minds was why Buhzid and Bhutto were so determined to protect the man, who had lowered his arms, his fat face expressionless.

The Death Merchant and the rest of them found out in a very short time when Fazal Bhutto turned to the group. "Sahazaba Daltizeb was *Malik* Khair Ghazi's chief agent in

Kabul," Bhutto said placidly. He smiled at "Lard Butt" who returned the smile with a toothy grin that spread across his pumpkin-sized face. "He is the man who gave us the information about your two friends, the two men you came to rescue from this place of evil—Hadji Wakul and Sinah Mugamkurl."

Elrod Kinsey nodded. "Fritz Werholtz and Stewart Hemschire," he said softly.

"The men were saying that they found it difficult to believe that Daltizeb was an agent," Bhutto explained to Camellion. "You see, he is a well-known torturer. I explained to them that if he had not given pain to the prisoners, someone else would have. In torturing prisoners, *kuvii* Daltizeb secured his cover with the Russian dogs and convinced the KGB he could be trusted. We have just seen the proof."

Thinking that the Afghans often went to extremes in many matters—*Lard-Butt certainly did!*—Camellion said matter of factly, "We owe a great debt to *kuvii* Daltizeb. Please thank him for us!"

"What proof?" inquired Hooppole suspiciously, his cool eyes going from Lard Butt to Bhutto and Buhzid.

Fazal Bhutto laughed. "Tell him yourself, *kuvii* Camellion. He speaks your language. You can also give your appreciation for his saving the lives of Fritz Werholtz and Stewart Hemschire. It was he who assigned them to work projects; otherwise they would have been executed."

For the first time, Sahazaba Daltizeb's face became expressive—now with satisfaction. "The proof is in the four dead KGB guards in the anteroom of the stairs area," he said to Hooppole. "I killed them. Three were Russians. The fourth was an Afghan."

Still suspicious, Hooppole glanced toward the open steel door north of the day room. *Mujahideen* were clustered around the opening, peering inside, their weapons ready to fire.

"Don't worry," Daltizeb reassured the group. "I've locked the main door at the bottom of the steps. The enemy cannot get out of the basement—not that Major Sogolov wants to. They could return to the administration building through the tunnel. But how far could they get? The building has been destroyed."

"Tunnel?" exclaimed the Death Merchant.

Daltizeb explained, adding that there was still a large group of Russians and Afghans in the basement, toward the east end. "They have a light machine gun and are determined to kill as many of you—of us—as they can before we kill them. They are also hoping that help will arrive in time. That is not possible though."

"Is there any chance that they might surrender?" asked Wesslin.

"None. Absolutely none."

"Why not get the inmates out, then blow up the entire prison?" suggested Jay Bunker. "I suppose we don't have enough bang stuff to do the job."

"We don't," Camellion said. "The only way to waste those pig farmers is to go in there and do it in person."

There were twenty-seven wide steel steps to the bottom of the basement, to the floor of the 11' X 14' room that, on the east side, contained the steel door that opened to Unit-K. With a dozen men around him, standing guard with SMG and assault rifles, the Death Merchant placed a half pound block of C4 against the bottom of the door and another half pound block against the south wall, in the center, five feet above the floor. In each package was a remote-controlled detonator.

Jugen Wesslin eyed the packages of explosives skeptically.

"Even with this stuff, it's going to be a risk getting to the swine! Grenades will cut down the odds."

"There isn't any other tactic we can use," Camellion said.

After the explosives were in place and the group had returned to the stair room and the day room, each man prepared himself, making sure that his weapons had full magazines. The Death Merchant checked the batter in the R-C unit; he didn't want any misfires at this stage in the game.

Forty men would comprise the first and the main assault force—Camellion, Kamal Din Buhzid, some of the *mujahideen,* and the group working for the Central Intelligence Agency. All except Elrod Kinsey. The Death Merchant had forbidden Kinsey to go, telling him, "If we get killed below, someone will have to make a complete and concise report to the Center. You're the man to do the job, if it comes to that."

The force was ready. So was the Death Merchant. He looked around the edge of the doorway at the top of the stairs, drew back, and firmly pushed the red button in the remote control detonation unit.

The two half pound blocks of C4 roared off with a power that pushed against the entire prison building, the double blasts throwing the steel door twenty-five feet inward and tearing open enormous holes in the thick concrete walls on the east and the south sides. Fumes and smoke were so thick that the Death Merchant and John Smith could hardly see through the drifting clouds of blue and gray as they leaned around the doorway and tossed controlled fragmentation grenades down the stairs, at the openings made by the C4.

The four grenades roared off, throwing their spirally wound prefragmented steel coils of shrapnel all over the place, including through the two large gaps in the walls. No sooner had the shrapnel pinged-pinged-pinged against the steel steps than Camellion and Smith were rushing down the stairs. A MAC-10 SMG was in the Death Merchant's left hand, a .44 Alaskan Auto Mag in his right. In Smith's big hands were a .45 Safari Arms MatchMaster and a MAC-10. Behind them came the rest of the assault force, Jay Bunker, Kamal Din Buhzid and Jugen Wesslin out in front.

Camellion jerked to a stop by the left side of the blasted hole in the east wall, while Smith darted across the area to the left side of the smoking maw in the south wall. Smith saw at once that the mouth of the square tunnel was ten feet to the west.

"Get some men over here," Smith yelled. "I can see the end of the tunnel. It's lit up like a Christmas tree. I don't see any of the enemy."

Camellion motioned to Kamal Din Buhzid with the Auto Mag, waving the long stainless steel barrel toward the south wall. "Take several men with RAWs and bring down the ceiling in the tunnel, at its first curve."

By now the Russians and the Afghan traitors with them had begun a heavy firing, using AKM assault rifles, PPS43 SMGs and a light ShKAS machine gun, the latter on a tripod just outside the door in the southwest corner of the large torture chamber situated in the northeast section of K-Unit.

One of the Afghans, running toward Smith with four other men, cried out, jerked and dropped, several Soviet 7.62mm projectiles in his side. A hailstorm of enemy slugs slammed through the large rupture in the east wall, dug hundreds of holes in the concrete of the opposite wall and effectively pinned down the Death Merchant and his assault force.

So far there were only eighteen men in the room at the bottom of the stairs. The rest of the force could not come down the steps until there was room for them. The hole in the east wall was vast and too many men in the room meant that many of them would not have any place to hide and would be exposed to enemy fire.

Zinggggggg! A ricocheting bullet from the west wall zipped back to the east wall and dug a tiny crater a few inches above Camellion's head. All Camellion could do was stay down and wait for the firing to cease—it did, as suddenly as it had started. No fools, the Russians didn't intend to waste ammunition.

Rod Hooppole, next to the Death Merchant, grimaced. "They could keep us here until the Second Coming. According to Lard Butt, the main torture chamber is too far to the east for grenades to be effective. The RAW devices would be too powerful, wouldn't they?"

"We'll soon find out," Camellion said dourly. "The RAWs are the only thing we have that can get us in there. Without them, we'd be cut down before we moved six feet."

He leaned out, looked past Hooppole and saw that Jay Bunker was carrying a rifle/RAW, plus his two Smith & Wesson .38 pistols and a Valmet "Bullpup." Next to Bunker was Fawin Ja-Kusi; he also had a M16 A1E1 automatic rifle with a RAW attached to it.

"Tell them to pass the RAWs to me," Camellion whispered to Hooppole. "We'll make short work of those pig farmers back there."

A minute or so later, after Camellion had the two RAWs, he leaned around the edge of wall and fired the first one, holding the rifle four feet above the floor and sending the "ball," with its explosive, straight into Unit-K. The RAW ball struck the west wall of the "main interrogation room" and went off with an ear-shattering explosion that tore out half of the wall and killed with concussion the three men grouped behind the ShKAS light machine gun. Ten men inside the torture chamber were also killed—smashed by chunks of concrete that hit them with the force of cannonballs. Included in the ten was Evhen Kovalev, the warden of the penitentiary.

192

Major Sogolov and five other men, behind a large water tank in the east end of the room, were unhurt, except for being severely stunned.

To the west, the big blast shook concrete dust from the ceiling, the wall of pure noise a tight vise on the consciousness of the Death Merchant and his group.

Kamal Din Buhzid, crouched in the corner, called out impatiently to the Death Merchant, "Why are we waiting? Why do we not charge?"

Camellion turned and looked at the perplexed Afghan. "We wait," he said, his voice low and deadly. "Let them have a chance to realize what's happening. Then we'll hit them with the second one. The instant it goes off, we do it." He said to Hooppole. "Pass the word. See to it that it gets to the men on the stairs and waiting in the room above."

He waited several minutes, until his order had been carried out. Carefully, he thrust the M16 A1E1 rifle around the edge of the hole, this time holding the weapon so that the explosion would take place in a different place. He pressed the trigger and fired the rifle. A blink of the eye and the RAW-ball rocketed from its launcher.

BLAMMMMMMMMMMM! The remains of the west side wall of the torture chamber bloomed with a giant flash of fire and were turned into large pieces of shrapnel that slammed into seven Russian and three Afghans, killing four pig farmers and one cockroach.

The thunderous sound of the explosion was not quite dead as the Death Merchant and the others stormed through the two holes in the walls. More men started down the steps. To the south, four *mujahideen* entered the mouth of the tunnel, two carrying Heckler & Koch assault rifles, the other two M16 A1E1s and RAWs.

Darting, weaving, and running in a zigzag, Camellion and the force of liberators were three quarters of the way to the torture chamber by the time the enemy had recovered sufficiently to offer any kind of defense. Submachine guns and assault rifles from both sides roared, the hot muzzles spitting out projectiles.

Kamal Din Buhzid stopped as if he had collided with an invisible wall. Hit in the stomach and chest by a stream of 7.62 military-ball slugs from a PPS43 SMG, Buhzid was chopped apart by the projectiles, and was dead before the impact could begin knocking him to the floor.

Igor Dyazhny, the pig farmer who had killed Buhzid, didn't live long to celebrate his victory. He was swinging the barrel of his AKM to the right when three of Hooppole's H/K A-R slugs popped him high, the 7.62mm projectiles zipping through his upper chest and lower throat and jerking him like a puppet. Four Afghans went down in death, all four wearing KGB uniforms. Lamiz Junikiz tried to duck and failed. Most of the 9mm projectiles from Anatoli Bok's Vitmorkin machine pistol missed. One didn't. The projectile struck Junikiz above the left eye. The bullet bored through the orbital bone, traveled three inches through his brain and stopped. So did Junikiz. He sighed, dropped and died.

With the roaring of weapons loud and furious, the Death Merchant and his men closed in on the last of the defenders of Kabul Central Prison. Camellion, spotting an Afghan swinging an AKM Kalashnikov A-R in his direction, jerked mightily to his right in time to avoid a river of 7.62 (x 38mm) semi-spitzer projectiles, most of which slammed into Muammer Geris and pitched him back. Three of the steel cored slugs came too close to the Death Merchant for him to feel comfortable about it. One zipped across his left side, below his armpit, leaving a short burn mark on his black coveralls. The second one cut a tenth of an inch of leather from the outside of his left side Auto Mag holster. The third bullet zipped through the holster and struck the "Alaskan," just above the trigger guard, Camellion hearing the faint *clank* in spite of all the noise around him.

Richard Camellion had a rare gift, a talent for total honesty and realism. For these reasons, he frankly admitted to himself that he enjoyed killing, particularly since he never wasted anyone who wasn't trying to kill him and who didn't deserve to be scratched into oblivion; and he derived triple joy from blowing up a son of a bitch who did him personal injury, of which harming his weapons—any weapon—topped the list.

Torith Lirorth, the Afghan *"Rance Galloway"* piece of trash who had failed to put Camellion to sleep, would have been better off paralyzed in the lower part of Hell. He tried frantically to swing his AKM toward the Death Merchant and reshoot. He failed. His Time had come. Camellion's right leg came up in a very powerful Tae Kwon Do Hyung *Chungdan*

Ap Changi middle front snap kick, the toe of his boot connecting solidly with the little finger side of Lirorth's right hand that was wrapped underneath the AKM, his finger on the trigger. The assault rifle and Lirorth's arms flew upward, the AKM roaring out a stream of projectiles that zipped into the ceiling. Tilted backward, Lirorth didn't have a single chance to pull back and lower the A-R—even if his right hand hadn't been broken.

The Death Merchant shot Lirorth high in the right leg with the last three MAC-10 .45 slugs. At the same time, he lowered the Alaskan Auto Mag in his right hand, tilted the muzzle steeply upward and pulled the trigger. The big weapon boomed, the 250 grain .44 flat-nosed projectile tearing off Lirorth's right hand at the wrist and wrecking the AKM, the impact kicking the assault rifle almost to the ceiling. With his right leg almost shot off, Lirorth screamed and crashed to the floor on his left side.

Let the scum bleed to death, and I hope he bleeds very very slowly!

Camellion darted to the left, his keen eyes watching his front and both sides. All around him men were yelling, crying out in pain and hate, and dying. Cihat Esenbel went down with Sergei Rogon, a bushy-haired Russian, a smile frozen forever on the dying Esenbel's face, his left hand with a death grip on the handle of the *Hazka*, the long blade of which was buried in the KGB guard's stomach. At the last moment, as the sharp blade was slicing into his stomach, Rogon had managed to press his Makarov pistol against Esenbel's side and fire twice.

Rod Hooppole would have been next to go bye-bye if Jugen Wesslin hadn't spotted Gorkin Yezheyshuk and Vasali Boyanus aiming down on the British merc and Jay Bunker, Boyanus using a Stechkin machine pistol, Yezheyshuk a PPS43 sub-gun.

Having exhausted the ammo in his "Bullpup," Wesslin had drawn his Smith & Wesslin .41 mag M-57 revolvers. Up came both mags, and he squeezed the triggers, the large revolvers roaring. One two hundred forty grain swaged projectile struck Boyanus just below the left ear and literally blew his head off. The second .41 flat-nosed bullet hit Yezheyshuk in his left side, just above the belt of his uniform coat. The slug cut all the way through his body, the TNT impact lifting the pig farmer on his toes before kicking six feet to the right.

Wesslin cried out in pain, feeling a sharp, burning pain streak across his right rib cage; yet experience told him that he hadn't been shot. He had been "almost" shot, the graze so deep that he could feel the hot blood pouring out of the cut; from the pain when he moved, he knew that a rib had been clipped and was fractured. Wesslin did the only thing he could do: wincing in pain, he fell flat, his eyes only partly open, a .41 mag in each hand.

It was Jay Bunker who had saved Wesslin's life and, in a sense was responsible for the West German's fractured rib. Bunker had spotted a Russian KGB guard raising his AKM toward Wesslin and had instantly fired both Sig-Sauer auto-pistols, the two 9mm hollow points crashing into the pig farmer's side and destroying his plan to kill Wesslin. Shock had set up a reaction and the dying man's finger had jerked against the trigger. The assault rifle had roared. Most of the projectiles had hit the floor. One didn't. It had stung Wesslin.

Bunker, John Smith, and the Death Merchant were now very close to the blasted west wall of the torture chamber, so close that they, as well as the enemy—the pitiful few that were still alive—were stumbling over large chunks of concrete on the floor.

Forty feet to the east, Bunker spotted several men leaning out from a tank four times the size of the average water heater. One of the men, to Bunker's left, was poking out the barrel of a 9mm Vitmorkin machine pistol; the other man was trying to get a PPS43 SMG into action. Bunker let experience take over. He "body pointed," fired both Sig-Sauers—and missed! The slugs glanced from the tank with screaming whines; yet they did force the two men to jerk back behind the tank.

Mentally spitting on his bad luck, Bunker dropped flat behind a pile of concrete blasted from the wall and waited. In his opinion, he was having a pee-poor day. . . .

John Jerrold Smith, six feet to the left of the Death Merchant, was also earning the $4,285.00 per month the CIA was paying him to do its dirty work and "wet affairs." His MAC-10 had long since eaten up its ammo and he was using two .45 Matchmasters. He too had detected the cruds behind the tank that supplied water for the "Waterwheel," a form of torture in which the victim was tied to a large wheel that was slowly turned, submerging the poor devil in a square tub of water. Major Sogolov and the other KGB sadists liked the Waterwheel almost as much as they enjoyed watching a naked man or woman jerk, jump and scream on the ''electric bed,'' or shrieking out their souls while being submitted to the foot, knee, or elbow crusher. Sogolov's favorite method was pouring boiling urine into a victim's nose, or bubbling and boiling lye into the anus.

There were only three Russian KGB guards in front of Camellion and Smith, among them Anatoli Bok who died when a .44 Alaskan bullet exploded his chest. The two other pig farmers went down .45 MatchMaster projectiles in their bodies.

''Behind the tank ahead!'' yelled Smith to the Death Merchant and the others. Once more the two men tried to fire from behind the water tank; they were too slow. Hooppole, Smith, Bunker and five Afghans fired, but the Russians had ducked back too quickly.

The Death Merchant dropped behind a pile of jagged concrete and fired the last three .44 rounds from his Alaskan AMP. At the same time, Jugen Wesslin began tossing slugs with his .41 S & W magnum revolvers. The .44 and the .41 projectiles cut through both sides of the thin steel as though the tank were made of cardboard. Major Andrew Sogolov, to the group's left, dropped the Vitmorkin machine pistol and died when a .44 bullet hit him in the stomach, broke his spine and took its exit from his back. He was sagging, his eyes wide open, as a .41 slug hit him in the right side of the neck and made his head bob.

Konstantin Zaostrevy, the KGB officer to the right, screamed when an Alaskan .44 bullet hit him in the left leg, just above the knee, and twisted his body to the right. He had sagged halfway to the floor when the next .44 round popped him in the right hip and dug a tunnel through his intestines.

Josef Chogevenhok, the chief guard, was the third man behind the tank. Paralyzed with terror, he had not fired a single shot. He never would. Two of Jugen Wesslin's .41 slugs slammed into his chest and shoved him violently against the wall. Dead, he hung there, braced between the wall and the tank through whose sides water was pouring, long streams from the bullet holes.

Smoke, the smell of burnt gunpowder, silence, and the stink of death. The Death Merchant and the other men looked cautiously around them. Upstairs they could hear the sounds of happy men . . . yelling and shouting . . . the sounds of *free* men.

"They've freed the prisoners," Smith said to Camellion, who was getting to his feet.

"I know." Camellion sounded angry. "We had better get up there. We'll never find Werholtz and Hemschire in that mess."

After going to the Day Room upstairs, Camellion was glad to see that he was wrong. Stewart Hemschire was sitting on a chair/ Next to him stood Fazal Bhutto and several other Afghans, a large half moon smile on Bhutto's face.

"This is *kuvii* Sinah Mugamkurl, the one you call Stewart Hemschire," Bhutto said.

Camellion looked sharply at Hemschire whose clothes were filthy. All skin and bones, his face a living skull, Hemschire couldn't have weighed more than 110 pounds.

"Who are you?" Hemschire asked in a weak voice, looking up at the Death Merchant.

"I'm one of the men who came to rescue you," Camellion replied.

Hemschire managed a smile. "What took you so long?"

"You know how it is, with coffee breaks and stopovers for beer. Where's Fritz Werholtz?"

"He's dead," croaked Hemschire. "He died last night— overwork and not enough food. His heart said 'the hell with it' and quit beating."

Camellion said to Fazal Bhutto, "We must move back into the mountains as quickly as possible. It won't be easy, not with all the wounded we have."

Bhutto nodded, a forlorn look falling over his smoke-smudged face.

"It will be easier for us than for the men we have freed from the cells. We can't take them with us. They are too weak and we don't have the supplies. Allah will have to protect them."

Uh huh . . . and if Allah's so good, why didn't he prevent the Russians from invading your land in the first place?"

The Death Merchant merely said, "Yes, *kuvii* Bhutto. Allah will look after them. . . ."

After the Russians return and blow their heads off!

AFTERMATH

15.00 hours. Four days after the attack on Kabul Central Prison.

The helicopters had not come from Pakistan to lift out the Death Merchant and the other Company men. *Too dangerous!* the agent had said from the *Redwing* station in India. *You'll have to walk out. Mockingbird, we have a coded message for you from a Higher Authority.*

The price of the attack had been very high. Not only had the attacks against Soviet headquarters and the Soviet airbase failed, but the grand flop had cost the lives of 3,900 *mujahideen*.

Khair Ghazi was dead.

Torak Adjar had been killed by a bursting shell.

Abdullah Saljoonque was wounded—head and stomach—and wasn't expected to live.

Of the three leaders only Mohammad Malikyar was in good health.

Ismail Mohammad Ghazi was dead. He had survived the battle against General Pavel Mozzhechkov's headquarters and had pronounced himself leader after the death of his father.

Sebghatullah Mahlik had promptly killed Ismail with a SMG burst.

Rod Hooppole put down his tin cup of cold tea and reached for the last cigarette in his pack. "I'm told we should reach Kukimac tomorrow night. It's only a few klicks from the Pak/Afghan border."

The other men, grouped under the enormous ledge and eating, didn't answer.

On the second day, Stewart Hemschire had died from exhaustion. He had died easy. He went to sleep and didn't wake up. . . .

The Death Merchant, sitting on a rock, thought of Rumania, his next stop after he got to India and flew to London.

Damn it! He pulled the .44 Auto Mag from the left holster, turned over the large stainless steel pistol and looked in dismay at its underside. The steel-cored 7.62mm AKM projectile had made a tiny crater in the steel, in front of the trigger guard.

I should have choked that cockroach to death!